WILDINGS

Eleanor Glewwe

VIKING

VIKING
An imprint of Penguin Random House LLC
375 Hudson Street
New York, New York 10014

First published in the United States of America by Viking,
an imprint of Penguin Random House LLC, 2016

LIBRARY OF CONGRESS CATALOGING-IN-PUBLICATION DATA IS AVAILABLE
ISBN: 9780451468857

Printed in the U.S.A.

1 3 5 7 9 10 8 6 4 2

For Nathaniel

As the train hurtles along the rails, I press my face to the window. The flat countryside stretches to the horizon, interrupted only by a few twisted trees, their black branches still bare. The fields are patched with snow. There is nothing to see in this empty landscape, but I can't tear my eyes away. After four dark years, I am on my way to Ashara at last.

"Mind your cello, Rivka," Father says without looking up from the newspaper he is reading on the velvet seat opposite me.

I grip the handle of my cello case. The porters wanted to put it in the baggage car with our trunks. They assured Father that many Atsani magicians had entrusted their instruments to their care, but he wouldn't hear of it. His own flute case lies beside him.

I will the drab fields and dirty snow to fly by faster, but instead the chugging of the wheels eases. The train's whistle emits a long shriek. Why are we stopping?

Father looks up. "We've reached the border."

My heart leaps. We're about to cross from Atsan into Ashara. In a moment, I'll be in the same city-state as my brother for the first time in four years. Excitement and yearning well up in me until I feel like I'm going to burst, but I'm careful to gaze calmly out the window.

Father retrieves our passports from his briefcase on the overhead luggage rack. We have to wait a while before border control reaches the first-class cars. At last, an officer in a black uniform enters our compartment.

"Ambassador Kadmiel," he says with an Ashari accent, almost bowing to Father. I watch him curiously while he examines Father's passport. Surely he is a kasir? But anyone can be dressed in a uniform, and so much has changed in Ashara since the Assembly was overthrown that I suppose anything is possible. Even halani checking passports at the border.

This is all a formality. Our papers are obviously in order. Everybody at the station must know this is the train on which the new Atsani ambassador to Ashara is arriving. But the officer must do his duty, so when he has finished with Father, I hand him my passport.

"My thanks, Gadin Kadmiel," he says.

I nod, feeling very grown up. I am an ambassador's daughter now.

The train starts to move again, and my heartbeat accelerates with the rhythmic clatter of the wheels. I can scarcely believe I've made it to Ashara. My hands tingle as it sinks in how close I am. I've been determined to go to Ashara since the night Mother died, but I had no illusions about the likelihood of my being able to travel that far on my own before I had at least finished secondary school. So when Father knocked on my bedroom door one evening a few months ago, I had no idea that my chance was about to arrive early.

"Come in," I said, my stomach tightening.

The door swung open, and Father approached my desk. I kept my head bent over the musical score open before me. I knew Father was scrutinizing the music, noting the architecture of the spell, the nuances built into each part to shape the magic in subtle ways.

"Rivka, I have some news for you," he said at last.

His grave tone made me look up. I couldn't imagine why he should sound so serious, unless . . . Was he going to remarry?

"I have been appointed ambassador to Ashara," Father said.

I was certain I'd misheard. "To where?"

"Ashara," Father repeated. Was he gauging my reaction? I had to pretend Ashara meant nothing to me.

"That's wonderful, Father." My voice sounded mechanical. I couldn't betray my eagerness to go to Ashara, but I couldn't let him think he could leave me behind either. "Does this mean we're moving to Ashara?"

"Would you be very upset to have to move?" Father asked.

"I don't know." I twisted around to face him. "When do you start?"

"In the spring, around the time you would be starting at Heshom." Father's gaze strayed to the envelope from the elite secondary school that was still sitting on my desk. It contained the acceptance letter I had received last week.

"I would go to Ashara with you," I said.

"I do not want to uproot you from your life here and force you to grow up in a foreign city, Rivka," Father said.

"You know I resigned as ambassador to Kiriz when you were born." The words rolled smoothly off his tongue, as though it was only ever me that was born.

"I'm older now, Father. I can come with you."

"It is because you are older that I felt I could accept, knowing I might leave you in Atsan," Father said.

My heartbeat quickened. I had to convince him to take me.

"I don't want to stay here without you." I had to be careful not to overdo it, lest he wonder at my sudden excessive attachment.

"My sister will be your guardian," Father said. "She has already agreed."

I teetered on the verge of panic. He wasn't listening to me.

"Of course, you will board at Heshom," he continued, "but you could spend holidays with—"

"Father, I would rather go with you. Truly."

I detected a hint of surprise in his eyes, but it was a pleased surprise.

"My appointment may last for many years, Rivka, and we would not visit Atsan often. I don't want to take you away from your friends."

Inwardly, I snorted. What friends? Out loud, I said, "I understand. I still want to go with you. I'd like to see more of the world."

I held my breath, worried I'd gone too far, but Father didn't look the least bit suspicious. He almost looked approving.

"Very well. If you are sure, I will make arrangements to take you with me."

"I'm sure, Father."

He nodded. "There is a fine kasir school in Ashara called Firem. I will see about enrolling you there."

With that, he left my room. The moment the door clicked shut, I jumped up from my chair. I didn't know what to do with myself. I felt like I'd been set free from a cage. Finally. *Finally*. Years sooner than I had ever thought possible, I was going to Ashara.

⤛ ⤛ ⤛

A whistle blast draws me back to the present. I am abruptly aware of the tension of countless spells in the air, a sort of sticky thickness I last felt in Atsan. It was absent in the barren countryside between cities, but now our train is pulling into the station in Ashara. Outside the window, a cloud of steam obscures the platform. Then it drifts away, revealing the people gathered there to greet those arriving. Everyone is still dressed in the black wool coats of winter.

Hefting my cello, I follow Father out of the car and climb gingerly down the steep steps onto the platform. I pause to loop my arms through the shoulder straps of my case and lift it onto my back. Father is already plowing his way through the throng. I hasten after him, the bottom of my cello case whacking my legs at each step. We pass through the station's high-ceilinged waiting room and emerge on a sidewalk. A line of black automobiles is idling along the curb. By the light of their headlamps, the cobbled street shines with melted snow. Next to one of the autos, a man with a gray beard and a floppy brown cap holds a sign that reads *Ambassador Kadmiel*.

"Father, what about our trunks?" I ask.

"They will follow us," he says impatiently, approaching the chauffeur.

Once Father and I and our instruments are settled in the automobile, we drive away from the train station. The sun has long since set, and so my first glimpses of Ashara are steeped in shadows. We pass rows of narrow town houses, their balconies trimmed with fir boughs for the new year. These soon give way to larger buildings with shops on the ground floor, all shuttered for the night. A few autos rumble by, but I see no people, until our driver turns down a new street and stifles an exclamation.

I lean forward to peer out the windshield. At first, I can make little sense of the scene ahead. An auto parked slantwise in the middle of the street. A shattered storefront window. Silhouettes of men darting back and forth like phantoms, flashes of colored light springing from their hands. The air is sharp with the scent of freshly stirred magic.

"What is this?" Father demands.

Our driver, his posture stiff, noses the auto forward. Broken glass crunches under our wheels. As we pass between the stopped vehicle and the shop, I slide across the seat to my window. A broad-shouldered halan in a thick wool sweater stands in front of the damaged store, his hands raised, palms out. Two men loom over him, their backs to me, so close my door would hit them if I opened it. The shopkeeper pleads with the kasiri in words I can't make out. I glance up at a second-story window and see a woman holding an infant, her fist pressed to her mouth. Her fear rubs off on me.

"What are—?" Father breaks off as though he has realized something. But what?

The auto lurches as our driver slams the brake. Two wild-eyed boys flit around our front fenders, carrying wooden boxes from the shop to the other side of the street. Are they trying to save their father's wares? A figure chases them, hands outstretched, a dense swirl of darkness where his face should be. He looks like a creature from a nightmare. I hear a shout, and then I smell smoke, not the bitterness of magic but the scent of something actually burning. Our auto speeds down the block.

"Society," the chauffeur mutters. It sounds like a curse.

"What's going on?" I ask.

"Nothing," says Father.

"Nothing?" I say, my voice high. "That man's face—"

"An advanced masking enchantment," Father says, as though identifying a spell for a classroom of students.

"But, Father," I say, incredulous, "weren't those men attacking—"

"Rivka," he warns. I fall silent.

No one speaks for the rest of the ride. At last, we turn onto a wide street lined with limestone houses, each one flying a flag. I recognize the banners of Kiriz and Tekova, the black, silver, and red stripes of Xana, and the pine of Aevlia before spotting Atsan's yellow half-moon on a dark blue field. The driver parks in front of our new home, and Father and I get out.

A woman stands in the doorway of the embassy, a ring of keys dangling from her hand. She is as tall as Father but thin as a rope. Her charcoal dress, white apron, and bun identify her as a member of the halan household staff.

The chauffeur lifts my cello from the trunk and hands it to me.

"Thank you," I say to him.

"Come in, Gadin Kadmiel," the servant says. "Welcome to the Atsani embassy."

I mumble another thank-you, crossing the threshold with my cello. My winter traveling boots click on the gleaming hardwood floor. I squint up at the electric lights glowing steadily in the chandelier overhead.

"Good evening, Gadin Kadmiel," says an Atsani-accented voice. I start. There is another woman in the foyer. Her dark, straight eyebrows are hawk-like, but her expression is kind.

"My name is Talya Liron," she says.

I recognize her name. She's the Deputy Head of Mission and has been in charge of the embassy since the old ambassador returned to Atsan. Now that Father is here, she'll go back to being deputy.

"Pleased to meet you, Deputy Liron," I say.

She turns to greet Father as he enters the house. "I hope your journey was smooth."

"It was, until the very end," Father says. "We drove through some Society activity on our way from the station."

Deputy Liron frowns. "I'm sorry you had to see trouble on your first night."

"Is this sort of thing common?"

Surely kasiri don't often smash up halan businesses in Ashara. This never happened in Atsan.

"Common enough," Father's deputy says. "These halani won't stop trying to open shops on kasir streets or send their children to kasir schools when they have perfectly good ones in their own neighborhoods."

I blink, wondering if she and Father are talking about the same thing. Then I realize she means it's the halani's fault if their stores are destroyed. Now that I think about it, it is odd that a halan owned a shop in the wealthy district we were driving through.

"Thank you for waiting for us to arrive," Father tells Deputy Liron.

"You're most welcome," she says, buttoning up her coat. "Good night, Ambassador. And welcome to Ashara."

When the deputy has slipped out into the damp night, the servant introduces herself as Irit Yoram, the housekeeper. She leads us up the staircase to the second floor, which is a maze of hallways and office doors. This is still part of the chancery, the official part of the embassy where Father will spend his days with the diplomatic staff. The stairs to the ambassador's residence are hidden away in a corner.

At the top of the steps, Gadi Yoram flips a switch, and electric light floods the third-floor foyer. "The dining room and parlor are that way," she says, gesturing down the hall. "The bedrooms are upstairs. They have been aired out in preparation for your arrival."

Father nods in approval. "Rivka, go choose a bedroom. Meet me here in fifteen minutes. We will dine out tonight."

Hoisting my cello case onto my back again, I trudge up to the fourth floor. As I climb, I can hear Father instructing

Gadi Yoram in the times we will take our meals and other mundane household matters. Soon their voices fade. The residence is eerily quiet. For a second, I let myself imagine another way things might have been, if Arik had been a magician and Mother had not died. We might all be moving into the embassy tonight, Mother darting gaily from room to room, exclaiming over some exquisite wallpaper or a charming set of candlesticks, Arik and I peering into bedroom after bedroom until we found the ones that suited us best. The vision fades, and I'm left alone in the silent corridor, facing half a dozen closed doors.

After locating the largest bedroom, which Father will surely claim, I choose the room farthest from it. The bed is freshly made with white sheets and a blue coverlet embroidered with silver. An oval mirror hangs over the dresser, and behind thick winter curtains, a window seat overlooks the street.

A few minutes later, Father and I depart for dinner on foot. The early spring night is cold, and I bury my hands in the pockets of my wool coat as I struggle to match Father's long strides. The warm glow of the restaurant windows is a welcome sight.

A waiter ushers us to a table tucked behind a painted screen. The other diners take no notice of us. I suppose we fit right in with our black coats. It's a bit disappointing to find Ashara so much like Atsan so far. When our waiter recites the menu, though, his accent reminds me that I'm in a foreign country.

While we wait for our food, Father drones on about having me fitted for school uniforms and selecting my classes at Firem. I nod at appropriate moments to give the impression that I'm paying attention. In reality, I'm trying to figure out how soon I can start looking for Arik.

At a pause in Father's ramblings, I break in and ask, "What is the Society?"

My question doesn't seem to surprise him. "The Society for Accord and Harmony is an Ashari civic association," he says.

"Like your club in Atsan?" At home, Father joined other men of his station at a hotel once a month for dinner and conversation about politics. I don't see the connection between that and what we witnessed tonight on the way to the embassy.

But Father nods. "Somewhat like that. The Society is dedicated to keeping the peace and promoting social harmony."

Breaking shop windows hardly strikes me as keeping the peace, and Father must sense some doubt in me because he adds, "Someone must deal with troublemakers, Rivka. If the government is too spineless to confront social problems, it is the people's duty to take matters into their own hands."

Just then, the waiter appears with our stewed rabbit and roast potatoes, as well as a jug of red wine. Father pours a glass for himself and then, to my surprise, another for me. He raises his glass.

"Welcome to Ashara, Rivka."

In the morning, after a tailor takes my measurements for my Firem uniforms, I explore the embassy. The other bedrooms are crammed with the relics of past ambassadors and their families: a child's bookcase shaped like a birdhouse, a rock collection, a pair of worn binoculars. I descend to the third floor, testing the stairs for creaks so later I'll know how to go up and down silently. Then I venture down the hallway to the music room. An upright piano with ivory keys stands against one wall. A phonograph sits in the corner beside a small writing desk, where a stack of blank staff paper is waiting for a magician to begin composing spells.

The rest of the third floor consists of the dining room where Father and I ate breakfast, a parlor, a library, and a study. I steal down to the second floor. The offices that were dark last night are brightly lit today. I glimpse an embassy secretary in a black suit through a half-open door, but I hurry past and walk down the carpeted steps to the first floor of the chancery.

Past Father's and Deputy Liron's offices, I find a spacious drawing room. Between the silk-covered divans and wingback chairs are little end tables whose lower shelves are filled with books. Kneeling in front of one table, I notice a guidebook wedged between an orphaned encyclopedia volume and an ebony bookend. It is entitled *A Walker's Illustrated Guide to Ashara*. It's thirty years out of date, but I'm excited to find it. I need to start looking for Arik as soon as possible.

The book is organized by district. Every few pages, there is an illustration of some landmark: a covered marketplace called the Ikhad, a bridge over the Davgir River, the Assembly Hall. More useful are the neighborhood maps. Parts of the city seem to be missing, though, and at last I figure out why: at the edges of several maps are blank gray fields marked *Lower Classes*. In other words, halan neighborhoods. That's where I'll find Arik.

Taking the guidebook, I return to my bedroom to fetch my coat. As I come bowling back down the steps into the embassy foyer, someone says, "Rivka, where are you going?"

It's Deputy Liron, standing in the hallway that leads to her office.

"To ask Father if I can go out," I say, breathless.

"Alone?" she says doubtfully.

Has Father said I'm not to leave the embassy on my own? I've been allowed to go out by myself since I was nine, as long as I told someone where I was going.

"I just want to explore the neighborhood," I say politely. "I won't get lost."

"Won't get lost where?" Father says, walking up behind Deputy Liron.

I stand a little straighter. "May I take a walk, Father?"

"Ashara is an unfamiliar city, Rivka," he begins, but without exactly interrupting him, I manage to head him off.

"I found a guidebook," I say, holding it up. "I know how to read a map." I must win this battle. If I don't have free rein to walk about the city, I won't be able to accomplish what I've come here to do.

"Let me see," says Father.

I reluctantly hand him the guide, resenting this inspection. "It seems suitable," he says at last. "But don't stray too far."

Outside, the sun is shining, though the air still has a wintry bite to it. The embassy flags snap in the stiff wind. Following a map, I walk eastward, toward the Davgir River and my new school. A few minutes later, I reach a square, and Firem rises before me, all stone columns and oaken doors.

It's still the break between school years, and there are no students about. I open my walker's guide again and hunt for one of the gray areas marked *Lower Classes*. I find a map showing such a neighborhood to the south of Firem. All I have to do is follow a wide boulevard that leads out of this square. Tucking the book under my arm, I set off for the halan district, my heart beating fast. The possibility is small, but there's a chance I could find Arik today.

Limestone buildings line the boulevard, their ground floors occupied by shops and offices, with a café here and there. Though it is barely spring, some owners have already set tables outdoors. Kasiri wrapped in coats sip steaming glasses of rust-colored tea as they read the newspaper. The air smells of spices, but not the cardamom of home. A few autos creep up and down either side of the street, while in the middle, a shiny black streetcar rattles along tracks embedded in the cobblestones. There isn't much room left for those of us on foot, and people jostle me as they hurry past. I'm so glad to have escaped the embassy that I don't mind.

As in Atsan, the kasiri are dressed mostly in black, the women in ankle-length gowns, the men in felt hats. The halani wear more colors, and instead of buttoned coats they keep warm with rippling cloaks in brown and gray. I pass a florist and a tea dealer. Doors swing open as shopkeepers call out to delivery boys. The streetcar spits out its passengers, all halani, onto a platform in the middle of the street. It's the end of the line, at least for now. Ahead, dust-streaked workers are laying new tracks in the dug-up street.

A few blocks beyond the construction site, the neighborhood changes. The bustle of the city center is gone, and limestone yields to soot-stained yellow brick. I don't see any black-clad kasiri anymore, and I'm beginning to draw furtive looks from the halani. I keep moving, pretending I know where I'm going.

The street is missing cobbles in places, and tufty weeds stick out between slumps of gritty snow. The gutters gurgle with runoff from the shrinking drifts. There are no autos around, so children play in the streets without fear. Three girls in patched cloaks tear past me, caught up in a gleeful game of tag. They dodge a horse-drawn cart as it comes around the corner, and when the driver shakes his fist at them, they laugh.

I stop and look up at the windows of the apartment buildings on either side of me. Some are shuttered, some obscured by curtains, some even boarded up. A few are clear, but I can't see anyone inside. Suddenly, the task I have set myself seems impossibly daunting. This is only one halan neighborhood of many in Ashara, and even if I wander its streets all afternoon, how can I be sure of learning whether Arik is here or not? I can hardly go around asking if anyone knows of a family that adopted a wilding boy from Atsan about four years ago. To even utter such a question would be unthinkable. Nobody mentions wildings.

"Are you lost?"

I turn to face a girl my age. She wears a thick brown sweater and a knitted red scarf, and her long black hair is braided.

"No," I say. It's true. I know exactly what street I'm on.

"Are you sure?" she asks bluntly. "Because I don't think this is where you want to be. Can I help you find something?"

"No, thank you," I say with all the dignity I can muster.

The girl frowns. "Are you foreign?" Her tone softens. "You must really be lost. This is a halan neighborhood. The city center is that way." She points in the direction I have come.

I stand my ground, but I have the acute sense of being unwelcome and of being watched by more eyes than I can see. I'm not afraid, just frustrated.

"Where are you from, anyway?" the girl asks.

"Atsan."

She cocks her head. "Oh. Well, please take my advice,

and stay in the kasir neighborhoods. I'm sure it's obvious to you which ones those are."

With that, she hurries away, leaving me to puzzle over her bold words. Do I have reason to fear being in this part of the city? No one would dare hurt me. Still, this isn't where I belong. Neither is the embassy. Neither is Atsan. I'm not sure I've belonged anywhere since I lost Arik. The place I belong is wherever he is.

3

I was born seven minutes before my brother, Arik. My earliest memories are of running wild through our house in Atsan while Father was at work and Mother reclined on a divan, writing letters to her friends or reviewing the cook's menus for the week.

Like all kasir children in Atsan, we began music lessons when we were four years old. Father chose the violin for Arik and the cello for me. Arik took to the violin as if he'd been born to play it. Music flowed from his instrument like water from a spring. Our parents never had to urge him to practice; he would've played all day if he could have. For me practice was a chore, no matter how much I loved the cello.

As we grew older, Father began watching for the manifestation of our magical ability. Most kasir children show the first signs of having magic around eight or nine. Some of our classmates had already shown the signs, and it became a competition to see who would be next. It never occurred to us that someone in our class might not be a magician. We knew such a thing was possible, but it was something we'd only heard about vaguely, like a rare and unspeakable disease. There were words for such children. The official term was changeling. The more common one was wilding, like an apple tree growing in the wild from a seed escaped from the orchard. We didn't know any wildings. We certainly couldn't *be* wildings.

One day when we were eight and a half years old, Arik was watching me practice in the music room. I was staring at the sonata on my music stand. My teacher had assigned me the first movement for my next lesson, which was tomorrow, and I still hadn't mastered the huge shift in the opening phrase.

"Imagine it before you play it," Arik suggested. "Then it will come out perfectly."

"Just because I know how it should sound doesn't mean I can play it," I retorted.

"Want me to try?"

I shrugged and held out my cello. We had been trading since the beginning, and we'd managed to get pretty good at each other's instruments, though whenever Father caught us switching he'd grumble that we were wasting precious practice time on foolishness.

While my twin squinted at my music, I amused myself playing a waltz on his fiddle. I stopped when he raised my bow. The dreaded shift soared under his fingers, exactly in tune.

"Like that?"

"It's not fair," I said. "You might as well learn my sonata for me."

He laughed. "You know I couldn't. Try again!"

Sighing, I exchanged his violin for my cello. I played the

pick-up notes and then slid my fingers up the ebony finger-board toward the high note. I hit it just right, and it sang as I drew it out. Before I reached the tip of my bow, though, a hum began to fill the music room. For a second, I thought it was some bizarre harmonic coming from my cello, but the hum grew louder, engulfing me. I caught a whiff of something unfamiliar but pleasantly spicy. The gas lamps flared on the walls. The next moment, both sound and light subsided, leaving only the mysterious scent. My ears rang. I lowered my arms and stared at Arik, who stared back at me.

Then he grinned. "You're a magician!" He dashed into the corridor. "Mother, Father, come see! Rivka's a magician!"

Because we were twins, everyone expected Arik's magic to manifest soon after mine did. Father spoke of it as a sure thing. As the weeks slipped by, we had to let go of this idea, but Arik and I weren't worried. We weren't identical twins, after all.

I had more episodes like the first one. My lack of control frightened me, but slowly I figured out ways to channel my magic. I wasn't casting real spells, but I could make certain things happen at will. By playing a wrong note, I stumbled upon a particular musical phrase that made the air smell of cardamom. It became my signature trick, until Arik threatened to hide my cello.

"You're going to make me so sick of cardamom I won't be able to enjoy Cook's spice rolls anymore."

"But it helps me," I protested. "The more I do these tricks, the less it happens by accident."

"Fine," he said. "But at least do some of the other ones,

like turning the gaslights blue, or shooting sparks out of your bow."

Something dampened my high spirits. "Arik, I wish *you* could do magic."

My brother laughed. "Don't be so impatient, Rivka. My magic will come when it's good and ready."

He seemed genuinely unconcerned, but the same wasn't true of our parents. By the time we were nine and a half, they were truly anxious. Mother took to watching us in the music room, lying on the sofa next to the piano. While Arik and I practiced our scales together, she would eye my brother, her brow pinched. Her presence made me painfully conscious of every flaw in my playing, but Arik didn't mind. He played Mother's favorite pieces until her brow cleared. Her instrument had been piano, but she rarely played now. She was neither an accomplished magician—she never helped Father cast the wards that protected our house—nor an accomplished musician, but she loved listening to Arik.

When Father came to the music room, it was much worse. One afternoon, he walked in while Mother was dozing and Arik was listening to me practice an étude. I broke off mid–bow stroke.

"Rivka, let us see your sparks," Father said.

My heart sank. I knew what was coming, but I dared not disobey him. Swallowing, I played an aimless melody of lively triplets. Gold sparks popped above my bridge.

"Very good," Father said. "Now you try, Arik."

"I don't know what to do, Father," my brother said.

"Imitate your sister."

Arik's gaze crossed mine, and I saw the pleading look in his eyes. After all the times he'd helped me prepare for a lesson with my demanding cello teacher, now he needed my help, and I had nothing to offer him. I couldn't make the magic burst forth from him. The only thing I could do was make Father stop, and I was too much of a coward to try.

Arik raised his violin and played exactly the same notes I had. Nothing happened.

"Try again," Father ordered.

Miserably, Arik played the melody again. No sparks appeared. My face was hot with embarrassment for him.

"Are you really concentrating?" said Father, his sternness terrifying. "Again."

"Nechemya, leave the poor boy alone," Mother said faintly from her sofa.

"I cannot leave him alone when his tenth birthday is rapidly approaching," Father said. Our birthday was the deadline for completing our official magic examination.

Arik knew better than to appeal to Mother. She might defend him halfheartedly, but she would always yield to Father in the end. Arik played my tune again, improvising some extra ornamentation. Nothing.

"Why can't you be more like your sister?" Father said. I cringed. "Her magic manifested itself more than a year ago. I don't understand it. You're twins!"

"I'm trying, Father," Arik said in a fragile voice, his gaze fixed on Father's polished shoes.

"You're not trying hard enough. Forget about that concerto your teacher seems to think you should learn. This is far more important. Do I make myself clear?"

"Yes, Father." Arik's eyes brimmed with tears that he refused to shed, out of pride and fear of Father's disgust.

Father stalked out of the music room. Immediately, I set down my cello and darted to Arik's side.

"It's not your fault," I said in a rush. "He's making you nervous. Besides, you can't *make* yourself do magic. It just happens the first time. It'll come soon, I know it."

Arik nodded slowly. He looked toward the sofa where Mother lay, but her eyes were closed, and she was pinching the bridge of her nose, no doubt plagued by a headache.

"He's gone now," I said, as though Father wouldn't return tomorrow or the day after. When that didn't reassure my twin, I said, "Play something for me."

Arik closed his eyes and launched into the piece he'd performed at his last recital. As he played the broad, majestic strokes of the opening, he seemed to grow taller. By the time he reached the fast section, his eyes were open, and he was smiling as his bow leaped joyfully across the strings.

Music might have been the balm that soothed Arik's hurt, but it could not erase the reality that we were almost ten years old and he still hadn't shown the slightest sign of having magic. While Mother kept insisting he was just a late bloomer, Father continued to watch us from the doorway of the music room, his expression stony.

One night, after we had gone to bed, Arik spoke through the darkness of our room.

"Rivka, I don't think I have magic."

"Don't say that!" I said fiercely. "It's not true."

"It is," he insisted. He didn't sound upset or afraid but instead almost peaceful.

"That's impossible." I turned onto my side to face his bed, though I could barely see him. "We're twins. We're Kadmiels. No one in our family has ever not been a magician."

"How do you know?" Arik asked.

Fear fell like a shadow over my heart. He was right. If there had ever been a child without magic in our family, nobody would have told us. Nobody would have spoken of it at all.

"Anyway, I can feel it," said my brother. "I don't have magic."

"What do you mean you can feel it?"

"It's . . . I think it's the other sense."

I shivered. The other sense was an uncanny ability to know things one had no way of knowing naturally. It was a gift all halani, and only halani, possessed. If Arik had it . . . I refused to consider what that meant.

"You *have* to be a magician," I whispered through the dark. "If you're not . . ."

I couldn't say it. We both knew what would happen. The government would take him away, and he would be adopted by a halan family. He would be given a new name. He would no longer be a kasir. His old life would fade away. I shied away from these thoughts. Arik and I had shared everything our whole lives. It was unthinkable that one of us might be a kasir and the other a halan.

"I don't want to leave you and Mother and Father," Arik said in a small voice. For the first time, he sounded scared.

"You won't have to. It's going to be all right."

"But what if it's not? What if they take me away?"

"They *won't*, Arik."

He was silent a moment. Then he said, "We should make a plan, just in case. So we can find each other again."

"Stop it." I would burrow my head under my pillow if he kept this up.

"You have to listen, Rivka," my brother said. "Please, let's pick a meeting place. How about the arch bridge over the river?"

It was the oldest bridge in Atsan, built in the time of the kingdom of Erezai, before the cold times began and the north lands split into the different city-states. Every year at midwinter, it was hung with lanterns, and at midsummer, children dropped paper boats from its railings into the water.

"The arch bridge, at ten o'clock on Seventhday," Arik said.

"All right," I said, even though everything in me rebelled against contemplating a future in which Arik and I were separated. "I'll come every Seventhday until I find you. I promise."

The week before our tenth birthday, Father took us to the local Precinct Office for our magic test. An official in a black suit exactly like Father's welcomed us into his office. He seemed not to notice how tense Father was or how frightened Arik and I were.

"I've never tested twins before!" he said with delight. "Who is older?"

"I am," I said.

"We'll test you first then, shall we?" He beckoned me and reached for his shiny horn, which was resting on a soft cloth on his desk. I stared at its twisting pipes and valves. It looked terribly complicated to play.

The official stuck his hand in the bell of the horn, brought the mouthpiece to his lips, and began to play the spell. A bead of silver light appeared in midair and drifted toward my chest. A hum built in the room, amplifying the full, round timbre of the horn. My heart pounded, and my palms grew sticky even though I knew I had magic. When the light hovering in front of me turned green, I couldn't help smiling. I was a magician.

The official lowered his horn. "Congratulations, my dear."

Father pulled me back and nudged Arik forward. I wanted to hold my brother's hand, but we were too far apart. The examiner began to play again. Arik's back was to Father and me. His shoulders were hunched, as though he was bracing himself for pain. The hum built again, and wild hopes swooped through me. Surely Arik would be a magician too. Surely we had worried for nothing.

As the sound grew, Father strode around Arik in order to see the bead of silver light floating in front of him. I darted after him in time to see the light turn an icy blue. Blue meant halan. It meant no magic. It meant adoption. I stared at that light, unwilling to believe my eyes. Then my gaze rose to Arik's face. There was no surprise in his expression, only despair.

The examiner looked in horror from my brother to our father. "The boy is not a magician," he stammered. I realized then that he knew who Father was, knew Father held an important position at the Foreign Office and had once been ambassador to Kiriz. He was afraid to be delivering bad news, though it hardly needed delivering.

"I'm sorry," the official added.

Father unsewed his lips. "This was not unexpected."

His words dismayed me. Had he *known* Arik wasn't a magician? And done nothing about it?

Arik was still staring numbly at the spot where the bead of blue light had been. I threw myself at him, determined never to let go. He staggered under the force of my embrace, but then he held me too.

"He'll be taken to a special dormitory tonight," the official was telling Father. "They'll match him with a halan family soon."

"Isn't he coming home first?" I demanded.

"No," Father said. Arik flinched in my arms.

"What do you mean?" I cried. "He has to. He needs to pack . . ." How could I even talk about Arik packing up his life and leaving us?

"No, he doesn't." Father spoke as though Arik weren't there. "He will not bring anything with him."

"It's better this way, child," the examiner said. He looked anxious. The first pair of twins he'd ever tested for magic, and this had to happen.

"No!" I shouted. "How will Mother say goodbye to him?"

"She . . . she won't," Father said, the hardness in his voice wavering for the first time.

"That's not right!" I was close to panic. They were going to take Arik away right now? I couldn't believe this was how it was done.

Father reached for me, but I backed away, shielding my brother with my body. Something dripped from my chin, and I realized tears were rolling down my cheeks.

"Rivka, stop this nonsense at once," Father said. "You're making a scene."

He came over to pull us apart. I stuck to Arik like a leech, but Father was too strong. As he pried me off, my brother was still, and suddenly I was enraged. Why didn't he fight? Why didn't he hold on to me too?

"Let me go!" I shouted, wriggling. Father's hands on my

arms were like shackles. "The test was wrong! It was a mistake!"

"It's time to go home, Rivka," Father said woodenly, shaking me a little as he hauled me out of the office. The door closed over my brother's face. I let out a sob.

In the auto, I lay sprawled on the backseat while Father drove. I wasn't crying anymore. I was in shock.

After a time, Father said, "I hope you're pleased with your behavior. You profoundly embarrassed me."

I was so angry I thought I would explode. "I don't care," I said. Let him punish me when we got home. Nothing mattered anymore.

Instead of yelling at me, Father sighed. "This is going to be a difficult time for all of us, Rivka. You're turning ten next week. You're not a little girl anymore. I need you to be strong for Mother."

Be strong for *Mother*? Arik was *my* twin, not Mother's. Why was I the one who had to be strong?

At home, Mother was waiting for us in the sitting room. I rushed to her chair and took her hand. "Mother, they kept Arik. Please, we have to bring him back."

She looked beseechingly up at Father, who had come in behind me.

"He is not a magician," Father said simply.

Mother seemed to crumple in her chair. "Oh, Arik, my son . . ."

She sounded as though she'd received news of his death. But he wasn't dead. He was at the Precinct Office.

I turned to Father. "You can make them give him back

to us. You're important. They'd make an exception for you. Besides, we're twins. They can't do this to twins!"

Father's jaw tightened. "No one is above the law, Rivka."

"It's not fair!"

"Be quiet." Father knelt in front of me and took my hands in his. "You are old enough now to understand that this is the way things are. Arik is not the same as you and me and Mother. He is not a magician. He will grow up among people like him."

"You mean halani," I said. "Arik's not a halan!"

"He will be," Father said. "This is for the best. Arik would not have been happy staying with us. He belongs with a halan family."

"But then . . . he's going to be poor?" I said, the full meaning of Arik's adoption beginning to sink in. I couldn't describe it, exactly, but I knew my brother didn't belong among halani. Not only did they have no magic, not only were they poor, but they were . . . less. Everyone knew that. They lived in cramped apartments in run-down neighborhoods. They didn't go to university, usually, and most of them worked in factories. Was that to be my twin's fate? It was the height of injustice.

"I know it's hard to understand right now," Father said. "You're sad and you're going to miss your brother very much, for a while. But you must learn to forget him. The less you think about him, the less you will miss him. Arik is not part of our family anymore."

He spoke gently, but his words broke my heart. I fled upstairs to our room. When I burst through the door and saw Arik's bed, neatly made that morning, it was too much to bear. I threw myself onto my own bed and cried until I gave myself a headache. Nobody came to comfort me.

In the morning, I found Father in the dining room. He was reading the newspaper, a steaming cup of coffee held between his thumb and index finger.

"Father," I said, my voice still watery from all the tears I'd shed the night before.

"Good morning, Rivka," he said without looking at me.

"Isn't there anything we can do about Arik?" I asked.

Father set his coffee cup on its saucer with a click. "Rivka, the matter is closed. I forbid you to mention your brother to me again. You do not have a brother."

I was stunned. In a trance, I walked to my parents' bedroom and knocked on the door. A weary voice said, "Come in."

I padded across the thick carpet to the bed. Mother lay against a great many pillows, her hair loose and limp like riverweed. She was having one of her episodes. It might be days before she rose from her bed. Normally, Arik and I tiptoed down this corridor when Mother was ill, but today I didn't have time to wait for her to feel better.

"Can't you talk to Father about Arik?" I said, looking into her pale face. "He won't listen to me."

She shook her head. A few tears leaked from her eyes, and she lifted a handkerchief to dab them away. "This is the way it has to be, my sweet."

"But don't you love Arik?" Why was no one willing to fight back? Mother had always been meek, but I had never doubted she was on our side. Now my faith in her was shaken.

"Shhh. Come here." Mother stretched out her arms, and I fell into them, half lying across the bed. "I know it's hard. But Father's right. Arik will be better off with his new family."

"That's not true." I struggled out of her embrace. "We need each other."

"You'll understand when you're older," Mother said. "For now, you must do as Father says. Don't talk about Arik. Try to forget him."

She was regurgitating Father's words, and it made me want to die, or else break something expensive. I left her bedside bitterly disappointed.

Betrayed by both my parents, I wandered into the music room where my twin and I had spent so many hours practicing. I found myself fumbling with the clasps of Arik's violin case, tightening his bow, resting his instrument on my shoulder. I began to play the slow movement of an old concerto meant to evoke winter, and with my eyes shut, I could believe Arik was standing beside me, ready to correct me when I played a wrong note. I didn't hear Father's footsteps approaching.

"What do you think you're doing?"

In my fright, I nearly dropped my brother's instrument. Before I could say a word, Father yanked the violin and bow from my grasp.

"Don't you dare touch these," he said, his voice crackling with rage. "Get out."

I hesitated, but when he took a step toward me, I bolted.

The next day, when I came home from school, Arik's violin was gone.

5

Though Mother had told me to forget about Arik, she didn't seem able to take her own advice. Four days after the disastrous magic test, she had grown so lethargic that Father summoned a quartet of healers to play strengthening spells for her. I watched the musicians set up in Mother and Father's bedroom. A maid helped carry in the harpsichord, which one magician painstakingly tuned while his colleagues, a cellist, a violinist, and a recorder player, arranged their chairs and stands. When they began to play, it was the first time I had heard polyphonic spells being cast, and despite my devastation over Arik and my worry for Mother, I was curious. The music was different from the kind I heard at concerts. The spells sounded more mathematical, somehow, composed not to be melodious but instead to shape magic into powerful currents.

The quartet played for an hour. Mother didn't show any improvement.

I remembered the promise my brother and I had made and waited for Seventhday. That morning, the healers came to play for Mother again. I asked Father if I could go for a walk. Distracted by Mother's condition, he gave me permission without paying much attention to my request.

We lived in a neighborhood just north of the city center, and the way to the Sohadir River was familiar to me. I reached the busy street along the water, where flower vendors weaved among automobiles driving in both directions. I crossed with a halan nurse and her tiny kasir charges and walked along the wall overlooking the river. Below me, halan men fished on the banks. I passed the automobile bridge and several iron footbridges with wooden planks. Then ahead of me, I saw it: the stone arch bridge built in the days of the kingdom of Erezai. I broke into a run.

The bridge was crowded with kasir families enjoying the fresh air above the water. I stood in the middle of the bridge and stared down at the swirling brown current, ignoring the people around me. As long as I didn't look, I wouldn't see that Arik wasn't there. I would wait until I heard him call my name, felt his hand on my shoulder. Then I would turn and tackle him in a jubilant hug. Our reunion was so clear in my mind.

But my brother's voice didn't come. No one touched me except to brush past me in their hurry. The hands on the clock tower on the south bank swept past eleven o'clock, twelve o'clock, one o'clock. Finally, I had to accept that Arik wasn't coming. I tried to contain my disappointment. There were all kinds of reasons he might not have been able to make it. It was only the first Seventhday since he'd been taken away.

Nevertheless, I trudged home in a state of utter gloom. When I reached our house, I half expected one of the servants to tell me that my parents were beside themselves and

I'd better have a good explanation for where I'd been all day. But no one came to scold me, and the house was strangely silent. I crept down the hallway to my parents' bedroom. The musicians were gone, but I heard voices. Father was speaking to Mother, too softly for me to make out the words. I couldn't remember when she had last been this ill. I was afraid, but my heart ached so much for my twin that this new fear could not make me much more hopeless than I already was.

Arik did not appear at the arch bridge the following Seventhday, or the one after that. As the weeks passed, I became accustomed to disappointment, but I did not give up hope.

Father continued to summon healers to play at Mother's sickbed, but she wasn't getting better. I knew in my heart that she was distraught over Arik, but she and I didn't speak of him, even when we were alone together. Father's authority was too strong. I hated him for making her suffer in this way, for everything he had done. I hadn't forgiven him for dragging me from the Precinct Office or for ordering me never to say Arik's name in his presence again.

Then one Seventhday, as summer was turning its face toward autumn, I came to the arch bridge and saw Arik there. His nearly black hair, the same shade as mine, had grown long, and he wore the brown trousers and cream shirt of a halan boy, but it was unmistakably him.

I ran, heedless of the automobile barreling up the street. The driver honked furiously at me, but I dodged the gleaming silver bumper and kept on. I reached the bridge and pounded across the flagstones. As if he could sense me coming, Arik turned around. His eyes widened.

Then we were hugging each other, and I was laughing as tears sprang into my eyes. I pulled away to look at him. He looked funny in his halan clothes, with his hair in need of a trim.

"Arik!" I said, still smiling. "You're here! You've never been here before."

His face fell. "I'm sorry, Rivka. It was hard to—"

"It doesn't matter. You're here now!" I hugged him again. "Oh, *Arik.* It's been so horrible. Mother and Father won't talk about you. Father—he didn't send you your violin, did he?"

"My violin? No."

"I knew it," I said, stamping my foot. "He sold it. I hate him!"

Arik just stood there, looking lost and forlorn, and suddenly I was angry.

"Why didn't you fight?" I demanded.

"What?"

"At the Precinct Office. Why did you let them take you?" My anger boiled hotter. "You didn't try to hang on to me when Father pulled me away!"

Arik didn't say anything, and that infuriated me even more. I shoved him, wanting him to react, to say *something.* He stumbled against the bridge railing, staring at me in shock.

"Why didn't you try?" I said, on the verge of tears. "Did you want to leave me?"

"No, Rivka, how could you think that? I've missed you so much. I've . . ." He started to cry.

Horrified, I put my arm around him. Passersby were staring

at us, and I suddenly felt very exposed. We were an odd sight: a kasir girl and a halan boy clinging to each other in the middle of the oldest bridge in Atsan. I tugged Arik toward the south bank. We walked to a park a few blocks away and settled onto a stone bench hidden behind the trunk of an enormous oak tree.

By then, Arik had gotten ahold of himself. "I'm sorry about that day, Rivka. I didn't think there was anything to do."

"It's all right," I said, regretting my outburst. "Tell me what happened after."

Arik leaned against the tree. "After you left the Precinct Office, they drove me to the Hall of Records, by the Senate. There was a little building there, sort of like a school, but really only a waiting place. I stayed there almost a week. Then one morning, a lady brought me to a room where a halan couple was waiting for me. After signing the adoption papers, they took me home."

"Who are they?"

"The Yadons. They own a dry-goods store. They don't have any other children."

"What is it like?"

"It's not so bad." He gazed up at the oak leaves shading us. "I mean, besides the worst parts. I miss you so much, Rivka. I miss Mother. I miss our house and playing the violin. And I hate my school. The teachers are mean, and the other children make fun of me for being a wilding."

"What's not so bad, then?" I said, dismayed.

"My new parents are kind to me. The lady at the Hall of Records told them they couldn't let me talk about my old life, but when I'm homesick, they let me be. They try so hard to make me happy. They're saving up to buy me a violin."

I started to fear that Arik would want to stay with his new family. After all, it sounded like the Yadons were being much nicer to Arik than our parents had been lately.

"You do want to come home, don't you?"

He hesitated. "I do, but I can't, Rivka. We're not supposed to see each other. They told me that at the Hall of Records."

"Well, we don't care about those rules, do we?" I said fiercely.

"No," he agreed. "I'll keep sneaking away to meet you. Every week. Forever. But we can't get caught."

In that moment, I believed we could do it. Though we might grow up in different neighborhoods, attending different schools, the bond between us would never be broken. We sat beneath the old oak, talking and talking, making up for the months we had spent apart. We didn't notice the shadows growing long around us.

Then a group of people came around the tree, and someone said, "There they are."

We froze. Two middle-aged kasir women in plumed hats were regarding us with puzzlement and concern. Accompanying them was a grave-faced police officer.

"I think that's the boy," he told the women. "Thank you for your help."

Before we could run, the police officer grabbed each of us by the arm.

"Do you know the trouble you've caused?" he asked Arik, shaking him. "And you," he said to me, more gently, "who are you? Do you know this boy is a runaway changeling? What are you doing mixing with halan children?"

"He's my brother!" I said hotly. It was the worst thing I could have said. The two ladies gasped in horror, and the policeman swore.

He dragged us to the neighborhood police station. Neither Arik nor I struggled. There was no point. I was furious with myself for letting our first reunion go so badly wrong.

At the station, the policeman sat us down on a bench and made several calls on the heavy metal telephone on the counter.

"Are they going to arrest us?" I whispered to Arik as the officer barked into the mouthpiece.

"I don't know." He was plainly terrified of the police officer, which I didn't understand. Mother and Father had taught us that the police were here to protect us.

After making his telephone calls, the policeman asked me if I wanted anything to drink. He invited me to sit in a chair behind the counter, but I wouldn't leave Arik's side. He didn't offer Arik anything. I couldn't understand why he was treating us so differently when we had committed the same crime. I was still trying to work it out when Father burst into the station, his face dark with rage.

He looked at both of us huddled on the bench but then turned deliberately away from Arik, refusing to see him. All his attention focused on me, and the anger in his eyes made my insides turn to liquid. I pressed myself against Arik, but Father seized me by the arm and lifted me to my feet. With the police officer looking on, I dared not resist. Father curtly thanked the policeman and pulled me toward the exit. I twisted around at the last moment and locked eyes with Arik.

"The bridge," he mouthed.

At home, Father took me directly to my room. I sat on my bed, eyes downcast, while he interrogated me.

"You two planned this, didn't you?"

Though I was shaking with fear, I kept my mouth shut.

"Answer me, Rivka!" he shouted. "And don't lie or I'll take you straight back to the police station."

Would they throw me in a cell? Cowed, I reluctantly said, "Yes."

"Yes, what? You had set a time and a place to meet?"

I nodded.

"This is why you always 'took a walk' on Seventhday?"

I nodded again, miserably, because I was giving everything away. How would Arik and I meet again? Surely now Father would lock me in my bedroom every Seventhday. At least he didn't know where we'd arranged to meet. We'd been found in the park, not on the bridge.

"I'm ashamed of you, Rivka," Father said. Even though I hated him, his words still made me feel worthless. "I thought you had grasped how the world worked. Evidently you have not, so listen to me. You are a kasir. You are a magician. You are not like the halani. They are not like us. None of them. And we do not mix with halani. Do you understand?"

What I heard was: *Your brother is a halan. He is dead to us. You are never to see him again.*

"Do you understand?" Father demanded.

"Yes," I lied.

He wasn't done. "You broke the law today. You were lucky to be let off this once, but if you do it again, you will be sent to prison. *Him* too. You will be punished like criminals."

I started to tremble again. Arik had said what we were doing wasn't allowed, but we hadn't truly known how much we were risking. How long would we be jailed for? Years, I expected. Yet even the threat of prison couldn't quench my desire to see Arik again.

Atsan was blanketed in snow before Father let me leave the house alone again. I regained his trust by being a model daughter. I was meek and obedient. I never spoke of Arik. I earned excellent marks, practiced diligently, and put on a cheerful face at dinner. Inside, I was grief-stricken, but my hatred of Father and my determination to find Arik again allowed me to pull off this massive charade.

That winter, I played it safe at first. Whenever I went out, I told Father exactly where I was going and proved it when I returned, showing him some new hair ribbons or a book borrowed from the library. Gradually, he grew less concerned about my whereabouts. I started going back to the arch bridge. Winter turned into spring, and Arik was never there.

I started the next year at school. Since Arik had been taken away, our old friends had treated me gingerly, as though my family's misfortune might rub off on them. Our teachers had briefly announced Arik's departure and told us, as Father had told me, that we were to forget about him. This effectively prevented my classmates from even expressing their sympathy, but I didn't want their pity anyway. I wanted their righteous anger on my behalf, and that was something

I would never receive. So I drifted away from them, and they let me go.

A year after Arik and I had reunited on the arch bridge, Mother's health entered into a steep decline. I watched doctors and healers come and go with a growing sense of dread. One evening, I was in the music room practicing the newest spell students in my year were expected to master. It was a freezing spell, and I had set a glass of water on the floor in front of me. I could play the notes of the spell perfectly, but no matter how hard I concentrated, the water stubbornly remained liquid.

"Rivka."

I looked up to see Father standing in the doorway. From his expression, I knew he was about to share bad news about Mother. I clutched the neck of my cello.

"The doctors say Mother does not have much time left with us," Father said, each word falling from his lips like a block of lead.

"How much time is not much time?" I heard myself say.

Father swallowed, his hand gripping the doorjamb. "Perhaps a week."

A week. Numb, I lifted my bow again and went through the motions of the spell. With a crack, the water in the glass turned to ice.

I stayed home from school after Father's announcement. We took turns sitting at Mother's bedside. One afternoon while I was with her, she woke.

"Is Nechemya here?" she murmured.

"Father's in his study," I said. "Should I get him, Mother?"

"No," she rasped, struggling to sit up. "Come here, Rivka."

I approached her, though her bloodless cheeks and agitated eyes frightened me.

"I'm so sorry to leave you, my sweet," she whispered. There was a lump in my throat, and I couldn't speak.

"I need . . . to tell you something," she went on. "Your father . . . wouldn't want me to . . . but I think . . . you deserve to know."

"Know what?" I said, disturbed.

"After last fall, they sent Arik . . ." Her eyes fluttered shut.

"Where?" I seized Mother's hand. "Where did they send him?" I had feared that Arik had stopped trying to find me, that he had decided it was best if we forgot each other after all. Now I shivered with new hope.

"Your father . . . was afraid you would find each other . . . again. So he asked the government . . . to send Arik away from Atsan."

I was floored. My brother had been sent to another country?

"He's in Ashara," Mother said.

"Ashara? Are you sure?" It was one of the other city-states of the north lands. Like Atsan, it had once been part of Erezai, before the cold times came and broke up the kingdom.

Mother nodded. The effort of saying so much had exhausted her, and she sank back against her pillow. I held her hand, turning her words over in my mind. This was why we hadn't found each other. Arik hadn't forgotten our pact. And neither had I. But halani weren't usually allowed to travel between city-states. So one day, I would go to him.

Mother died in the night. The funeral was three days later. It was attended by a handful of Mother's friends, most of whom I barely recognized, Mother's brother and his wife, Father's sister, and a number of Father's colleagues from the Foreign Office. After the burial, Father and I returned to a silent house filled with flowers. Their scent was suffocating.

"Well, Rivka," Father said as we shed our coats in the entryway, "it is just you and I now."

It was the closest he'd come to speaking of Arik in over a year. He didn't sound so much sad as lost. But I found it difficult to feel any compassion for him. Mother had died of a broken heart, and I placed the blame squarely on him. He had given up Arik, had *wanted* to be rid of him, and he hadn't understood Mother's love for her son. As far as I was concerned, he'd destroyed our family. What was left was just two people, a former diplomat and his eleven-year-old daughter, living in the same grand and empty house.

6

On my first day of school in Ashara, I walk to Firem in my new uniform: black skirt, white blouse, and black jacket with the Firem Secondary badge. I report to the auditorium where we are to receive our class schedules. Among the first years, it's clear who has gone to Firem since preparatory and who has come to Firem Secondary from another primary school. The students from Firem Primary gather in clusters, exchanging rumors about the teachers their older siblings had. The new students sit by themselves, rubbing their Firem badges as though to reassure themselves that they deserve a place here.

I sink into a velvet-lined seat, dropping my shoulder bag. A girl sitting halfway down the row eyes me, but I pretend not to notice her. Eventually, she comes nearer.

"May I sit next to you?"

I nod, though I don't particularly want to talk to anyone.

She plunks herself down beside me. "You didn't go to Firem Primary either, did you?"

I shake my head.

"My name is Hilah," she says.

"I'm Rivka." Before she asks about my accent, I add, "I'm from Atsan."

"Oh! Did you just move here?"

I nod again, wondering when she's going to stop asking questions. I know she's only being friendly, but soon she'll be asking me things I can't answer.

"Why?"

"My father is the Atsani ambassador to Ashara."

Her jaw drops.

Our conversation has attracted the notice of a girl standing in the aisle. She squeezes her way down the row toward us. Behind her, two other girls are dabbing at one of their blouses with their handkerchiefs, but when the first girl approaches us, they follow. By the way all three move in unison, I can tell they've known each other a long time.

"I'm Merav," says the girl in the lead. She gestures to her friends. "This is Kelilah, and this is Ronit."

"Hello," I say, though Merav's friends aren't paying attention.

"It's no good," Ronit says, examining a spray of grayish spots on her shirt. "That stupid sparker!"

"Did you say your father's an ambassador?" Merav asks me, her light eyes alive with interest.

"Yes," I say. "My name is Rivka Kadmiel."

"She just moved here from Atsan," Hilah says eagerly, but Merav hardly spares her a glance.

"Atsan?" Ronit says, glancing up. "I bet in Atsan sparker delivery boys don't splash you with filthy water on your way to school without even stopping to apologize!"

"Um . . ." I stare at her stained blouse, unsure what to say.

"It's true," says Merav. "You're lucky to be from Atsan. No one's overthrowing governments there."

"Have things changed a lot since the revolution?" I ask. Four years ago, Ashara was struck by a terrifying plague whose cause no one could discover. When it came out that the city's leaders were behind it, and that it had been unleashed to destroy Ashara's halani, there was a rebellion that toppled the Assembly. The new government created in the aftermath gave Ashari halani more political power than halani have anywhere else in the north lands.

Kelilah sighs dramatically. "Halani don't know their place anymore. No wonder, when they got two-thirds of the seats in the United Parliament just like that."

"Wasn't it in proportion to their population?" I dimly recall Father telling me that once.

"Yes," Merav says, "but just because there are more of them doesn't mean they should be in charge. What do halani know about governing?" She gestures at Ronit. "They can't even push a cart around a puddle."

I don't want to keep talking about halani, so instead I introduce Hilah. Merav, Kelilah, and Ronit greet her politely but coolly. Then Merav turns back to me.

"We've been going to Firem since preparatory. We'd be happy to show you around."

"Thank you," I say.

Kelilah and Ronit giggle. Heat creeps up my neck. What did I do?

Merav laughs too. "In Ashara, we say 'my thanks.'"

"Oh."

"I'm going to find Ilanah," Ronit announces. "She's good at stain-removal spells."

I stare after Ronit as she shuffles off. Do Ashari really put spells to such frivolous use? Isn't it for servants to get stains out of one's clothes? An Atsani magician would be embarrassed to cast such a trivial spell in public.

Merav and Kelilah sit with Hilah and me as the headmaster of Firem Secondary calls us to order. The head teachers read off their class rosters and lead their students out of the auditorium. I'm listening so hard for my name that I don't notice any of the other names on the same list until Merav excitedly grips the armrest between us.

"We're in the same class! Kelilah and Ronit too." She beams, and I try to look happy.

We file out of our row. When I notice Hilah following us, I realize she must also be in our class. I feel guilty about the other girls slighting her in my favor, so I wait for her. She smiles briefly but does not speak as we trail after the others.

We enter a classroom and choose seats among the wood and wrought-iron desks. Our head teacher steps onto the platform at the front of the room. He is a slight man of at least sixty years.

"Welcome. I am Aradi Noach, and this is History of the North Lands Novel."

As Aradi Noach writes the title of a book on the blackboard, I hear whispers and catch one of my classmates pointing at a skinny boy sitting in the front row. I can't see his face, but his hair is dark brown. The sleeve of his black jacket is streaked with white dust. It makes him look careless.

The murmurs subside when our teacher turns around. Underlining the title he wrote on the board, he says, "The History of the North Lands Novel begins with this work."

After lecturing for an hour, Aradi Noach dismisses us to morning recess. I follow the pack out into an arcade that borders a sun-soaked courtyard.

Hilah comes up behind me. "Shall we join them?" she asks, nodding at Merav and her friends.

"I guess."

When we approach, Merav is complaining about the boy everyone was whispering about. "I can't believe he's in our class! He's got nerve, sitting at the front like he has more right to be here than anyone else."

She looks pointedly across the courtyard, and to my horror, I see the boy walking right past us, well within earshot. He's carrying a book under his arm, as well as a slate dusted with chalk. That explains the white marks on his sleeve.

"Merav," I murmur, nodding in his direction.

"Oh, he can't hear us, Rivka," she says loudly.

"I think he can," I say, still in an undertone even though the boy hasn't glanced our way. He sits down on the step of the arcade and opens his book. His black uniform doesn't quite fit him, and his badge looks somehow wrong.

Merav gives me a condescending smile. "Rivka, he's deaf."

"Deaf?" I say, astonished. How could a deaf student have followed Aradi Noach's lecture? And how does Merav know he's deaf anyway? "Do you know him?"

Ronit can hardly contain herself. "Rivka, that's *Caleb Levi*."

The name is obviously supposed to mean something to me, but I don't know what. Except Levi was the surname of . . .

"Marah Levi's younger brother," Kelilah says gleefully.

Hilah breathes in sharply. For a second, I cannot breathe at all.

"Marah Levi has a kasir brother?" I finally manage. Marah Levi, the halan girl who found the cure to the dark eyes plague and brought down the Assembly of Ashara four years ago? Her younger brother is a kasir? Did Marah get to keep him?

"What? No," Merav says scornfully. "He's a halan. Can't you tell?"

I steal another glance at the boy. She's right. His hair would be a little long for a kasir boy's. And his uniform is not only ill fitting but rather shabby. He probably got it secondhand.

"He doesn't even go here, really," Kelilah says. "My father works at the Education Bureau and told me everything. He's just taking a couple of classes."

"Halani can do that?" I ask.

Merav sniffs. "Technically, Firem's integrated, but everyone knows that's not really true. He's only being allowed to take classes here because he's Marah Levi's brother. She's how he got into the school for the deaf too. That's also a kasir school."

"And even that wasn't good enough for him," Kelilah says.

"I can't believe he goes here," I say. Merav nods approvingly, assuming I share their outrage, but that's not what I mean. I can't believe I'm in the same class as the brother of the most famous girl in the north lands. Marah Levi is a legend. She may be a halan, but she, along with a kasir boy named Azariah Rashid, saved Ashara from the plague and revealed to the world that the Assembly was carrying out a decades-old plan to exterminate the halani of Ashara. And she was my age when she did it.

"Should we introduce ourselves?" Hilah asks, looking at Caleb.

Merav, Kelilah, and Ronit gape at her.

"Have you lost your mind?" Merav says. "Why would we talk to him?"

Hilah returns Merav's gaze without flinching, and I feel a spark of admiration for her. "Why not?" she says. "He *is* our classmate."

"He is not our *classmate*," Merav says. "He's an interloper." Her eyes narrow. "Who are you, anyway? What's your surname? What primary school did you go to?"

I'm startled by the sudden interrogation, which seems needlessly aggressive.

"My surname is Menachem," Hilah says. "My mother is the governor of Orev County, and I grew up in Daresh. There's no kasir school in Daresh, so I've had tutors until now."

Merav clicks her tongue. "Daresh? That's a village in the middle of nowhere, isn't it? Were there even any other kasiri there?"

"Just the constable's family," Hilah says.

"No wonder," Merav says, her tone a mixture of pity and

contempt. "You're in the city now, Hilah. We don't talk to halani."

Hilah frowns. "They're not another species, you know. All my friends growing up were halani."

I wince. Ronit and Kelilah give little shrieks, and Merav's expression is one of naked disgust.

"You were friends with halani?" she says in a hushed, dangerous voice.

Hilah flushes. "There was no one else to play with. Nobody minded, as long as we all came home for dinner."

There is an ugly pause, and I can tell Merav is dragging it out, trying to strike fear into Hilah's heart.

"Wait," Ronit says, suddenly suspicious, "you don't think kasiri and halani *should* go to school together, do you?"

"Of course not!" Hilah says, too quickly.

"If you want to belong here," Merav says, "stay away from the sparker." Her friends don't even flinch to hear her call Caleb that name.

Kelilah laughs nervously. "You don't make friends with halani in Atsan, do you, Rivka?"

"No," I say automatically. It's true; back home, I hardly ever spoke to halani other than our servants. But I regret my swift answer. I'm just piling onto Hilah, and she doesn't deserve it. I try to give her a sympathetic smile, but she's gazing at her shoes.

7

After recess, my class has Magic, but I'm exempt because I'm an Atsani magician and we don't cast spells the Ashari way. Father is taking it upon himself to see to my magical education while we're in Ashara. I'm not looking forward to evening lessons with him twice a week, but for now, I have a free period, so I make my way to the library. I push open the heavy door and find myself in a reading room furnished with long tables, straight-backed chairs, and electric lamps with emerald-green shades. Through the doorways to my right and left, I can make out the stacks. Behind the librarian's desk, a young woman is perched on a stool.

The only other student in the reading room is Caleb Levi. Of course he has a free period too. A halan wouldn't be taking Magic. If he hasn't gone back to the school for the deaf, it probably means he has Epic Poetry with us next period and doesn't have time to return to his other school between our two literature classes.

I sit down two tables away from him, take out a notebook, and ponder the exercise Father set me for our first lesson tomorrow evening. My task is to compose a spell to strengthen glass. Doodling in the margins of my notebook, I recall other strengthening spells I've learned, for sewing needles, earthenware, wood. They're all in A major, so I should probably stick to that key. Glass is made of sand. Will I need to take that into account?

The period is almost over when two boys enter the library. They head toward the stacks, but then one of them catches sight of Caleb.

"You! Levi!" he says in a loud whisper.

Caleb has gone very still.

"Sparker boy! We're talking to you!"

Caleb sweeps his books into his schoolbag, gets to his feet, and starts to walk toward the library door. The boys cut him off. He stops, uncertain. Something about the way he doesn't try to sidestep them suggests he knows it won't be so easy to get away. They're both a head taller than him.

I look quickly around the reading room. The librarian sits at her desk, absorbed in a book.

One of the boys says something I can't make out to Caleb. He shakes his head and offers up his slate with the piece of chalk tied to it. Smirking, the kasir boy takes the slate and scrawls something on it. His companion snickers. Part of me wishes I could see what he's written, and part of me is glad I can't.

Caleb stares at whatever the boy wrote on his slate. He doesn't react. After a few seconds, he tries to take the slate back, but the kasir boy doesn't let go. Instead, he brings the slate down hard against his thigh, breaking it in two.

I'm disgusted with myself for watching while doing

nothing, but I can't confront those boys. I'm not afraid of them turning on me. I'm afraid of them asking themselves why a girl like me would come to a halan's defense. Still, since they're making a disturbance, I approach the circulation desk.

"Excuse me?"

The librarian's head snaps up. "Yes?"

"Um . . ." I peer over my shoulder. The kasir boys have Caleb Levi backed up against a table. His broken slate lies on the floor.

The young woman follows my gaze and then looks back at me. "Is there a problem?"

For a moment, I think she's just unbelievably obtuse. When the truth hits me, it takes my breath away. Two boys are about to attack a first year in the library, and she has no intention of doing anything. No prizes for guessing why.

The bell chimes, signaling the close of second period and distracting Caleb's tormenters. He wriggles free of their grasp and dashes out of the library. The boys let him go, laughing.

As I suspected, Caleb is in my next class too. The Epic Poetry teacher doesn't write a single thing on the blackboard the entire period. Even though Caleb sits in the front row, I wonder how much of the lesson he can follow. Is someone taking notes for him?

After Epic Poetry, it's lunchtime. The dining hall is a dark-paneled room with a vaulted ceiling and tall windows that let in the spring sunshine. While I wait in line with Merav, Kelilah, Ronit, and Hilah, I look around for Marah Levi's brother, but he has disappeared.

Halan women behind the kitchen counter fill our plates with roasted potatoes, glazed asparagus, and herb-crusted fish, and we help ourselves to cookies flecked with lemon peel. Then the five of us claim a round table. Immediately, the girls start peppering me with questions.

"What is Atsan like?"

"What's it like being the daughter of an ambassador?"

"Have you traveled all over?"

I answer as best I can, unaccustomed to being the center of attention and not enjoying it much.

"Your accent is so charming," Kelilah says.

"What does your mother do?" Merav asks, taking a dainty bite of fish.

"My mother died a few years ago," I say.

There is an awkward pause.

"I'm sorry," Merav says, the required response.

"Was it the . . . ?" Kelilah begins.

"Don't be stupid," Ronit hisses. "They didn't have the dark eyes in Atsan."

"Oh, right," Kelilah says, embarrassed. "I forgot your family wasn't here then. Only, that's what everyone thinks of first now . . ."

How strange it must be to live in the shadow of a plague.

"Do you have any brothers or sisters?" Hilah asks.

The question is perfectly ordinary, but it feels jarring. At home, everyone knew about Arik, and people were scared to even mention brothers in my presence. That meant I rarely had to lie about my twin. But now I must.

"No," I tell Hilah. Surprisingly, it doesn't hurt to deny

Arik. I've kept my love for him a secret for so long that it feels almost natural.

"You're going to be here a long time, aren't you?" Ronit says.

"Probably," I say. "I'm sure I'll at least finish secondary school here. After that, I might go back to Atsan for university." But maybe not, if I find Arik. If he's made his life in Ashara, I will too, so we can be together.

"Shouldn't you learn Ashari magic, then?" Merav says.

I shrug.

"What's your magic like?" Kelilah asks. "Will you show us a musical spell?"

"Show you?" I say hesitantly. These Ashari seem so casual about their magic. In Atsan, spells have a more ceremonial quality to them. Magic is a serious discipline, almost an art, not something to be used for every little thing. One-voiced spells aren't even considered to be of much importance. It's the elaborate polyphonic spells that are the real measure of a magician's skill, both in composition and casting.

"Do you need your instrument?" Hilah asks. "What do you play?"

"Cello," I say. "Our instruments are amplifiers. They make spells stronger. But I don't need my cello for a little spell."

"Well, show us something!" Merav says. It's almost a command.

I can't decide whether Father would be horrified at my casting a pointless spell like a dog performing tricks or pleased at my representing Atsan. What would it hurt to show them one simple Atsani spell though? I glance over the table, taking in the plates scraped clean of potatoes and fish, the rumpled napkins, the cookie crumbs. Then my eyes light on Merav's glass of water.

I fix my gaze on the water and clear my mind of all distractions. Between the sound of voices, the clink of cutlery, my discomfort at being watched by four Ashari girls, and my misgivings about casting the spell at all, it's not easy. Finally, I find my focus. It's a feeling of simultaneously narrowing my concentration onto one object and opening my mind to the magic around me.

I sing the wordless melody of the Vapor, a basic spell I learned years ago in primary school. It appears as a motif in ancient, multi-voiced spells once used to bring favorable weather to the fields. As I sing, the water in Merav's glass trembles, then bubbles, then boils violently. Steam curls up from the glass. Within seconds, the water has evaporated.

My Firem classmates look suitably impressed.

"Let me show you an Ashari spell," Merav says.

She holds out her right hand, her thumb and ring finger pinched together, and pronounces an incantation. Her empty glass lifts from the table and hovers before her at eye level. A smoky scent overpowers the smell of fish. She utters another phrase, and the scent grows spicier, though the floating glass stays where it is.

Merav waits for my reaction, and I make myself smile, though I'm distracted by her spell. Up close, it's startling how different Ashari magic feels. It works, undeniably, but the way it pulls on the surrounding magic is somehow off. The sensation is like lacing my fingers with the other thumb on top, or trying to play the cello left-handed.

Idly, I hum the melody of the levitation spell I know. Merav's spell shivers, and I break off in astonishment. It was like I was intruding into the spaces between the currents of magic she'd established. Curious, I sing quietly again, but not any particular spell. I choose the notes I need to worm my way into the weak spots of the Ashari spell and burst them apart with music. Merav frowns, and the next instant, the glass falls to the table with a crack. Everyone jumps.

"I'm sorry!" I say. Luckily, the glass didn't break.

"What did you do?" Merav demands.

"I—I don't know," I stammer. "I was just improvising . . . I didn't mean to break your spell."

Merav says nothing, her expression still resentful.

✢ ✢ ✢

The next day, Caleb Levi is back at Firem with a new slate. He sits in the front row in History of the North Lands Novel and Epic Poetry and talks to no one.

"He won't be able to keep up," Merav says at lunch as she slices into her chicken. "What's the point of taking these classes when he can't even hear what the teacher is saying?"

"Maybe he can lip-read," Hilah says.

Merav ignores her. "Don't they teach literature at the school for the deaf? I don't see why he should get to come to Firem."

"Mother was so upset when I told her he was in our class," Ronit says. "She says at this rate it won't be long before there aren't any good schools left in Ashara."

"Firem can't get taken over by the likes of Caleb Levi,"

Merav says, scandalized. "The whole point of Firem is that it only takes the best."

"Right," says Kelilah. "Why should we share our school with the sparkers? We made Ashara what it is. They should be grateful."

Merav looks expectantly at me, waiting for me to agree with them, but I can't. Arik is a halan, and he's brilliant and talented. Of course, he's different from other halani because he was first raised a Kadmiel, but I can't deny that he's living among halani now. That means Merav and Ronit are talking about him, and I can't bring myself to match their disdainful remarks with one of my own.

At last, Merav clears her throat. Kelilah and Ronit look at me accusingly. At the same time, something like satisfaction glints in their eyes. Merav reached out to befriend me, but she has found me wanting, and I stand no chance in the competition for her favor. I don't care. I didn't come to Ashara to make friends. I came to find Arik. And once I do, I won't need friends anyway.

8

The first weekend after school starts, Father hosts a party at the embassy. The guests include the leaders of Ashara's United Parliament, officials from the Department of Foreign Affairs, and other ambassadors.

Around seven o'clock, I change into a dark red dress and put on a pearl necklace I inherited from Mother. Then I glide down the steps to the chancery drawing room. Father is greeting a regal, middle-aged woman, kissing her on both cheeks as though he does this every day. While he's talking to her, three men in black suits come in. They might be Ashari parliamentarians. A ruddy-faced gentleman with hair the color of dead grass and eyes the color of the sky follows on their heels. He must be a foreign ambassador, perhaps from Aevlia, where people have eyes that blue and hair that light. Immediately after him comes another foreigner with dark brown skin and black hair like moss. The Fadran ambassador, I'd guess.

As the room fills, two maids weave through the throng, offering everyone glasses of wine and miniature meat pastries. I hover by the mantel and watch Father move easily among his guests until he beckons me to his side.

"You look very nice this evening, Rivka," he says. "I would like to introduce you to Shimshon Omri, from Foreign Affairs."

I turn toward the gentleman he was talking to and stretch my lips into a smile.

"I understand you're in the same class as my daughter at Firem," Banar Omri says.

I have no idea whose surname is Omri.

"Merav," he supplies, his eyes twinkling.

"Oh," I say. What has Merav told her father about me?

Before I can find out, Father whisks me off to more introductions. Soon, I've met everyone except for a handful of local officials huddled in one corner. Once, I notice Deputy Liron making polite and, from the looks of it, forced conversation with them, but when I glance back, she's gone.

When it's time for dinner, we move to the dining room. A shimmery cloth covers the long table, and each place is set with gleaming silverware and a crystal wine glass. I slip into my assigned seat, where I find myself surrounded by parliamentarians and officials whose names I have forgotten. As the maids come around with shallow, gold-rimmed bowls of velvety mushroom soup, they begin talking to me.

"I've heard so many good things about you, Gadin Kadmiel," the white-haired parliamentarian on my left says. "Like what a talented musician you are."

"Your father is so proud of you," the tiny woman on my right adds.

I smile shyly, but I don't believe any of it. Father's not

proud of me. He uses my accomplishments to prove what a good daughter he's raised. All he cares about is the Kadmiels being seen as the perfect Atsani family.

"And you were admitted to Firem too," the man next to Banar Omri says. "What do you think about having Marah Levi's brother there this year?"

"It's exciting," I say without thinking. Everyone looks taken aback.

"Exciting?" the white-haired parliamentarian asks, lifting one eyebrow.

"I mean because he's Marah Levi's brother," I say. I glance nervously at Merav's father. Surely she gets the ideas she spouts at school from him.

They all laugh at me in the indulgent way that adults laugh at children, and I'm too relieved that they don't suspect me of harboring halan sympathies to feel annoyed.

"So Marah Levi is famous even in Atsan?" the small woman says.

"Of course!" I say. "She and Azariah Rashid are heroes. Everyone knows that."

"True," the old parliamentarian says. "But they set events into motion that led to far more drastic changes in Ashara than were needed. Certainly the Assembly was full of dangerous madmen who had to be stopped. But Marah and Azariah did not understand what they were doing. They upended the order of things in Ashara when ousting the Assembly leaders would have been enough."

Is that true? I try to remember the story of how Marah and Azariah saved Ashara, but the details are hazy. I know they cured the dark eyes and prevented the extermination of the halani. Did they really bring about too much change? The Assembly was going to let the halani die of the dark eyes. When it came to light that the plague had been created precisely for that purpose, everyone was outraged. In Atsan, people wondered how things could have gone so wrong in Ashara. If I were a halan and the people running my city were trying to kill me, I'd certainly want to be in charge.

But maybe the problem wasn't kasir rule. After all, kasiri brought the north lands through the cold times and the collapse of the kingdom of Erezai. They know what they're doing in the other city-states. There are things I'd change, with the kidnapping of children like my brother at the top of the list. But as long as the leaders are good, does it matter if they're all kasiri?

"The way I see it, we should be grateful she got her brother in," the woman on my right is saying. "This way, Firem can say it's integrated, and those radicals at the Education Bureau won't harass the headmaster about breaking the integration laws."

One halan student in the entire secondary school hardly makes Firem look integrated, especially not when that student is only part-time and happens to be the brother of the most famous halan in Ashara, but maybe it's the gesture that counts.

"You have a point," Banar Omri says grudgingly. "Caleb Levi may be the only thing standing between students like my daughter and Rivka and a whole swarm of halani at Firem."

I hunch over my soup, resenting being grouped with Merav.

"If the boy is as intelligent as they say, I am not opposed to his taking classes at Firem," the old parliamentarian says, sounding as though he expects to be congratulated for his generosity. "There will always be a few extraordinary halani who can thrive at an elite school. But schools like Firem should not be forced to lower their standards for the sake of integration."

"Integration would not force Firem to lower its standards," a new voice says. Everyone at our end of the table turns to face the woman who has interrupted our conversation. She is about sixty years old, and her gray hair falls in a straight curtain behind her shoulders. I haven't been introduced to her yet tonight.

"All integration would do is require Firem to consider both halan and kasir students," she continues. "They could still take the best."

"Impossible," Merav's father says. "Halan and kasir primary schools are not comparable. Even a halan student with perfect grades will not be as well prepared as the average kasir student."

"True, because halan schools have far less money than kasir schools," the woman replies. "But halani and kasiri all take the same secondary-school entrance exam. Why not just use those scores?"

The adults around me fall into a hostile silence, and it finally dawns on me that this woman must be a halan. I can't believe Father invited any, but perhaps there are halan leaders in Parliament he can't afford to offend. Before she entered the conversation, the guests were talking as though there were no halani present. I feel embarrassed for them, but none of them seem the least bit sorry.

There doesn't seem to be any way for this conversation to end well. Fortunately, the maids begin serving the next course, an Atsani lamb stew with mint sauce. The halan settles back into her chair, and the kasir officials turn their attention to the food.

⤳ ⤳ ⤳

After the party, the invitations come pouring in. Father doesn't eat another meal at the embassy the entire weekend. On Tenthday afternoon, while he's visiting a parliamentarian in the suburbs, I set out from the embassy in my least fancy clothes to search for Arik again. Beyond Embassy Row, I follow the throngs heading east along the river to a huge marketplace. Under a roof on stilts, vendors are selling everything from sausages to straw hats. The aisles are packed with halani and kasiri alike.

Hovering at the edge of the square, I consult my Ashari guidebook. This is the Ikhad, and the book mentions that Tenthday is the busiest market day here. Why didn't I think to visit before? Given how many halani there are, it doesn't seem unlikely that Arik might come here too.

I'm tempted to stay and look for my brother, but I can come back to the Ikhad whenever I want. I should take advantage of Father's long absence this afternoon to venture farther afield. Peeking in the walker's guide, I locate another lower-class district and start walking east.

I know when I've reached the halan neighborhood because it looks the same as the first one I visited. The apartment buildings are worn and darkened by time. The snow is almost all gone, leaving patches of salt, sand, and dirt crusted on the cobblestones. What must it be like to live in a place where everything is grimy and the buildings themselves look exhausted? I hate to think of Arik having spent the last four years somewhere like this.

I walk up and down the streets of the neighborhood, noting every person I see. Two young women in bright knit shawls, shopping baskets bouncing on their arms. A gaggle of children in an alley building a fort out of crates bristling with rusty nails. An elderly man smoking a pipe on a bench. Then I have the bad luck of crossing paths with a woman I've already seen this afternoon. I recognize her green scarf. She gives me a funny look, and I decide it's time to leave. I haven't seen a single halan boy my age. Feeling defeated, I return to Embassy Row.

9

At lunchtime on Firstday, Merav, Ronit, and Kelilah are all aflutter about some party coming up. My attention drifts in and out of the dining hall as I ponder where to look for Arik next.

"Mother says we can use the drawing room," Merav is saying. "My older brother's going to teach us a new card game. And there will be chocolate."

According to the walker's guide, there's a halan quarter on the north bank of the Davgir.

"Chocolate!" Kelilah says rapturously. "I can't wait."

But maybe I should go back to the Ikhad instead.

"Rivka."

I look up, jolted from my reverie.

"I'm having a party this weekend," Merav says. "You're invited."

"Oh." I wasn't expecting that. I can't remember the last time I went to a friend's house in Atsan. After Arik was taken away and things became awkward between my school friends and me, I began to decline their invitations to come over. After a while, they stopped asking me.

"Will you come?" Merav presses me.

I glance at Hilah sitting beside me. I may have been daydreaming, but I'm pretty sure Merav hasn't invited her.

"It's on Seventhday afternoon," Merav adds.

Seventhday afternoon. The walker's guide said Seventhday is another Ikhad market day. If I go to Merav's, I won't have much time to look for Arik there. Besides, I don't really want to go to her party if I'm going to have to eat chocolate while listening to her pour contempt on halani.

"Thank you for the invitation, but I can't," I say. "My father and I have plans for Seventhday already." I'm scrambling to think of what those plans might be, but she doesn't ask. She just looks down at her beef stew without saying anything.

When I come home from school, Deputy Liron is in the chancery foyer inspecting the mail. She looks up from an envelope splashed with a bright red seal and smiles. "How was your day, Rivka?"

"Fine." I'm eager to go up to my room, but politeness prevents me from scuttling away.

Father's deputy appears to be in no rush to return to her office. "How are you adjusting to life in Ashara?"

I'm at a loss as to how to answer. If I give a cheerful reply, she probably won't believe me. I can hardly tell her the truth, though. Her kindness seems genuine, but it makes me uneasy. I can't be sure Father hasn't put her up to this.

"I'm doing all right," I say. "I'm certainly not unhappier than I was in Atsan. At least I feel like I'm in the right place."

"It must be hard to see so much less of your father," Deputy Liron says. At my blank expression, she adds,

"Because being ambassador keeps him so busy."

Does she imagine we used to spend cozy evenings together in Atsan? Father and I talk exactly as much as we did before we moved, which is to say very little. His many absences are actually a relief since I have to be constantly on my guard around him.

"You aren't lonely?" Deputy Liron says gently.

Her words are jarring. Back in Atsan, I spent almost all my time alone. Of course, classmates swirled around me and Father saw me every day, but I wasn't really *with* these people even when in their presence. I've been lonely since Arik left, and nobody has ever thought to ask me if I wanted not to be lonely anymore.

"I'm all right," I tell Deputy Liron again, fidgeting with the shoulder strap of my schoolbag.

"I can't help noticing that you don't send or receive any mail from Atsan," she says, waving the stack of envelopes. "Are you not keeping in touch with your friends back home?"

Why is she so concerned about my social life? She's Father's deputy, not my mother.

"There's no one I really want to write to," I say shortly.

"Are you making friends at Firem?"

Are Merav, Kelilah, and Ronit my friends? Merav did invite me to her party, but I can't forget the look she gave me that first day when I accidentally broke her spell. Then there's Hilah, who sticks to me like a burr and whom the others barely tolerate.

"There are some girls I sit with at lunch." If she were Father, I would say no more, but something makes me go on.

"I think they only want to be my friends because Father's an ambassador though."

Deputy Liron smiles sympathetically. "Once they get to know you better, I'm sure they'll appreciate you for who you really are."

I drop my gaze. Nobody is ever going to appreciate me for who I really am. Who I really am is Rivka Kadmiel, sister to Arik Kadmiel, a halan. And I can't tell anyone that.

"You're allowed to invite friends to the residence, you know," Father's deputy says.

Determined to end this interview, I put on a sweet face and say, "Maybe I will."

* * *

The second week of school comes to an end. On Seventh-day, before Father leaves for morning coffee with the Kirizi ambassador, I tell him I'm going out walking. I spend most of the day at the Ikhad, wandering up and down the aisles and watching the sea of faces in hopes of glimpsing a familiar one. Whenever I see a boy about my age from behind, my body tenses in anticipation, bracing itself for disappointment. I can't rest until I've gotten a look at his face. There are boys dressed in expensive black wool coats or white shirts made of the finest cotton. There are boys from the countryside with homespun shirts and callused hands, selling cheese and eggs. The few city halan boys I see are never Arik.

Short of going door to door in halan neighborhoods, I don't know how I'm going to find him. I don't know which part of the city he lives in. I don't know what his new name is. It's looking more and more like I'll have to wait for our paths to cross accidentally. The idea makes me grit my teeth. It's not good enough.

After a frustrating day at the market, I still have to face my magic lesson with Father. Tonight I'm to assist him in renewing a ward on the embassy. This is no practice spell but a real enchantment that guards the house. Father has never called upon me to help cast the wards on our home before, either here or in Atsan, and I know it's both an honor and a test. I'm afraid of bungling my part even though I've been practicing the cello music feverishly all week.

We unpack our instruments in the music room and carry them down to the chancery foyer. As the entryway to the whole house, it's the best place to cast protective spells. Father and I sit opposite each other on armless chairs. While he plays warm-up trills on his silver flute, I smooth the music on my stand. The ward takes up an entire page.

"So," Father says, lowering his flute, "remind me what this ward is."

"It guards against rot," I say, staring at the thick clusters of notes.

He nods. "And how does this two-voiced version differ from the monophonic version I cast by myself when we first moved into the embassy?"

He's checking how much I remember from my lesson on Secondday. Speaking slowly so as not to blurt out something wrong, I explain the advantages of the more complex ward. As I talk, my awareness of the layers of spells around me grows increasingly sensitive. Most of the time, I don't pay much attention to the net of wards cast on the house; it's like a faint background noise, easily tuned out. But now that we're preparing to modify the enchantments, I can feel each current of magic like a taut rope.

When Father is satisfied that I've mastered the theory of rot wards, he straightens his music and asks, "Are you ready?"

I wipe my damp palms on my skirt, and we begin to play.

Afterward, when the spell has been successfully cast and we're putting our instruments away, Father says, "You did well, Rivka."

"Thank you, Father," I say, pleased but mostly relieved.

He closes his flute case and turns to me. "I am speaking before Parliament tomorrow. Would you like to accompany me?"

"What?" I say, startled by the invitation.

"Someone at the embassy party suggested you might be interested in observing a session of Parliament."

I must have made a good impression on his dinner guests. "What are you speaking about?"

"Smuggling across the Atsani-Ashari border. The United Parliament has some questions, which I will answer on behalf of the Senate."

"I see." I think quickly. I could spend tomorrow wandering around another halan district, but the thought exhausts me. And I am curious to see how Ashara's United Parliament works.

"I'd like to come," I tell Father.

In the morning, the embassy chauffeur drives Father and me to Parliament. I recognize the building as the one my walker's guide calls the Assembly Hall. I follow Father through the huge carved doors, across a soaring atrium with a green floor, up a grand staircase, and into an enormous, windowless chamber. A gold-carpeted aisle slopes down to the front of the room, where three ranks of wooden desks are arranged in a semicircle. On either side of the aisle are rows of benches. Below the parliamentarians' desks, a handful of young men and women sit on wooden chairs, sorting paperwork.

"I'm going down there," Father says, pointing to the front bench. "You should find somewhere else to sit."

He marches down the aisle, leaving me to fend for myself. The benches on either side of me are already half-filled, and there is a stark divide: halani on the left, kasiri on the right. I shuffle into an empty bench toward the front of the kasir section and fold my hands in my lap.

The halan side of the chamber is much emptier than ours. There are a few old women in embroidered shawls and a handful of bearded men kneading their flat caps. The only bench in their section that is even close to full is one near the front, where a group of young men and women old enough to be done with secondary school are sitting together.

A few rows in front of me sits a young man with curly black hair. He's about the same age as the halan youths across the aisle, and I notice him glancing their way every few seconds.

I crane my neck to see where Father has gone. He's sitting in the front row, behind a desk that faces the parliamentarians' seats. Besides him, three other people are waiting to testify. Two of them look like government officials, but the last is a young halan woman. Her dark brown hair hangs in a braid down the back of her blue cardigan. My curiosity spikes. What could she have to say to Parliament?

A door at the front of the chamber swings open, and the parliamentarians file in. There are twenty-one of them. I recognize several from the embassy party, including the halan woman who argued with the kasir guests about school integration. Today, her gray hair is plaited in a braid that reaches her waist. The brass nameplate on her desk reads *Ayelet Nitsan, Horiel District*.

A different parliamentarian rises and declares the session under way. "First order of business: approving funding for the new eastern streetcar line."

The representative from Gishal District introduces a proposal to allot a certain amount of money to building the streetcar line. A heated argument immediately breaks out over whether the cost is too high, the number of stops planned excessive, and the construction workers' wages too generous. Within minutes, I'm fighting to stay awake.

I rouse myself when the presider announces the second order of business. "This is a citizen's petition." He nods at one of Father's seatmates, and the young woman stands up. As she walks to the testifier's desk, the gaze of every parliamentarian follows her. The chamber has become very quiet.

The presiding parliamentarian clears his throat. "Please state your name for the record."

The girl raises her head, and her dark brown braid slides down her back. "My name is Marah Levi."

10

I gasp, and I'm not the only one. Only the parliamentarians do not look surprised that the girl who saved Ashara from the dark eyes is here today. Caleb Levi's older sister. She looks so ordinary.

"Good morning," Marah Levi says, gazing up at the rows of parliamentarians. "I've come today on behalf of a halan family I know. Their oldest child was found to have magic this past week, and she is due to be taken from her family on Firstday and placed with adoptive kasir parents."

A whirring sound starts up in my ears. Marah Levi is talking about a wilding. Father would never have brought me to Parliament today if he'd known someone would testify about *this*. I must not look his way. I don't know what he'd see in my expression.

"I'm here to ask you not to take this girl away from her parents," Marah Levi continues, her voice thin but unwavering. "They love her and don't want to give her up. I realize that special favors are more likely to be granted to me and to those I speak for. So what I'm really asking is for you not only to let this girl stay with her family but also to end all forced adoptions. It's cruel to take children away from their families over a question of magic."

The chamber rings with a stunned silence. What Marah Levi is requesting is enormous.

"I know what I'm asking requires the law to be changed," she says, her voice growing stronger. "So I would like to make a smaller request, namely, that forced adoptions be temporarily suspended while Parliament considers changing the law. To be clear, I would like this girl to be able to remain with her halan family legally for now, and I would like other children whose magical status doesn't match their parents' to be able to do the same."

Half a dozen parliamentarians jump to their feet, burning to speak. The presider first gives the floor to a white-haired man who I think is a kasir.

"Gadin Levi," he says, "you are in essence asking Parliament to stop enforcing a number of the Family Laws."

"I understand that," Marah Levi replies. Everyone seems to expect her to go on, but she doesn't, and her silence strikes me as powerful.

Another parliamentarian I don't recognize speaks next. "It would be foolish to allow mixed families. Halani and kasiri are fundamentally different and have lived apart for centuries. The United Parliament exists to mediate between us and make sure everyone is treated fairly, but blurring the lines between our communities would only lead to more conflict."

"I completely disagree." It's the halan parliamentarian from the embassy party. She tosses her gray braid over her shoulder and looks squarely at her colleagues. "Keeping our communities separate is holding us back from real equality. To become a truly united society, we should start by refusing to sort our children into opposing camps."

A kasir parliamentarian pounds his fist on his desk. "Mixed families would spell Ashara's doom. It would dilute the gift of magic in the population until magicians simply died out."

Marah Levi leans forward across the testifier's desk. "I don't see how allowing a girl with magic to grow up in her halan family would dilute anything, sir."

"What would she be?" the kasir demands. "Not a halan, since she's a magician. But if she isn't raised by kasiri, she won't be a kasir either. She'll grow up confused. And anyway, ending adoptions would almost certainly lead to intermarriage. But perhaps that is your hope, Gadin Levi?"

To my surprise, Marah Levi does not reply. Her posture is rigid, and there is something sour about the silence where her answer should be.

"Take care, Parliamentarian Zevulun," Horiel's representative says to the kasir legislator. "Your talk of dilution sounds very much like the Assembly's line about kasir blood."

All the parliamentarians tense. It takes me a moment to understand what she means. Then I remember why the Assembly tried to kill off the halani with the dark eyes plague. They were afraid halani would one day so outnumber kasiri that magicians would go extinct in Ashara.

Zevulun's face darkens. "How dare you? I have nothing but contempt for the Assembly and their plot. Of course Ashara needs its halani. But it also needs its kasiri, and the only way to preserve a thriving population of magicians is with the Family Laws."

"There will always be magicians in Ashara," the parliamentarian from Horiel says.

"Indeed, Parliamentarian Nitsan? Look around you!" Zevulun gestures at their colleagues. "Today kasiri make up one-third of Parliament. How many years before that is only one-quarter, only one-tenth? How many years before we are squeezed out entirely?"

"Have you lost your mind?" Nitsan demands. "The Assembly didn't create the dark eyes in order to wipe out the *kasiri*! Just who do you think should be worried about their continued existence in this city?"

"Colleagues, we are getting bogged down," the presider says. "I would like to bring the discussion back to Gadin Levi's petition. Speaking of which, Gadin Levi, is there any proof of the facts you have presented?"

"I requested that the examiner's report from the District Hall be available this morning," Marah Levi says. Immediately, a young man seated below the parliamentarians' desks leaps up and delivers a document to the presider.

The presider scans the page. "This confirms that Samira Harun was tested and found to have magic on Secondday. The examiner referred her case to the Office of Family Affairs, recommending, of course, her removal from the household of her parents, Mahir Harun and Nadia Daud . . ."

Murmuring breaks out among the parliamentarians as well as among the public. The names are Xanite. Marah Levi is fighting for a Xanite family. We have Xanite immigrants in Atsan too. The kasiri tend to be viewed with resentment and distrust while the halani are seen as backward, a burden on the city. If attitudes are the same in Ashara, I wonder if Marah has any chance of success now.

"Excuse me!" a parliamentarian interrupts. "The adoption process is supposed to be anonymous. The family that adopts the child is not allowed to know her birth name. Yet Gadin Levi has just revealed it to all of us!"

"If my request is granted," Marah Levi says, "there will be no need for secrecy since Samira will be able to stay with her parents."

My heart swells. I could hug her for refusing to give in to the silence that would erase this little girl's name.

"Their names will be struck from the record," the presider says impatiently. "Gadin Levi, please finish your remarks."

She draws herself up. "I have visited the Haruns twice in recent days. Samira's parents and siblings are devastated, and she is terrified of leaving home. Her family does not love her any less because she is a magician. Imagine how you would feel if Samira were your daughter. Or perhaps you don't have to imagine. Perhaps some of you have been in that position."

She pauses, and I could swear no one in the chamber is breathing, so stunned are we that she would so directly prod the taboo subject of wildings. I'm surprised Father hasn't dragged me from the chamber already.

"Years ago, when my brother was tested for magic," Marah continues, "I accompanied him to the examiner's office. He'd shown no sign of having magic, but I was afraid of losing him all the same. Why should anyone have to experience that fear? For Samira's sake, for the sake of every child like her, I ask Parliament to suspend all forced adoptions immediately. Let Samira remain with the family that loves her."

I grip the edge of the bench to keep my hands from trembling. In Marah's words, I hear her defending Arik's right to stay with our family, defending my right to keep my twin. Why couldn't she have been there to speak up for us when we were tested for magic?

Nitsan, the gray-haired representative from Horiel, stands up, and the presiding parliamentarian acknowledges her.

"My thanks for your moving testimony, Gadin Levi," she says. "I would like to propose halting all forced adoptions for the time being while Parliament engages in a full debate about the Family Laws."

The presider receives her proposal expressionlessly. "Are there three members who will support bringing this measure to a vote?"

"Once a moratorium like that is in place," a kasir legislator says, "there will be no turning back. Does anyone seriously believe that after several months or years of debate it will be possible to remove a child who should've been removed long before?"

"A good point," another parliamentarian says. "If in the end we decide to continue with adoptions as before, we will have raised the hopes of parents like the Haruns only to dash them again later."

"If ten years old is not too old to be taken from one's family, why should eleven or twelve be?" Horiel's representative says dryly.

"Parliamentarian Nitsan," says the presider, "how long will the full debate you mentioned take? We should not proceed with a moratorium on forced adoptions without knowing when the issue will be resolved."

Nitsan is unfazed. "I agree. After we declare the moratorium, I suggest we assign a committee to study the impact of forced adoptions and make a recommendation to Parliament by a certain date. At that point, we can revisit the moratorium and decide whether forced adoptions should resume or be ended for good."

"A committee requires a chairperson," the presider says.

"I volunteer," says Nitsan.

"You will need three more halani and two kasiri to complete the committee."

Two halan parliamentarians offer to join Nitsan at once. Then Zevulun, the kasir who said mixed families would spell Ashara's doom, offers to join the committee, and Nitsan accepts him even though everyone knows his position on forced adoptions. Finally, another halan and another kasir step forward.

The creation of the committee and the promise of a firm end date seem to have reassured some of the parliamentarians about putting forced adoptions on hold. After some negotiation, they decide to reconsider the question of adoptions in four months' time. Then three legislators—all halani, I think— express their support for bringing the moratorium to a vote. The presider asks the parliamentary pages to distribute the ballots. The young people waiting below the desks spring to action, passing out small cards to each representative.

"Please vote yes or no on the question of whether or not to declare a moratorium on the family reassignment of changelings," the presider says. "Fourteen or more yes votes are necessary for the proposal to pass."

The legislators hunch over their cards. Some of them seem uncertain, and the voting takes a while. At last, when everyone has laid down their pens, a page collects the cards and brings them to the presider's desk, where another young man joins her. As she holds up each card, he reads off the votes in a clear voice.

I feel hot and cold at once and can scarcely concentrate on the tally even though I'm breathless to know the outcome. I want Parliament to vote to stop forced adoptions. I know nothing about this Samira Harun, but nobody should suffer the fate Arik did, nor should her siblings have to bear the pain that I bear.

The counters reach the bottom of the pile. The silence in the room tells me nothing.

Then the presider says, "Fourteen yes votes, four no votes, and three abstentions. The proposal passes. All reassignments of changelings are suspended, effective immediately. In four months, we will gather again to make a final decision about forced adoptions."

I feel a flood of relief and a surge of triumph. Relief that Samira will not be taken away from her family. Triumph that Marah Levi won. She may be one of the saviors of Ashara, but she's still only eighteen or nineteen, and she just convinced Parliament to halt forced adoptions for now.

The presider calls a recess for lunch, and the chamber fills with the hum of voices. Marah Levi leaves the testifier's desk, a dazed look on her face. Beaming, the halan youths spill out of their row to embrace her. Across the aisle, the young kasir looks elated. His eyes are on Marah, but he hangs back from her and her friends.

"Rivka." Father is standing at the end of my bench, his expression grim. A chill spreads down my arms.

"We are leaving," he says. "This instant."

Father doesn't say another word until we are seated in a restaurant six blocks from Parliament. The moratorium is all I can think about. Marah Levi's victory already feels like a dream, and so every time I remember it was real, another spurt of euphoria jolts through me. The problem is masking my true feelings from Father. Luckily, waiting in dread for the explosion of his fury makes it easier.

Father unpurses his lips to give the waiter our order, and then we fall back into an agonizing silence. Does he expect me to say something first? The matter of Arik sits like a boulder between us.

Only when the endive salad arrives does Father finally ask me what I thought of the morning session. I feel out of control. How do I convince him I don't wish Arik were still my brother without making him suspect I'm lying? I decide to approach the subject indirectly.

"I can't believe Marah Levi was there," I say, unable to keep from breaking into a smile. "I never imagined I'd get to see her!"

"That girl." Father slashes an endive in half. "No single person should have that much sway over Parliament. You saw how she had them eating out of her hand."

I see Father's point. It wouldn't be right if Marah Levi could expect Parliament to do anything she asked just because of who she was. But she didn't strike me as taking her influence for granted. If anything, she seemed hesitant to be speaking publicly.

"I trust you are not so blinded by her celebrity that you fail to grasp the foolishness of what she convinced Parliament to do?"

"The—the moratorium?" I stammer.

"Yes," Father says, watching me. "What do you think?"

I'm almost too scared to breathe. Hiding the fact that I still think about my brother constantly was easy when Father never talked about him. Now he might as well be asking me point-blank how I feel about Arik's adoption these days.

"It doesn't seem like a very good idea," I hear myself saying, my voice sounding like it's coming from far away. "I don't see how children with magic could grow up happily with halani, or the other way around. If the child has magic, the rest of her family will envy her. If she doesn't, but they do, she'll feel bad about herself. I'm sure it would be hard at first for the girl Marah Levi was talking about, but in the end she'd be better off. And her family would be sad, but eventually they'd come to understand." I look up at Father, desperate for some sign that he believes I'm sincere. I hesitate before uttering my last line. "After all, I did."

Father regards me without blinking. Will he realize that everything I've spouted is embroidered from things *he's* said? At first, his face is unreadable, but gradually I detect a subtle satisfaction there. I've passed the test.

"You've grown into a mature and sensible young woman, Rivka," Father says. "I don't think I'd realized quite how much until today."

I bask in his pride for a few moments before the warm feeling starts to trouble me. I shouldn't crave Father's approval. Not when what he approves of are the awful lies I've just told. If understanding that kasiri and halani can't be brothers and sisters makes me mature and sensible, then I don't want to be.

Suddenly, I have an idea for how to show him I'm not unrealistically immune to memories of Arik and throw him off the scent of my quest in Ashara all in one stroke.

"Did you think of him today, though?" I ask. I don't need to explain who "he" is. Father's eyes darken, and I have the sensation of walking across a barely frozen lake. "When Marah Levi started talking, I couldn't help wondering how he is, back in Atsan."

Father gives no hint that he knows Arik isn't in Atsan. "I too thought of him this morning."

My stomach clenches. He hasn't acknowledged Arik in my presence since the day we were ripped apart for the second time.

"It was difficult not to," Father continues irritably. "But I am content knowing he is exactly where he belongs, and inexpressibly grateful that there is no United Parliament in Atsan."

✦ ✦ ✦

On Ninthday morning, the front-page story in the *Journal* is about the new policy on forced adoptions. I wait until Father has left the breakfast table and then pour myself another glass of tea so I can read the article.

At Levi's Urging, Parliament Imposes Moratorium on Forced Adoptions

I skim the beginning since, after all, I was there yesterday, but then a paragraph about Marah Levi catches my eye.

> Levi, eighteen, is a social worker with the Department of Social Welfare. It was not clear whether she came to know the family on whose behalf she testified through her work or not. Since her ascent to fame four years ago, Levi has largely stayed out of politics. Eighthday marked the first time she has testified before the United Parliament and the first time she has spoken publicly since the hearings that took place after the fall of the Assembly.

I can't believe yesterday was her first time speaking before Parliament. She spoke with such assurance, even when Zevulun attacked her proposal. If she prefers to stay out of the public eye, the fact that she made an exception for Samira

Harun means she must feel very strongly that forced adoptions are wrong. She would understand about Arik, I'm sure. She might even want to help me find him.

This thought electrifies me. *She might help me find him.* Lurking at the Ikhad and haunting halan neighborhoods aren't getting me anywhere. I need someone more powerful on my side.

Suddenly, I know I have to meet her. And I can think of only one way to do that.

11

Sitting in the library during my free period, I watch Caleb Levi page through a book. Despite my eagerness to talk to him, I'm reluctant to approach his table. What if the librarian wonders why I'm talking to the halan? But my brother is somewhere in this city, and I swore I'd find him. This is why I accompanied Father to Ashara.

I stand up and cross the reading room, my shoes clicking on the polished floorboards. I stop across the table from Caleb and wait until he glances up. His face is expressionless.

"Hello," I say. Can he understand me? Is Hilah right that he can read lips? I reach tentatively for the slate next to his book, and he abruptly pushes it toward me.

My name is Rivka Kadmiel, I write with the stub of chalk. *I'm in your class.*

When Caleb reads what I wrote, he looks startled. He scribbles a reply.

You're the Atsani ambassador's daughter.

I didn't expect him to recognize my name. "How did you know?" Belatedly remembering he can't hear me, I write the question out.

I'm not the only one here everyone's heard of, Caleb writes. He doesn't bother introducing himself.

There is a moment's pause. Finally, I pick up the chalk again and write, *Can I sit with you?*

Caleb stares at the question and then looks coldly at me. He writes a single word on his slate. *Why?*

Heat rises in my face. It didn't occur to me I might not be welcome. I'm about to slink back to my table when Caleb nods stiffly. Surprised but relieved, I drop into a chair, planning what to say next. But Caleb pulls his slate close and bows his head over his book. This is no better than before.

How can I get him to talk to me? And what should I say? I can't ask straightaway to meet his sister. It would come off as rude.

After a few minutes, I notice that Caleb's only pretending to read. He's staring fixedly at one spot in the text. I lightly tap the table near his book. He grudgingly looks up.

"What are you reading?" I ask.

He must understand because he lifts the book so I can read the spine.

"I don't know that author," I say.

Do you read much halan literature? Caleb writes.

What's halan literature? I write. As soon as I show him the slate, I know the answer, but it's too late.

Caleb's eyes have gone cold again. *Believe it or not, halani write books.*

I'm about to lose him again. I have to write something, anything, to keep him talking to me, but Caleb holds the slate out of my reach and scrawls a new message.

Why are you here? What do you want?

I'm hurt by his distrust and hostility, but my heart quickly hardens. If he wants to be direct, I'll be direct.

I want to meet your sister.

His mouth forms a tight line. *You and every other person in Ashara.*

Please, I write. *It's important.*

Caleb presses the chalk so hard against the slate that a chunk of it snaps off. *If it's so important, go find her yourself.* He gathers his books and stalks out of the library.

When the bell rings, I trudge to Epic Poetry. I'm too drained from my unsuccessful conversation with Caleb to notice that nobody except Hilah has spoken to me all morning. At lunchtime, I wait for Merav and the others at our usual table, but instead of joining me, they march past me with their plates. Merav leads Kelilah and Ronit to another table whose occupants immediately make room for them.

It's clearly a deliberate slight. I'm not hurt, exactly, but while I don't mind eating alone, I mind being conspicuous. Hilah, who has just gotten her food, starts to cross the dining hall. To my surprise, Merav waves at her.

"Hilah, join us," she says, scooting her chair over to make space.

Hilah stops in her tracks, her expression confused. When she spots me sitting by myself, understanding dawns on her. And to my astonishment, she walks over to me.

"You don't want to eat with them?" I say.

Hilah looks incredulous. "Of course not."

"They won't be happy."

She shrugs. "They never liked me anyway. And I only put up with them so I could sit with you."

"Really?" I say, taken aback. I thought I'd been the one doing Hilah a favor, trying to include her despite Merav and the others' unfriendliness. It never crossed my mind that she was the one choosing me.

"What did you do to upset them?" Hilah asks.

I glance over to where Merav is sitting. Kelilah and Ronit are giving me dark looks. Bewildered, I stare down at my food. "I wish I knew."

Not until the end of the day do I learn what I've done. As I'm passing through the arcade on my way out, I catch my name. Two girls in my class are standing in the courtyard on the other side of an archway. I pause in the shadows to listen.

"—saw her at the Ikhad on Seventhday afternoon."

"Why does it matter if Rivka was at the Ikhad?"

"Because she told Merav she couldn't go to the party because she had plans with her father! Adina said she was definitely alone, just walking around the market."

I go cold. I don't think I was doing anything obviously strange at the Ikhad, but the idea that someone was watching me without my realizing it is unsettling.

"Ronit says she's really stuck-up," the first girl says. "When they'd try to talk to her at lunch she would just stare at them, like she couldn't even be bothered to answer."

"Well, if Merav Omri isn't good enough for her, nobody is."

I've heard enough. I steal through the arcade and run out the school doors. Being called stuck-up stings. It was a mistake to lie to Merav. I should've been more careful. But just because my classmates discovered I'd made up an excuse, they decided I'd snubbed her? It's absurd.

The next day, I try to join Merav, Kelilah, and Ronit at lunch. Without a word, they pick up their food and move to another table, leaving me alone again. A few minutes later, Hilah sits down beside me.

"Why did you try to sit with them?" she asks, sounding genuinely puzzled.

I shrug. I wanted to blend in. I doubt sitting with Hilah is going to do the trick. She's already scandalized our entire class by telling Merav all her friends in the countryside were halani.

As if she can read my thoughts, she says, "Should I go?"

"No, no," I say hastily. I can't let my isolation become complete. Hilah is better than nobody.

* * *

On Sixthday morning, after a week of my being shunned by my classmates, Aradi Noach holds me back at the end of History of the North Lands Novel. When the room has emptied, I nervously approach his desk. He returned our second weekly composition today, but I did well, so I can't imagine what he wants.

"I have a favor to ask of you, Rivka," my teacher says, closing a notebook.

"Yes?" I say uncertainly.

"Would you be willing to help Caleb Levi with this class?"

The question is so unexpected I don't know what to say.

"To be clear, he is an excellent student," Aradi Noach

says, "but his first two compositions have not been up to my standards, and the reason is simple. There is a great deal of lecture and class discussion he is not following."

Our essays are supposed to draw on our classmates' ideas and the historical context Aradi Noach provides, so I can understand why Caleb might be doing poorly on them.

"I was told he could lip-read, and I have tried to face him as much as possible and to write more than I normally would on the blackboard. When I spoke to him yesterday, though, he told me he still cannot understand everything I say. And class discussions are impossible, of course. In short, Caleb needs someone to fill him in on what he is missing. I wonder if you would share your notes with him and summarize the discussions for him."

I can't believe it. He's offering me the perfect opportunity to talk to Caleb again. But I mustn't look too eager to spend time with a halan, so I bury my excitement and chew my lip.

Aradi Noach sighs. "It's up to you. You would not be the first student to say no. But I understand both you and Caleb have a free period after this class, so you would not have to meet with him after school."

He's right, of course. It makes perfect sense for me to be the one to help Caleb, which I hope will make fewer people question why I'm doing it.

"Caleb is intelligent and hard-working, but he will not succeed at Firem without someone's help." Aradi Noach studies me. "You are doing well, Rivka, and if I may say so, you seem less prejudiced than some of the other students."

His last words make me slightly uneasy, but I think I've

feigned reluctance long enough. "I'll help him, sir."

Aradi Noach smiles. "My thanks. It is very good of you."

During morning recess on Firstday, Aradi Noach introduces Caleb and me to each other. We don't mention that we've already met. After explaining what he expects of us, our teacher sends us off to the library. Caleb doesn't stop in the reading room but disappears through one of the doorways to the stacks. There are study alcoves furnished with tables and chairs built into the walls. An older girl with short hair is reading in one of them. I follow Caleb to a different one, and we sit down opposite each other.

I try to smile, but at Caleb's closed expression, I falter. His parting words from last week stick in my throat like a fishbone. *If it's so important, go find her yourself.* I dare not bring Marah up again right away. I need to win Caleb over first.

I pass him my literature notebook. He accepts it stiffly and begins to copy my notes. While he writes, I contemplate the subject of our next composition, which Aradi Noach assigned this morning. Caleb interrupts my musings to ask me to explain an obscure phrase in my notebook. Then I start to tell him what our classmates argued about during the class discussion. He asks a lot of questions, and the more we write back and forth on his slate, the less distant his manner becomes.

Do you think she was selfish to leave her fiancé like that, without even a note, to go back to her village? Caleb asks, referring to the main character in the book we're studying.

I struggle to answer. I want to explain that I understand how the character felt during the years she lived away from her family. I understand what it's like to feel that your heart is with someone you love, in a place that seems impossible to reach. But I can't tell Caleb that without revealing my secrets.

Instead, I write, *I know how it feels to long for another place.*

Caleb peers at my response, then looks very seriously at me. *You're homesick.*

I hesitate. I don't miss Atsan. Well, I miss not having an accent and not being ostracized by my classmates, but there was nothing left for me there.

Did you want to move? Caleb asks.

That at least I can answer truthfully. *I wanted to come to Ashara with my father.*

What about your mother? As Caleb hands me his slate, his expression wavers, as though he can guess the answer.

My mother is dead.

I'm sorry, he writes. *My father died when I was four.*

I'm sorry.

He shrugs. *I was very young. I barely remember him.*

My mother died when I was eleven.

Caleb looks up from the slate, his eyes full of sympathy. We're actually talking like normal people. It's like he's forgotten I'm a kasir.

Do you have any siblings? Caleb asks.

It's a natural next question to ask. It feels particularly wrong to lie to Caleb about the very reason I need to talk to him, but I'm not ready to tell him about Arik. My heart heavy with guilt, I write, *No.*

✦ ✦ ✦

"The highest mark this week," Aradi Noach says as he returns our fourth composition, "went to Caleb Levi." He pauses at Caleb's desk and lays down his paper. "An original idea and a convincing argument. Well done."

An ugly silence follows the teacher's announcement. The looks my classmates give Caleb are truly poisonous, but sitting in the front row he can't see them. I wish Aradi Noach hadn't said anything.

The repercussions are not long in coming. Compositions are due at the beginning of the week. When I walk into History of the North Lands Novel on Firstday, three of my classmates are looming over Caleb's desk. Several other students are gathered in a ring around them. My stomach drops.

"We want your essay," the girl standing over Caleb says as I lower my schoolbag.

"Aradi Noach thinks you're brilliant," one of the boys says. "So let's see what you've written."

"He can't hear you, you know," Merav calls from across the room.

"He can lip-read," the girl retorts. "Can't you?"

Caleb says nothing. His gaze flicks from side to side, and his eyes meet mine. I break eye contact at once. Shame splashes over me, and I look back, but Caleb is staring at the girl again.

"Give me your essay," she repeats.

Caleb shakes his head. A murmur of excitement ripples through the classroom, and the girl's face fills with rage. She lunges for his schoolbag, and when Caleb dives for it too, one of the boys barks an incantation. A spray of fiery sparks explodes around Caleb's hands, and he jerks back with a yelp.

Before I realize what I'm doing, I've stepped into the ring. I don't stand between Caleb and my other classmates, though. Instead I keep to the side.

"Is copying off a halan the best you can do?" I say.

A thick silence blankets the classroom. I've succeeded in drawing the three students' attention away from Caleb and onto myself, but the hatred in their eyes makes my knees shake. What have I done? I hope nobody thinks I meant to defend Caleb. And I hope he couldn't read my lips, because I insulted him as surely as I insulted his tormentors.

"What's going on here?"

The crowd parts for Aradi Noach. Our teacher looks from me to the three students glaring at me to Caleb, who is cradling his right hand. He frowns slightly and continues on to his desk.

"Find your seats," he says. "We have much to do."

After class, as I hurry off to the library, I hear my classmates muttering in my wake. I can't rid my mouth of the taste of the awful words I said, but I would feel even worse if I hadn't said anything.

When I join Caleb in our nook, he is examining an angry red streak on the back of his hand. I catch my breath. I reach toward him just to get his attention, but he flinches, and I grab his slate instead.

Someone should look at that, I write. *Go to the infirmary.*

He shrugs, as if to say it isn't that bad, but the tightness of his mouth tells me his hand hurts more than he will admit.

I recall the basic healing spells we were taught toward

the end of primary school, the building blocks of the more complex spells like those used to treat Mother before she died. I'm not sure which one is right for a magical burn, but I could at least cast a cooling spell to soothe the pain. When I offer to, though, Caleb shakes his head vigorously and snatches his hand back, as though I suggested cutting it off. I stare at him, wondering what he's so afraid of. Not meeting my eyes, he grips the chalk in his injured hand and scrawls a message on his slate.

You didn't have to step in earlier.

I look up at him, indignant. Not only does he not want my help now, but he's also not the least bit grateful I stopped our classmates from hurting him even more badly? It dawns on me that he might have caught what I said, and I feel bleak.

Wouldn't you think less of me if I hadn't? I write.

He looks troubled. *Let me take care of myself.* It's not really an answer. I think he *would* think less of me, but he also doesn't want me to defend him. So I can't do anything right.

Why didn't you show them your essay? I write in frustration. *How could they have stolen your work in only a few minutes anyway?*

I don't know, he writes, his expression irritable. *Maybe with a spell to change my name to theirs or to change the handwriting without messing up the paper. I don't know what all you can do.*

He lumps me with Ashari kasiri without even thinking, but I'm impressed by his imagination, and by what it implies about our classmates' resourcefulness when it comes to magic. It would never occur to me that I could transform someone else's schoolwork into my own. I can't even think what spells I would use to accomplish such a thing.

And then, Caleb continues, setting his jaw, *I wouldn't have had an essay to turn in, and I would've gotten a zero for the week. I can't afford that. Firem only needs the slightest excuse to kick me out.*

Why are you even taking classes here?

I want to study literature at university, Caleb writes. *Firem will prepare me for that far better than the school for the deaf can.*

Study literature at university! Do halan universities even have literature departments? Or does Caleb aspire to a kasir university? That goal is so lofty it's laughable.

It's also to take a stand for integration, I guess, Caleb adds. *Sometimes I'm not sure if I'm doing this for integration or because it makes sense for me.* He rubs at the chalk letters, as though surprised he has said so much. Wiping out the part about integration, he adds, *I'm just so tired. Going to hearing school is so much work.*

I have nothing to say to that, so I just hand Caleb my notebooks. He's been reading my notes for Epic Poetry too, even though as far as I know the Epic Poetry teacher has shown no interest in how he's faring. After half an hour, he sets the notebooks aside, and we talk about the new novel Aradi Noach has started us on. It caused a stir in class today because the first chapter describes the narrator's childhood friendship with the son of her family's housekeeper.

Do you think kasiri and halani can be friends? I ask Caleb.

He smiles uneasily. *Believe me, it's going to go sour.*

In the book. But what about in real life? I think of Hilah and her halan playmates in Daresh.

Caleb is no longer smiling. *It's possible. But rare. And it's always hard.*

I'm certain he's thinking of someone in particular. I'm equally certain it's not us.

Your sister and Azariah Rashid? I write.

He nods. I don't ask him whether we're friends yet. I know the answer is no.

We work quietly for a while. The silence between Caleb and me feels comfortable now. Comfortable enough that I'm working up the courage to ask about Marah again. I'm fearful of bringing back the hostile, taciturn Caleb, but I need to get on with my search for Arik.

Hesitantly, I reach for the chalk. *I'd still like to meet your sister.*

Caleb's stillness after he reads my note is different from his stillness before. He meets my gaze, and I'm surprised to notice the faintest hurt there.

At last, he writes, *Why?*

The inevitable question. I can think of no reason besides the truth. But I'm afraid to talk about wildings within Firem's walls.

I can't tell you here, I write.

Caleb frowns, then scribbles something on his slate. *Are you free after school?*

12

The school for the deaf is a narrow brick building on Harish Street, not far from Firem. When I come to meet Caleb, students are still trickling out. A girl coming down the front steps taps a boy on the shoulder, and when he faces her, her hands move in a series of complex gestures. It's much livelier than the careful hand shapes Ashari magicians use to cast spells. It's not only her hands that move, but also her arms, her shoulders, her head. Her facial expression keeps changing. Then the boy is answering her in the same way. Up and down Harish Street, students in black uniforms are silently jabbering with one another. It's mesmerizing.

I spot Caleb standing with three other students on the sidewalk. One girl is talking rapidly with her hands, and when she pauses, Caleb responds with his own quick motions. I always thought sign language consisted of making primitive gestures in painfully slow succession, but what Caleb is doing is swift and fluent. He has shed the slight hunch he always has at Firem, and he looks carefree and at ease. Almost like he's a different person. Even as the only halan among all these kasiri, he clearly belongs, while I feel woefully out of place. I wonder how this can be. Does being deaf create a bond strong enough to overcome the divide between halani and kasiri?

When Caleb notices me, he bids his friends goodbye and motions for me to follow him. The red mark on his hand has faded to a less noticeable pink. Either it improved on its own or he has a friend here he trusted more than me to heal his burn.

We walk to a park tucked between two limestone apartment buildings. It has no fence, just a hedge of prickly barberry. A man is reading the *Journal* on one of the benches, and a halan nurse is watching a chubby boy toddle across the grass. Caleb and I settle onto the bench at the far end of the park, in the shade of a towering spruce. He twists around to face me.

"The way you talk!" I exclaim before he can take out his slate. "Those signs . . ." I must look awed because Caleb smiles.

It's Ashari Sign Language, he writes. *I learned it when I came to the school for the deaf.*

I wait for him to look at my face and ask, "When was that?"

When I was ten. I didn't start there right away. I went to Horiel Primary for a while first. The spring after the dark eyes.

I frown. That was only four years ago. "You didn't go to school before that?"

He shakes his head and taps his ear.

"What did you do before you learned sign language?" I ask, unable to contain my curiosity. His brow wrinkles. When

I realize he hasn't understood, I write my question down.

I wasn't born deaf. After I lost my hearing, I had a different way of talking with my family. I still use it with Mother. My sister's learned sign language pretty well.

"Can you talk?" I blurt out before it occurs to me it might be rude to ask. I half hope Caleb failed to read my lips, but the flicker of annoyance in his eyes tells me he understood.

I don't like to, he writes. *Only my family understands me very well. But at school, they push us to.*

Because your classmates are kasiri! I write, realization dawning. *They need to be able to talk to cast spells.*

They don't, actually. They have a way of using signs instead of incantations. I've seen it. But the teachers don't think it counts. I thought you wanted to talk about my sister. He looks up.

"Oh, yes," I say, flustered. "I need—I want to talk to her."

It was clever, agreeing to help me with my classes just to get to her.

I bristle. What he says is close to the truth, but the way he puts it twists everything around. I don't just see him as a means to an end, not anymore.

I don't understand why you want to meet her, he continues. *You're a kasir. You're not even Ashari. Do you know how many people have asked me to introduce them to Marah? If I did it for everyone who asked, she'd kill me.*

I glance across the park. The man reading the newspaper has left, but the nurse and her charge are still here. They're probably out of earshot, but I still hold out my hand for Caleb's slate. Somehow it's easier to write what I need to tell him than to say it out loud.

I want to ask her for help.

Caleb looks skeptical. No doubt he's wondering what kind of help an ambassador's daughter could possibly need from his sister. *She doesn't do political favors or anything like that.*

She just did.

That was the first time ever, Caleb writes. *And probably the last. She doesn't like politics.*

I don't need her to make Parliament do something for me.

Then what do you want? Caleb writes, exasperated.

Taking a deep breath, I grind chalk to slate. *My twin brother is a wilding. He's in Ashara, and I want to find him.*

I hear Caleb's sharp intake of breath as he reads. He looks up, his expression a mixture of shock and pity.

I'm sorry I lied about not having any siblings, I add.

Caleb shakes his head, stricken. *Don't be sorry. You're supposed to lie, aren't you?* He clears space on the slate and writes, *How do you know he's in Ashara?*

My mother told me before she died.

His eyes widen. *Why would they send him here?*

Telling the truth is getting easier. *Because we found each other once, after they took him away the first time.*

Caleb stares, first at the words, then at me. Then he writes, *I can see where this is going. But Marah only persuaded Parliament to suspend forced adoptions. She can't make them reverse an old adoption.*

I don't need her to reverse the adoption, I write. *I only want her help finding records. I've tried looking for my brother, but the city is too big. I need to find out who adopted him, or what his new name is. Your sister works for the government, right?*

Not in a records office.

But she's Marah Levi. Can't she go anywhere?

Caleb looks unhappy about this for some reason, but he doesn't deny it.

Will you ask her if she'll meet me? I write. *You can explain. And I don't expect her to help me for nothing. I'll do anything I can in return.*

There is a long pause. Then Caleb nods.

Immediately, I feel ten times lighter.

I can't promise anything, Caleb writes, *but I think Marah will help you. I know how she is about brothers.*

"Thank you, Caleb!" I say.

We get up from the bench. The little grass-stained kasir boy and his nurse are gone. As we pass through the hedge, the red barberry leaves blood-lit by the slanting sunlight, I turn to Caleb. He faces me.

"Please don't tell anyone," I say.

He nods solemnly.

I gently take the slate from him and write, *My father can't know what I'm doing.* Caleb must understand how secret this is.

He hesitates. *This is against the law, isn't it? Wildings aren't ever supposed to see their birth families again.*

Even after all these years, Father's words still echo in my head. *If you do it again, you will be sent to prison.* But I say, "I don't care."

I wouldn't either.

13

Three days later, when I reach our alcove in the library, Caleb pushes his slate across the table. *Marah says she'll meet you.*

At first, I'm too stunned to smile. Then my spirits soar. I feel like I've secured an audience with a queen.

Within a few days, it's all arranged. On Seventhday, Azariah Rashid will meet me at Firem and take me to the Levis' apartment in Horiel District. I'm mildly horrified by this plan, but Caleb says I'd stick out in Horiel if I came alone. The neighbors are used to Azariah. Meeting both of Ashara's saviors in one day sounds overwhelming, but I don't protest further. I've gotten what I wanted.

On the last day of school before the weekend, I slide the final piece of my plan into place. These days, Hilah and I always sit together in a corner of the dining hall, ignored by the rest of our class. Neither of us minds, and it's a relief to no longer be under Merav's scrutiny.

"Hilah," I ask as I spear a potato, "can you do something for me?"

"Of course," she says eagerly.

"Do you have plans tomorrow?"

"Just studying." She sounds hopeful, like she thinks I'm going to suggest we do something together, and I feel guilty for misleading her.

"If anybody asks later, can you say I was studying with you tomorrow afternoon?"

Hilah frowns. "You mean you're not actually going to be studying with me?"

"I . . . want to go somewhere, but I can't tell my father where."

Hilah catches on quickly. "So you'll tell him you're studying with me, and it's my job to cover for you if he ever asks me about it."

"Exactly," I say, relieved.

"Where will you really be?"

"Um, it's a secret."

Hilah looks expectant, until she realizes it's a secret from her too. "You want me to cover for you and you won't tell me why?"

"Please, Hilah?"

She gives in easily. "All right. Just promise me you're not, I don't know, doing something illegal."

My stomach turns over. "I promise," I say, forcing a grin. "Thank you, Hilah."

On Seventhday, Father goes out for lunch with several expatriates, Atsani citizens living in Ashara, which means I don't have to lie to his face. Instead, I tell Gadi Yoram, the housekeeper, that I'm going to study with a classmate who lives in the dormitory.

It is a warm afternoon, and ragged clouds are scattered across the blue sky like torn bread. At Firem, secondary-school boarders and university students are relaxing with their friends in the square. I'm not sure where to find Azariah, but then I spot a young man standing on the front steps in the shadow of a column. He's wearing a white button-down shirt and black trousers, with a black jacket folded over his arm. The spring breeze tangles his dark curls. His face is serious and somehow familiar. The more I look at him, the more convinced I am that he was the young kasir spectator in the Parliament chamber. Was *that* Azariah Rashid?

The young man catches me watching him and walks down the steps. "Are you Rivka?"

"Yes," I say. "Are you . . . ?" What should I call him? Azariah seems too familiar, Banar Rashid much too formal.

"Azariah," the young man supplies, nodding politely. "Pleased to meet you."

"Me too," I manage.

"Shall we be on our way?"

We walk down a boulevard heading south. Azariah seems untroubled by our silence, but I find it awkward. If it's like this with him, how much worse will it be with Marah Levi, who's not only as famous as Azariah but a halan as well?

"Are you at university?" I ask at last.

"Yes," Azariah says. "Studying history. I'm in my second year."

"Where?"

"Firem. I've gone there my entire life. Sometimes I think I'll never leave. How do you like Firem Secondary?"

"It's . . . fine. I mean, it's a very good school."

Azariah laughs. "You don't have to pretend to like Firem. It can be a difficult place. My brother hated it. They weren't too kind to Xanites or the children of kasir radicals, and we were both. Frankly, I worry about Caleb taking classes there, but he tells me everything's fine."

Azariah throws me a pointed look, and I sense his unspoken question. Has Caleb not told anyone about the insults and the harassment? If he's hiding it from his family and friends, I won't be the one to tell.

When I don't say anything, Azariah says, "Caleb's one of the first halani ever to go to Firem. The very first was Zeina Abid, who was a friend of Marah's at Horiel Primary. After the Assembly fell, when the provisional government insisted Firem integrate, they said they'd take the one halan with the best Secondary School Exam score in the city. That was Zeina."

"Did she even want to go to Firem?" I ask. It must have been terrifying to be picked like that, to bear the entire burden of integrating the most prestigious school in Ashara.

"She did," Azariah says. "She was ambitious. But she hated the way she was chosen, and that Firem made her do it alone. If she succeeded, it would mean she was exceptional, and if she failed, it would mean halani weren't as smart as kasiri. She was determined to prove she could do it, though."

"So she graduated?"

"Yes," Azariah says. "She survived. And she has the scars to prove it."

"Scars?" I say, aghast.

He doesn't respond right away. In the middle of the boulevard, the streetcar reaches the end of the line, and a bell clangs as the passengers spill out.

"Have you heard of the Society yet?" he finally asks.

"Yes." A sense of dread thickens in my chest, and my memory resurrects images from that first night in Ashara: jagged glass, sparks of magic, a face drenched in shadows, and two boys' fearful eyes. "My father told me about it."

"I see." Azariah eyes me curiously. "Well, the Society's main activity is terrorizing halani, and they're bent on blocking any kind of integration. When the first halani started going to kasir schools, the Society made sure it was hellish for them. Zeina's not the only other halan to have studied at Firem, but she's the only one who's graduated."

Each of his sentences is more ominous than the last, but I can't help asking, "What do you mean by *hellish*?"

"The Society sent her death threats. Zeina fought with her parents over whether or not to drop out."

"Nobody tried to kill her, did they?" I ask, alarmed.

"No, but she had to walk up the school steps through crowds of screaming demonstrators who threw things at her. Like rocks. And broken bottles. She has a scar here"—Azariah touches the back of his wrist—"and here." He traces his eyebrow. "Sometimes they even cast spells, despite the drastic penalties Parliament set for using magic against a halan student integrating a kasir school. There were days Zeina couldn't have gotten to the doors if there hadn't been kasir students around willing to break immobilization spells cast on her."

It occurs to me that Caleb is a halan integrating a kasir school. I wonder how much trouble the boy who burned his hand could've been in if Aradi Noach had seen him cast the spell, or if Caleb had told on him.

"People would have harassed Zeina anyway," Azariah

continues, "but the Society stirred them up and definitely made things worse."

"Why didn't somebody stop them?" I say.

Azariah sighs. "The trouble is the Society's a secret organization. People can guess who's in it, but it's impossible to prove that anyone is a member. Kasir parliamentarians like to say the Society is mostly harmless, but some of them probably belong to it themselves."

His words send a chill down my arms. If the Society is so violently opposed to integration of any kind, I have little doubt what they would think of mixed families or my trying to find my lost halan brother.

We're in Horiel District now, and the only other people in the street are halani. Azariah and I stick out in our tailor-made clothes, and passersby give us a wide berth, casting us wary glances. On the Street of Winter Gusts, Azariah stops in front of number five and pushes in the door. I follow him into the dim entryway and up the stairs.

By the time we reach the fourth floor, my stomach hurts. What if Marah Levi doesn't like me? Azariah knocks on one of the apartment doors. It swings open, and Caleb's face peers out. He grins at Azariah and waves at me.

"Hello, Caleb." It's strange to see him outside of school. Instead of his uniform, he's wearing gray trousers and a green shirt without a trace of chalk on it.

Opening the door wider, Caleb beckons us in. And there, sitting at a round table in the middle of the kitchen, is his sister, Marah Levi.

14

I recognize Marah immediately from Parliament. She's dressed in trousers and a light wool sweater, her dark brown hair in a braid.

She stands and greets Azariah, then turns to me. She's not smiling. If anything, she looks shy. "You must be Rivka Kadmiel."

"Yes."

"You were there that day. In Parliament."

I'm shocked. I had no idea she'd noticed me.

"Oh, now I see," she says. "Your father was testifying after me. Ambassador Kadmiel."

"You were brilliant," I blurt out as we all sit around the table.

Marah looks away in embarrassment. "Oh, no, I was just . . ."

"You were brilliant," Azariah says firmly.

"Would you like tea?" Marah asks me. "I'll put the kettle on."

While the water is boiling, a woman in a sober wool dress steps into the kitchen. There are lines at the corners of her mouth and strands of gray in her braid, but she greets

Azariah with a warm smile. Then she looks questioningly at me, her expression guarded.

Remembering my manners, I jump up from the table. "Good afternoon, ma'am. My name is Rivka Kadmiel."

My politeness seems to come as a pleasant surprise to her, but she still looks hesitant. "Welcome, Rivka. You're a classmate of my son's?"

"Yes," I say, wondering how much she's heard about me.

"Welcome," she repeats, and I can tell she means it, though there is still something reserved and sad in her gaze.

The teakettle whistles on the stove. Marah shuts off the gas and then lets Caleb take charge of the brewing. Their mother has a brief signed exchange with them and walks out the door. She must have to work on weekends. I'm relieved she's gone.

Caleb brings an earthenware teapot to the table and pours four glasses.

"So you're from Atsan," Marah says. She's talking to me even though she's looking at her brother. "What instrument do you play?"

"Cello," I say.

"Oh!" She smiles. "I play the violin."

Like Arik.

"She teaches too," Azariah tells me, though he also keeps facing Caleb.

"Barely," Marah says. "Once in a while old instruments fall into my lap, and I give them away to the children of the families I work with. I have a friend from school who fixes them up beforehand. Mostly they're violins, so I can teach the children a bit in my spare time. The schools they go to don't have medshas, and their parents are too poor to afford lessons, but I think they deserve to learn music as much as anyone else."

"What are medshas?" I ask.

Marah tilts her head in surprise. "The medsha is the traditional ensemble in Ashara. Twelve musicians, strings, flutes, horn . . . You don't play in medshas in Atsan?"

"No." With only twelve musicians, medshas are quite a bit smaller than our orchestras.

As Caleb replenishes our tea glasses, Marah's expression grows purposeful. "Rivka, Caleb told me why you wanted to see me. I can't reverse a forced adoption from four years ago."

Azariah nearly spits out his tea. "Wait, what?"

I stare at him and then throw Marah a panicked look. How could she reveal my secret in front of Azariah without asking me first?

Dismay spreads across her face. "Oh, I thought since Azariah was bringing you here that he . . . I'm sorry, Rivka." She glances at Azariah. "You can trust him, though."

I grip my scalding tea glass, still trying to quell my indignation. After our walk to the Levis', I do feel inclined to trust Azariah, but the choice should've been mine.

"My twin brother, Arik, is a changeling," I say at last. "He was sent to Ashara to live with halani four years ago."

"Your twin brother?" Azariah says, his face slack with horror. "God of the Maitaf, that's awful."

Quickly, I tell them what I told Caleb in the park earlier this week.

"I can't believe you found each other again in Atsan," Azariah says when I've finished. "That's unheard of."

"Maybe it happens more often than we think," Marah says. Her eyes linger on Caleb, her fierce love for him stark on her face.

"There's usually a lot of shame on both sides," Azariah says quietly. "And the law is a powerful thing. We know how people will follow the law just to be safe even when deep down they wish it were different."

Marah avoids his gaze and takes a long sip of tea.

"I don't need you to reverse the adoption for me," I say. "I just want to find Arik. You work for the government, right? Is there an office that keeps records on adoptions?"

Marah thinks for a moment. "There is an office for changeling records, but practically no one is allowed to see them. Birth families and adoptive families are absolutely prohibited from knowing each other's identities."

"They must find out sometimes," Azariah protests. "Children can't always keep secrets. I'm sure some wildings have told their adoptive parents their birth names."

"Maybe," Marah says, "but officially the confidentiality laws are very strict." She pauses to sign to Caleb, her hands moving almost as fluidly as the deaf students'. He nods, pensively tracing the frosted pattern on his tea glass.

"So who *is* allowed to see the changeling records?" I ask.

"Parliament can request the release of a record if they

have a good reason to," Marah says. "And Parliamentarian Nitsan's committee has probably been granted access to the records for their study of forced adoptions. Also, scholars can request to enter the archive for research. That's it."

While she and Caleb sign back and forth again, I sip my tea. Its bitter taste matches my discouragement.

Noticing my glumness, Marah says, "Maybe there's a different way. A wilding from another city-state is so rare that people must have noticed. If we ask around . . ."

"That'll take forever," Azariah says. "Besides, I think we can get into the archive."

I'm heartened by his eagerness to help me, but I don't understand his optimism. "How? We're not parliamentarians, or scholars . . ."

I trail off as Marah eyes Azariah in a peculiar way.

"I know what you're thinking," she says. "And I'm not sure I like it."

"I'm a scholar," Azariah says.

"You're a *student*," Marah retorts. Caleb touches her arm, interested in the sudden tension between her and Azariah. She signs to him, and then tells Azariah, "You study the ancient civilizations. No one's going to believe you need access to the changeling archive for your research."

"I'll make up a side project."

Marah shakes her head. "I doubt they let students go through the records. I'm sure you need an actual degree."

"They'd probably accept a signed letter of support from the head of my department," Azariah says blithely.

"And he would give you such a letter? For a fake research project?"

"No, I'd forge it. A quick copying spell should do the trick."

"Azariah!" Marah cries. "This is serious."

"I'm completely serious," he says. "It'll never get back to my department head. He's completely lost in his books, he'd never notice. I bet he *would* sign a letter I'd composed without even reading it because he likes me, but to be safe, I should reproduce his signature myself. Besides, I hate to say it, but the fact that I'm me will probably be enough to get me into that archive."

"I'm coming too," I say. "I know the most about Arik. What if they use some strange filing system? Like if it's by birth date, or district of birth?"

"Good point," Azariah says. "You need to be there."

"What's going to be your excuse for bringing her?" Marah demands.

"She'll be my research assistant," he says, grinning.

"She's a first year in secondary school."

Azariah glances at me. "She could pass for older. It's not inconceivable for a third year to be doing busy work for a university student."

"This whole idea is ridiculous," Marah says. "We're talking about gaining entry into a restricted government archive under false pretenses . . ." Caleb taps the table impatiently, and she begins to fill him in. At one point, she indicates Azariah and me with her chin, and Caleb interrupts. Marah shakes her head in an unmistakable refusal. Indignation flashes across his face, and he signs in protest. His sister doesn't yield. Caleb signs more, a stubborn gleam in his eyes. I'm not certain, but I think he wants to come to the archive with Azariah and me.

In a fit of frustration, he taps his ear and his lips and, a moment later, points at me. Marah frowns.

"Rivka has an Atsani accent," she says.

This stings, especially since I think it was Caleb who thought of it. He was one of the few people in Ashara who had never commented on my speech.

"If the archive staff guess who she is . . ." Marah begins.

"I'll keep my mouth shut," I say. "I'm coming no matter what."

Azariah and I sit in uncomfortable silence as Caleb and Marah continue to argue. Marah's expression is profoundly unhappy now, but she keeps shaking her head no. Finally, Caleb gives in, but he looks ready to storm from the kitchen table.

"So it's settled?" Azariah says awkwardly.

"It's settled," Marah says, avoiding Caleb's gaze. "You and Rivka will go to the archive."

"I'll find out what the hours are and check my schedule," Azariah says. "Can I write to you, Rivka?"

"No!" My hand jerks, and I almost knock over my tea glass. "My father sees all the embassy mail. If not him, then his deputy. They'd ask who was writing to me from within Ashara."

"Right. Then I'll send word through Caleb?" He signs haltingly to Caleb, who nods, less angry with Azariah than with his sister.

I suddenly realize that I didn't believe any of these famous people would actually agree to help me. Now they all are.

"Thank you," I say to Marah and Azariah, despairing at the inadequacy of these words. "How can I repay you?"

"Don't be silly," Marah says. "You don't have to repay us. I haven't even done anything for you."

"Are you sure?" I say anxiously. "If there's anything I can do . . ."

"No," Marah says, embarrassed. "We want to help you, Rivka. You have the right to see your brother again. Please don't feel—" She breaks off, suddenly thoughtful. "Actually, there might be . . . You play the cello, right? Have you ever taught?"

"No," I say, surprised that she would even think it possible. I'm still taking lessons myself.

"Would you like to try?" I must look lost because she laughs ruefully and says, "What I'm trying to say is, I need a cello teacher, and, well, here you are. Remember how I said I give away used instruments to my families' children? A month ago one of my old teachers gave me a half-size cello someone had donated to the school. It wasn't in great condition, but Shaul, a friend of mine from primary school, did some work on it, and I gave it to a girl who wanted it. Samira Harun, actually."

"The magician girl?" I say in astonishment.

Marah nods. "I showed her how to play, more or less, but I'm not a cellist. I'm afraid I'm setting her up with bad technique. And now you've come along . . ."

"You want me to teach Samira to play the cello?"

"Better you than me," Marah says. Hastily, she adds, "You

don't have to, of course. You might not want to, or you might not have time. But Samira's a wonderful girl, very bright, and she's dying to learn to play."

"Marah," Azariah says, "will the Haruns want a kasir giving their daughter cello lessons?"

If Azariah weren't a kasir himself, I'd be offended.

"Normally, I wouldn't consider it," Marah says. "Nobody in the slum trusts kasiri. But now that Samira's officially a magician herself, I think her parents might be a little more open to the idea."

"My father will never allow it," I say. Especially not if he hears Samira lives in the slum.

"Well, I didn't expect he would," Marah begins, but Azariah raises his eyebrows.

"You can't ask her to do this behind her father's back."

"She's already meeting us without his permission," Marah points out. "But you don't have to, Rivka."

Part of me believes Marah won't mind if I refuse, but another part of me worries she'll change her mind about helping me find Arik if I don't say yes. And then Azariah might change his mind. If I don't do her this favor in return, will they think I'm ungrateful? It would be another secret to keep from Father, but I already have so many.

"I'll do it," I say, feeling a thrill at plunging headlong into another risky endeavor.

"Are you sure?" Marah says, as if she regrets bringing up the idea in the first place.

"Yes." It's not a lie. I want to meet the first wilding to stay with her birth parents.

Marah beams. "My thanks! Can you meet me at the Ikhad at one on Ninthday? Or is that too soon?"

Ninthday is in two days. "That should work," I say recklessly.

"Excellent," says Marah. "There's one more thing. You'll have to wear halan clothes. It'll put the Haruns more at ease, and . . . there are people in the slum who bear a great deal of ill will toward kasiri. You'll be safer if you aren't dressed as one."

I hadn't thought of that, but she must know what she's talking about. It would also be disastrous if a Firem teacher or one of the embassy secretaries saw me with Marah at the Ikhad and informed Father. They're less likely to notice me if I'm dressed as a halan. There's only one problem.

"I don't have any halan clothes," I say.

Marah looks me over. "I wonder . . . Here, stand up."

I obey. Even though I'm four years younger than Marah, I'm already as tall as her.

"We're near the same size," she says. "What if I lent you a couple of things?"

I nod, and she disappears down the hallway. While she's gone, Caleb asks Azariah and me to fill him in on what I've just agreed to. His sister soon returns with a brown skirt and a pale blue shirt. I take them, dazed by this swift turn of events.

Caleb shows me out while Marah and Azariah wash the tea glasses. As we say goodbye on the landing, something stiff in his manner reminds me of his fight with his sister. I hold out my hand for his slate, and when he gives it to me, I write, *I wouldn't mind if you came to the archive.*

Judging by Caleb's grimace, I correctly guessed the subject of their argument.

My thanks, he writes. *It's not really the archive. It probably actually is better if I don't come. But she never wants me to do anything. Everything's always "too dangerous." But only for me, of course, not for her. Never for her.*

15

By evening, I'm beginning to think I was too hasty when I told Marah I would wear her clothes. Even if I manage to sneak out of the house unseen, I can scarcely walk down Embassy Row dressed as a halan. But by the time we reach the slum where Samira lives, I need to be wearing Marah's shirt and skirt. I don't see how it can be done unless I actually change in the street.

I'm still pondering this dilemma after dinner in Father's study as I wait for my magic lesson to begin. I idly turn the pages of the spell book on my lap. Since earlier this month, Father has had me choose a new spell to cast each week. To-night, I've picked a spell for brightening lamplight, another fairly straightforward enchantment I would be learning at school this year if I were still in Atsan.

Father is running late, and as I leaf through the book containing my chosen spell, I get an idea. What if I *could* leave the embassy unseen in Marah's clothes? Seized with in-spiration, I flip to the index of the book, searching for *invis-ibility*. Nothing. I jump up and grab several more spell books off the shelves. In the third book, I find what I'm looking for: a one-voiced spell and counterspell for invisibility. It's called the Veil. I notice a warning under the printed music: *The longer invisibility is maintained, the harder the counterspell becomes to cast.*

Just then, Father strides into the study. "My apologies, Rivka. Have you selected a spell?"

"This one." I show him the book. "I want to learn to make things invisible." I'm careful to say *things*, not *myself*, because he cannot suspect how I actually intend to use this spell. If he can teach me to cast it on an object, I'm sure I'll be able to cast it on my body.

Father raises his eyebrows. "The Veil? This is much more advanced than anything else you've chosen. Back home, you would not learn such a spell for several more years."

"I wanted to try something a little more challenging," I say innocently, making myself meet Father's gaze. I must tread cautiously because I have never before shown any interest in tackling hard spells. I mastered everything we were taught in school, of course. Being good at magic is a crucial part of my model-daughter act. But no love of magic ever stirred me to seek knowledge above and beyond what was expected of me. After all, it was magic that split Arik and me apart, binding me to the Kadmiel family while he was cast out.

Father studies me curiously. I hope he's pleased I'm finally demonstrating some ambition, not skeptical of my motives. At last, he smiles. This is such a rare event I almost drop the spell book.

"It is a difficult spell, to be sure," Father says, "but if you work hard, I believe you can cast it successfully. Shall we begin?"

I decide on a chair as my target. As always, I must learn to cast a new spell by singing it before casting it on the cello. The notes of the Veil aren't hard to memorize, but making it work is another matter. I've never attempted an enchantment so subtle. Casting it is like trying to balance my mind on the edge of a knife blade. After I've sung it a dozen times without success, my throat is dry, and I'm close to despair. Father offers more suggestions and easily sings the chair invisible and visible again, even though I've never seen him—or anyone—cast the Veil before. It's already ten minutes past when my lesson usually ends, but I won't rest until I've learned this spell. Father, delighted by my refusal to give up, hasn't even glanced at the clock.

I breathe in deeply and sing the spell again. All at once, the chair is gone. There is no gradual fading; one moment it was there, and now it isn't. I reach my hand out, and my fingers brush against unseen wood.

"Well done!" Father says. "Leave it alone for a bit while we consider the counterspell."

I break into a smile, my accomplishment finally sinking in.

I spend a few minutes memorizing the counterspell, stealing glances at the chair every so often to marvel at its continued invisibility. Father gives me some advice on making objects visible again, and then I sing the counterspell. The chair remains stubbornly concealed. I'm not too worried, since it took me quite a few attempts to manage the original spell. I try again. And again. Soon I've cast the counterspell twice as many times as I had to cast the invisibility spell, and nothing has happened.

Father looks pensively at the spot where the chair should have appeared. "We may have left it invisible a bit too long for your first time. The Veil's counterspell is tricky, and as the book says, it becomes harder to pull off the longer the invisibility lasts."

I also stare at the empty air where the chair is. It's stuck. With every passing minute, its invisibility becomes more permanent. That chair could have been me. It still could be, if I'm not careful. I start to sweat.

". . . cast the invisibility spell, your mind must be transparent, like glass, or better yet, air." Father is dispensing advice again, so I pay attention. "Now, your mind must be solid, like rock."

With his guidance, and after three more failed attempts, I finally bring the chair back. This time, there is no sweet taste of victory but only a wave of relief that feels more like queasiness. A faint hum drones in my ear.

"Good work, Rivka!" Father says. "How do you feel? Any lightheadedness? Nausea?"

I remember with a start that these are the symptoms of stretching one's magical abilities beyond their natural limits. I've never experienced them before. Could this dizziness be it?

"I feel fine," I tell Father. The buzzing noise is fading already. "Can I try again?"

⚓ ⚓ ⚓

On Eighthday, Father has a lunch engagement, giving me ample time to figure out how to make myself invisible without risking his walking in on me. In my bedroom, I practice making various objects—a book, my desk lamp, the wardrobe—disappear and reappear again before focusing the spell on myself. I succeed on my first try. When I look down at my body and see nothing but the honey-colored floorboards, I nearly fall over with the shock. I sing the counterspell at once, terrified of trapping myself under the shroud of invisibility. My limbs return, and I wait for my hammering heart to settle before plunging back in.

This time, I stay invisible for a whole minute. The clock on my nightstand ticks out each excruciating second. When I cast the counterspell, my body reappears without a hitch. Cautiously, I work my way up to three minutes, then five minutes. By the time Father returns, I can make myself invisible for fifteen minutes, more than long enough to escape the Embassy and meet Marah tomorrow.

At lunch on Ninthday, I tell Father I'm going to Firem to review for a test with Hilah. Up in my room, I wriggle out of my long black dress and throw on Marah's clothes. With a shiver of apprehension, I sing myself invisible.

A minute later, I'm out in the balmy spring air, striding away from Embassy Row as fast as I can. Clutched in my hand is the pendant watch I usually keep in my purse. I check it obsessively as I hurry through the cobbled streets.

Near the Ikhad, I wedge myself in a recessed doorway to cast the counterspell. By my watch, it's only been nine minutes, but I don't want to push my luck. The magic is difficult, sticking like a bad lock. Grimly, I remind myself that I didn't fail once yesterday, and at last I manage to shed the

Veil. I creep out of the doorway, expecting to attract attention in these unfamiliar clothes, but no one gives me a second glance.

Marah is waiting for me in the square, wearing a knapsack that makes her look like a schoolgirl.

"Rivka!" she says, waving.

"Hello," I say, breathless and a little woozy from casting the counterspell.

She looks me over and nods, satisfied. "Let's be on our way."

The walk to the slums is far longer than I expected, even at the fast pace Marah sets. I find myself wishing for the embassy auto and then feel ashamed of myself. Is this how halani get everywhere? Now I understand why Parliament is building streetcar lines.

We've long since left the grand limestone buildings of the city center. The last few neighborhoods have all been like Marah's slightly dingy halan district. I keep an eye out for Arik, but no one looks like my brother.

As we walk on, the four-story brick apartment buildings become dilapidated wooden houses with sagging porches and crooked gables. Children in much-mended garments scamper across the crumbling cobblestones and between wet shirts flapping on clotheslines. The houses strike me as surprisingly large until I realize by the number of women scrubbing sheets in metal tubs out front that each one is home to multiple families. I wonder if we've reached the slum, but Marah doesn't slow.

When the street peters out into a dirt road, she stops. "Do you mind if I braid your hair?"

"All right," I say.

Her hands make quick work of my thick dark hair, and she ties off the end of the braid with a bit of twine pulled from her skirt pocket. "There."

"I look like a halan now?"

"Oh, not up close. You still carry yourself like a kasir. But at least you won't stick out so much."

We pass the last boardinghouses and find ourselves amidst dwellings built of badly fitted boards and sheets of corrugated metal. Looking at some of the crude structures, I wonder how their inhabitants could possibly survive a north lands winter. It occurs to me that maybe they don't always, and I shudder.

"This is the slum," Marah says.

As we come tramping through, people emerge from their shacks. They light up at the sight of Marah. She smiles and greets them but doesn't pause to talk to anyone. I stick close to her as the slum dwellers stare at me.

Finally, we stop in front of a weathered hut. Fistfuls of dead grass are stuffed into the gaps between the boards. Marah knocks on the door, which hangs askew in its frame.

A woman in a sun-faded dress answers. She embraces Marah, greeting her in Xanite. Marah responds warmly in the same language and motions for me to follow her inside.

"You speak *Xanite*?" I mutter as we duck through the entrance.

"I studied it in secondary school," she says. "And I practice with Azariah sometimes."

The interior of the house is like a cave, dim and smelling of wet earth. It has only one room, barely larger than my bedroom. Two small children crouch in the corner, petrified, their eyes glued to me.

Opposite the door, an oil lamp sits on a piece of plywood laid across two crates. Two rolled-up reed mats lean against the wall next to a stack of folded blankets. Nearby is a wood-burning stove, and nestled in the far corner of the room is a worn canvas cello case.

"Rivka?" Marah beckons me and explains something to the woman in Xanite. I catch my name and try to smile. I hope my dismay doesn't show on my face. What am I doing in this place? Why did I agree to this?

"Rivka, this is Gadi Daud, Samira's mother," Marah says.

"Pleased to meet you," I say mechanically.

"Welcome," she says in Ashari. "I make tea."

"Oh, you don't have to do that," I say, but Marah elbows me, and I shut up. Gadi Daud opens the stove door to stoke the fire, then places a blackened teakettle on the burner. She turns to the two children and gives an order. The older girl runs out the door and soon returns with another child.

"Marah!" the new girl cries, a grin splitting her face.

"Samira," Marah says, opening her arms. Samira hugs her fiercely. The sleeves of her dress don't quite reach her bony wrists.

"I've found someone to teach you to play the cello properly," Marah says.

Samira turns to look at me. Her gaze is startlingly intense. I have the feeling she might recognize the clothes I'm wearing as Marah's.

"Who are you?" she says.

"My name's Rivka."

"You don't sound Ashari," the Xanite girl says. "Are you an immigrant?"

Gadi Daud starts to scold, but Samira doesn't seem to hear her.

"I'm from Atsan," I say.

"Atsan!" she says wonderingly.

"Come drink tea!" Gadi Daud interrupts, beckoning us to the makeshift table where she has set out three mismatched glasses. She quickly fills two of them and presses them on Marah and me. Since Marah accepts, I do too. Gadi Daud keeps the last, chipped glass for herself and her children, and they pass it among them. The tea is harsh and bitter, but drinking it makes me feel a little less out of place.

When we finish our tea, Marah pulls some forms from her knapsack to show Gadi Daud. Samira leans across the plywood to peer at them. "What are those ones for?"

"There's a new program for mothers with children under five," Marah replies. "I thought your mother should apply for Marwan."

"Will they give us more food for him?" Samira asks gravely, sounding much older than her ten years.

"If I can get your family enrolled," Marah says. "There's already a long waiting list, but it's worth trying. Why don't you and Rivka see what you can do with that cello?"

Samira darts to the cloth case in the corner and lays it on the dirt floor.

"Where do you sit?" I ask when she has unpacked the cello and bow.

She points to a crate standing on its short side, so that its length forms the height of the seat.

"Will it hold you?" I ask doubtfully.

By way of reply, Samira perches on its slats. They don't break.

I reach for her cello and pluck the strings, wincing at the warped intervals. Once I've coaxed the strings in tune, I check the straightness of the bridge and the condition of the bow before handing the instrument back to Samira. She already knows how to let out the endpin and tighten the bow's horsehair, but I help her adjust both. She has a lump of amber rosin Marah gave her, and I have her rub some on the bow hair. Then I teach her the names of the strings and show her how to tune them. I ask her to play an open string. She clutches the bow in a death grip. Patiently, I mold her hand into the correct bow hold. In the background, Marah is talking to Gadi Daud in Xanite.

I show Samira how to draw her bow across the strings, unbending her arm as she reaches the end of the horsehair. She catches on quickly, applying herself with a single-mindedness that impresses me. She seems so absorbed in following my instructions that I'm unprepared when she suddenly says, "You're a kasir, aren't you?"

I go still. My silence is her answer.

As though sharing a secret, she says, "I'm a magician."

"I know."

"They were going to take me away."

"You aren't going to be taken away," I say at once. It might be a lie, because the moratorium is only temporary, but I need to promise her this. "Play your open strings again."

She obeys, and for a while we practice smooth bow strokes.

"Rivka," Marah says from the plywood table, "we should leave in a few minutes."

I nod and turn back to my student. "You're doing really well. Play every day, if you can. Show me your bow hold one last time."

She sticks out her arm. I correct her grip once more, gently bending her knuckles.

"You'll come back, right?" she says.

I look at Marah, who looks as hopeful as the little girl. "Yes," I say. "I will."

I'll worry about keeping all this from Father later.

16

Midway through the week, Caleb tells me Azariah's request for permission to enter the changeling archive has been granted. The archive is open from eight to four every day, and Azariah proposes going on Seventhday at half past one. I agree at once.

At lunchtime on Sixthday, I ask Hilah, "Can I be studying with you again tomorrow afternoon?"

She looks amused. "You'll be somewhere else, I suppose?"

"Right," I say, gazing down at my stewed greens.

"What are you doing on Seventhday afternoons?" she says. When I don't answer, she says, "Nobody asked if you were with me last weekend. Not that anyone ever asks me anything."

"So it's not too much trouble?"

She shrugs. I'm afraid I've hurt her feelings.

"Would you like to come over on Eighthday?" I ask impulsively.

She breaks into a smile. "I'd love to!"

I feel relieved. Now the balance of favors between us won't be so lopsided. Better yet, I can introduce her to Father and Gadi Yoram so they'll have a face to picture whenever I tell them I'm spending time with Hilah.

✢ ✢ ✢

On Seventhday, I meet Azariah Rashid at Firem. We walk to the archive of changeling records, which is tucked away on a side street near Parliament. Azariah rings the bell. While we wait, I fret over whether I make a convincing enough research assistant. I'm suddenly tempted to cast the Veil over myself and follow Azariah into the archive unseen, but I can't risk staying invisible for more than fifteen minutes, and we're sure to be here far longer.

Before I can ponder this further, the door opens, and a man in a black suit pokes his nose out. "Yes?"

"I'm Azariah Rashid, the Firem University student who was recently granted permission to view the archive," Azariah says crisply.

"Ah, of course," the man says, looking us both up and down. "We are delighted to welcome such an illustrious guest to our humble archive. Come in and we'll review your paperwork."

There's no hiding now. I follow Azariah down a narrow hallway to a gloomy office illuminated by a single electric bulb. Heavy green curtains cover two of the three windows, and the block of sunlight that falls in through the third is thick with dust motes. The official bends over a cluttered desk, the tufts of his white hair bobbing as he searches for a document amid the disorder. At last he holds up a letter on fine stationery.

"Here it is." The official frowns at Azariah. "You're a bit young to be losing yourself in archives already, aren't you?"

"I'm helping a professor research families in which changelings have been especially common, historically," Azariah says. "He thinks it could shed light on how to reduce the number of changelings, which is something we'd all like, isn't it?"

His delivery is good, but I'm still alarmed. All it would take is one inquiry to the Firem history department for the archive keeper to discover that no such research project exists.

But the official nods and glances at me. "You've brought an . . . associate?"

My heart beats fast.

"She's a research assistant," Azariah says. "She's here to make the job go faster."

"Very well," the official says. "Follow me, please."

He approaches a door behind the desk and inserts a large metal key into the lock. The door opens with a terrific creak. We enter a chamber filled with wooden file cabinets. Sunlight slants in through a high window. It is as quiet as a library, but the silence is oppressive. I can feel the weight of all the paper kept here, paper recording the lives of hundreds of children who were wrenched from their families due to an accident of birth. My skin breaks out in gooseflesh.

"What era were you looking for?" our guide asks Azariah.

Azariah hesitates. To keep up the pretense of working on a historical project, we need to inspect old records, but in fact we've come for a very recent one. How are we going to find it if this leech-like official won't leave us in peace?

"Turn of the century," Azariah says finally.

The archive keeper leads us down a row of file cabinets and points to a number carved into the wood. "This is where the years are marked. Each cabinet contains five years' worth of records." He opens a drawer, revealing dozens of stiff brown files, each one marked with a name in spidery handwriting. "They're alphabetized by birth name."

"I see," Azariah says. "My thanks."

He waits to see if our guide is going to return to his dust-choked office. The old man doesn't move. My stomach clenches with the start of panic. How are we going to shake him?

Azariah clears his throat. "Rivka, why don't you start on this cabinet? We're looking for Gavriels and Yitzchaks, mainly. Pull out any Shachars too."

I slide open a drawer at chest level and cough as a cloud of dust puffs out.

"The archive seems quite neglected," Azariah remarks, looking askance at the dust coating everything. Wondering if this is a hint, I cough harder.

"May I bring you a throat lozenge, my dear?" the archive keeper asks me.

I nod.

"Perhaps we could all use one," Azariah says meaningfully.

"I'll fetch a handful," the official says.

As soon as he has tottered away, I stop coughing. "What are we going to do?" I whisper. "He won't let us out of his sight."

"We'll have to pretend to work for a while," Azariah says, listening for the returning footsteps of the archive keeper. "Then I'll try to lure him away so you can find the file."

"What if—?"

"Look busy," he hisses, yanking open another drawer.

I bend over mine, examining the contents. Some of the cardboard files are disintegrating at the edges, and I can barely make out the names. They're all terribly old-fashioned: lots of Mordokhais and Binyamins and Tsipporahs and Malkahs, all spelled the Ashari way, which makes them look doubly strange. Before I can speak to Azariah again, the archive keeper returns with the throat lozenges.

We work in silence for what feels like ages. I worry my lozenge with my tongue, knocking it against my teeth over and over. The official watches us with neither interest nor boredom. By some miracle, I actually come across a file bearing the surname Gavriel. I ease it out of the drawer and set it on the floor.

When we have collected a small stack of files, Azariah asks the official, "May I examine these in your office? The light is better there."

"Of course," the official says.

Azariah starts down the aisle, but when the archive keeper doesn't follow him, he stops. "Would you be willing to come with me? I might need your help figuring out what everything means, especially with these older records."

The official looks indecisively from me to Azariah. "I am at your service," he says at last, walking slowly after Azariah.

I wait until they're gone and then dart up the aisle in the

opposite direction. I follow the cabinets forward in time until I reach the second to last one. I check the numerals carved into the wood. This is it.

With trembling hands, I open the drawer at my waist and find myself in the right part of the alphabet. But when I find the place where Kadmiel should be, there is nothing.

Maybe it's been filed out of order. I glance over the whole drawerful and still don't see my surname. Desperate, I start to go through the files one by one. I can't find Kadmiel anywhere. Will I have to look through the entire cabinet?

Then something awful occurs to me. What if they filed him under the adoptive name he was given when he came to Ashara? That's not how the archive keeper said the records were organized, but Arik's case was unusual.

Suddenly, I remember that there's another name he could be filed under: his first adoptive name, the one he had in Atsan. That day in the park, he told me his new parents' surname was Yadon.

I shove in the drawer where Arik's record should've been and crouch to open a different one. I flip through the files, wanting to go faster, faster, but afraid of missing the name in my haste. And then I see it: *YADON, Malakhi*.

I tug the file free and open it, my heart beating wildly. The first thing I see is a palm-size photograph clipped to the first document. Arik's face stares out at me, unsmiling. It's my brother as I last saw him, at age ten.

I look at the document under the photograph. The first item is *Birth name*, which is listed as *Malakhi Yadon*, but there's a note scrawled in the margin: *Atsani adoptive name. Original Atsani birth name: Arik Kadmiel.* I steel myself and read his Ashari adoptive name. *Elisha Natan.*

Elisha. It's a nice enough name, but it belongs to a stranger.

I fumble in my purse for a pencil and a little notebook and scrawl down Arik's new name, along with the names of his adoptive parents, Ezra Natan and Hadassah Maor. Then I copy their address. When I get to the words *Horiel District*, I almost drop my pencil in surprise.

The squeal of neglected hinges echoes under the archive's soaring ceiling. I slap Arik's file shut, stick it back in the drawer, and walk swiftly back to where I was working. I pull open a cabinet drawer at random, my knees weak. A moment later, Azariah and the archive keeper amble up the aisle.

"How are things progressing?" Azariah asks, his tone detached. I meet his gaze and catch the silent question there. I jerk my head in a nod that could just be a twitch, but Azariah understands. His shoulders drop ever so slightly.

"It's all right if you haven't found anything more," he says. "We have enough for now."

"You're leaving?" the official says hopefully. I'm glad he's as eager for us to go as I am because I don't want to spend another minute in this dusty archive of horrors.

"Yes," Azariah says.

Outside, I gulp in fresh air and lift my face toward the sun. Then I turn to Azariah and grin. We did it.

⭑ ⭑ ⭑

At the Levis' apartment, Caleb and Marah are waiting for us, eager for news. Their mother doesn't appear to be home. Marah puts the teakettle on while Caleb offers us a plate of shortbread. I bite into a crumbly square.

"It's delicious," I say. "Who made it?"

After a moment, Caleb points to himself. I look at him in surprise. I assumed his mother or Marah had baked it.

"It's very good," I tell him. He grins.

We gather around the table, Marah tending the teapot. Smiling broadly, I take my notebook from my purse.

"My brother's adoptive name is Elisha Natan," I announce. "And he lives in Horiel."

"What?" Marah exclaims. She bends over my notebook, and Caleb comes around the table so he can see too.

"I know where that street is," Marah begins, but Caleb catches his breath. He signs to me.

"I know Elisha Natan," Marah translates.

I stare at Caleb. He signs more.

"He was at Horiel Primary when I was there," Marah says.

"Hang on," Azariah says. "Are we sure this is the same person?"

Caleb notices he spoke and frowns.

"Does he look like me?" I ask.

Glancing back at me, Caleb signs something that looks frustrated.

"Sorry," Azariah says, "we're all talking at once."

Marah signs to Caleb, and he returns to his chair.

"Tell me about Elisha," I say when he's watching me.

He thinks back, his brow furrowing. And then he tells me, as Marah interprets.

"I met him four years ago when I started school. Right after the Assembly fell."

"That's when Arik came to Ashara," I say, my heart racing.

"School was . . . hard." Marah's jaw tightens as she watches her brother sign. "Most of the teachers refused to do anything to make it easier for me to follow their classes. The only way I could talk to my classmates was by writing, and most of them didn't have the patience for it. They thought I was some kind of idiot. But then I started doing well, and they hated me for that."

I feel indignant on Caleb's behalf, but what does any of this have to do with Elisha?

"There was another boy in my class that everyone hated," Marah says as Caleb signs. "We weren't friends exactly. It was hard to talk, because we had to write, and he wasn't talkative. His name was Elisha Natan. I asked him once if he was new too, and he said he'd just moved to Horiel."

"Could you tell if he was a wilding?" I ask breathlessly.

Caleb shakes his head apologetically.

"I was missing so much of what was going on," Marah translates. "I saw our classmates taunting him, but I couldn't figure out why. He seemed unhappy, but he wouldn't explain."

"Did he play the violin?" I realize I desperately want this Elisha Natan to be my brother. But Caleb shakes his head.

"He wasn't in the medsha," Marah translates. "And I never saw him with a violin."

"It could still be him," Azariah says. "How many Elisha Natans can there be in Horiel? Rivka and her brother are the same age as Caleb. It fits."

"We should go find him," I say resolutely.

"You can't just go knocking on his parents' door," Marah says, alarmed. "How do you think they'll react if you show up without warning and announce you're their son's kasir sister from Atsan?"

"He's not their son," I say, recoiling. "He's my brother."

"He's their son," Marah says. "He's been their son for four years." Before I can protest, she continues, "And there's the fact that you're not allowed contact with him by Ashari or Atsani law."

Caleb's gaze darts from me to his sister, his forehead wrinkled in concentration. He signs to Marah.

"Caleb could find out whether Elisha Natan is really your brother," she says. "If he is, he could arrange for you to meet."

"That's a good idea," Azariah says, facing Caleb. "You're the only one with a connection to Elisha."

I almost choke. "*Caleb's* the only one with a connection?"

Azariah grimaces. "I didn't mean it that way. But your connection is to Arik Kadmiel. You'd never heard of Elisha Natan until today. Caleb knows Elisha, whoever he is."

"I think he's your brother," Marah says. "It can't be a co-incidence. But Azariah's right. It makes sense for Caleb to be the go-between."

I don't want Caleb to be the first one to talk to Arik after all these years. *I* want to be the one. But in the end, I agree to send Caleb to find Elisha Natan.

17

On Eighthday afternoon, the embassy doorbell rings. By the time I've raced down from the residence, Gadi Yoram is already inviting Hilah in.

"This is my friend Hilah from school," I tell the housekeeper.

"Welcome to the Atsani embassy, Gadin Hilah," Gadi Yoram says.

"My thanks," Hilah says.

I bring her upstairs and show her around, though I'm sure the county governor's house in Daresh is as grand as this one. In the music room, she brushes her fingers over the piano's ivory keys.

"Do you play?" I ask.

"I took lessons," she says. "But I stopped when I came to Firem."

"Play something."

"I'll embarrass myself," says Hilah, but she sits at the piano and plays a chord. "Oh, it has a nice touch." She launches into an unfamiliar impromptu, something light and frothy. She plays well, much better than Mother ever did. A dull pain flashes somewhere near my heart.

My classmate stumbles on an ascending run. "That's where I always get stuck. I haven't played in—" She falls silent, and I turn to see Father standing in the doorway.

"Is this your friend, Rivka?" he says.

Hilah looks mortified to have been caught playing the residence piano by the Atsani ambassador.

"Yes," I say. "We're in the same class at Firem."

My friend leaps up from the piano bench. "Good afternoon, Ambassador Kadmiel. My name is Hilah Menachem."

I can sense the good impression she's making on Father, and I could hug her.

"Welcome, Hilah," Father says. "I'm glad to meet Rivka's study partner at last."

Hilah doesn't bat an eye. It starts to sink in exactly how much I owe her.

"Rivka tells me your mother is the governor of Orev County," says Father. "You grew up in Daresh, then?"

"Yes, sir." Hilah says nothing about the halan friends of her childhood.

"Well, I'm glad Rivka has found a friend in you," Father says.

He means he's found her suitable. But he's right. I have found a friend in Hilah, or perhaps an accomplice. I'm not so sure Hilah has found a friend in me.

I take her to my bedroom. Gadi Yoram brings us a tray with a steaming teapot and two cinnamon buns. I serve the tea on my desk, and we savor the warm rolls standing up, catching crumbs in our palms.

"These remind me of our cook's cinnamon buns," says Hilah.

"Are hers as good as these?" I tease.

She looks thoughtful. "I think food from home always tastes best, don't you?"

I shrug.

Hilah puts down her half-eaten cinnamon bun. "I miss home. I miss my parents, and Daresh, and our cook's dishes . . . Are you ever homesick for Atsan?"

"No," I say honestly. Hilah turns away, but not before I see the disappointment and loneliness in her eyes. I regret my blunt reply, but I don't know what to do besides refill Hilah's tea glass.

We finish our buns and sit on my bed, afternoon sunbeams falling across our laps.

"So what is it you do when your father thinks you're studying with me?" Hilah asks.

I glance nervously at the door. Father and Gadi Yoram are probably downstairs, but I'm still wary about talking about this under the embassy roof.

Unlike at school, though, Hilah doesn't back down. "I pretended in front of your father, didn't I? You can trust me."

I don't want to lie to her. I lie enough to Father and the other girls at school and the rest of the embassy staff, and I'm weary of it. Hilah deserves better. But I keep silent.

"Come on, Rivka."

"I can't tell you," I say finally. "I'm sorry, Hilah." I expect her to retort that if I can't tell her I can't expect her to cover for me either.

Instead, she says, "Are you seeing a boy?"

"Am I *what*?" I almost laugh. "No, of course not."

Hilah looks unconvinced. "What about Caleb Levi?"

My heart stops for the space of three beats. Hilah has struck much, much too close to the mark. "Are you crazy?" I say. "Caleb Levi's a halan. And anyway, I'm not seeing anyone." I feel bad about dismissing Caleb as a halan like that, but it popped out of my mouth. Hilah looks as though she noticed, though, and a trickle of shame creeps down my back.

"The other week . . ." She traces the embroidery on my bedspread. "I was on my way to buy ink after school, and I saw you and Caleb in a park."

My blood freezes. If she saw us, who else might have?

"You were writing back and forth on that slate he always carries around," Hilah says. "It looked like you were friends."

I silently utter all the swearwords I know. "Aradi Noach makes me share my notes with him, remember?" I say. "We ran out of time in second period that day, so we met up after school. He was just asking me some extra questions."

Hilah hesitates. "That's not what it looked like."

"Hilah!" She draws back from me. "There's nothing going on between Caleb Levi and me. We talk about our literature classes. That's all."

"You don't have to pretend you're not friends," Hilah says, a touch defensive. "I told you all my friends from home are halani."

"All right," I say, dropping my voice to a whisper, "we're friends, but nothing more. And I do not see Caleb Levi on the weekends."

"Fine, I believe you," Hilah says. I hope she's telling the truth. That would make one of us.

18

I arrive at school on Firstday morning hoping Caleb will have news of Elisha Natan, but he doesn't. With each passing day, my impatience grows. Though I try to conceal it from Caleb, he can tell anyway.

I can't just knock on his apartment door, he writes in the library one morning. *One of his parents would probably answer, and then what would I say?*

You used to know him, I write back. *It wouldn't be that strange.*

But how would I have gotten his address? That would be strange.

Pursing my lips, I return to my biology homework.

On Fourthday morning, Caleb is waiting for me outside Aradi Noach's classroom. He looks up and down the empty hallway and then tilts his slate toward me. *It's him.*

I stare. A tentative smile spreads across Caleb's face, and I have the sudden urge to hug him. But our classmates start spilling into the hall, Merav in the lead. Caleb drops his head and moves past me, as if we weren't talking at all. Merav throws me a haughty look as she walks into the classroom.

Once Caleb and I are safe in our alcove in the library, I say, "Tell me everything."

As Caleb writes, my mind fills with memories of Arik. How much will he have changed? I'm bursting with questions, but they will only slow Caleb down. It's excruciating having to wait for him to write. I wish I knew sign language.

At last, Caleb passes me his slate.

After school yesterday, I walked to Dogwood Street in Horiel. I've been there every day, but yesterday a boy came along holding a violin case.

"He's playing again!" I murmur.

He looked a bit like you, but I wasn't sure. As soon as he stopped in front of the address you gave me, though, I knew. I walked up to him. I hadn't planned what I was going to say, but he recognized me. He said it was good to see me after all these years, and he invited me upstairs, as if I were an old friend.

"Of course he did," I say, unable to stop smiling. That's Arik, good to the core. I'm not surprised he was so glad to see Caleb, and I know he'll be even gladder to see me. I slide the slate back to Caleb, and he writes more.

We didn't go upstairs. I told him I go to the school for the deaf now. He goes to Kazeri, a halan music school. I didn't know how to tell him about you. Finally, I just asked him if he was from Atsan. He looked scared. It was pretty obvious the answer was yes. So I asked if he was a changeling. He was upset and asked if I'd always known. I said I didn't care if he was, I just had to make sure. He asked why, and I asked him if he was Arik Kadmiel. His eyes got huge. I told him not to worry, that I only knew because you were here looking for him.

As Caleb erases the slate again, the chalk rolls off the table. I lunge for it, starving for Arik's words.

At first, he couldn't speak. Then he said, "How?" I told him about your father being ambassador and us meeting at Firem. He looked like he'd been struck by a streetcar. Then he said Nechemya Kadmiel wasn't his father.

"What? He said that?" Then Elisha Natan can't be Arik. But then I realize he probably wouldn't even know Father's full name unless he was Arik.

I told Elisha you really wanted to see him, Caleb writes, *and he said he really wanted to see you too. I said I'd talk to you about figuring out how you could meet.*

He looks at me expectantly. I'm suddenly speechless. After years of dreaming and hoping, I'm finally only one person removed from my brother. Caleb spoke to him, actually spoke to him, only yesterday.

Where could we meet? I finally write.

My apartment, probably. We'd just have to pick a day when Mother's at work.

By the weekend, the meeting is arranged. Hilah agrees to cover for me again, though I can feel her reproachful gaze on me for the rest of lunch. I wake up before dawn on Seventhday morning, my whole body tense with anticipation. It's difficult to believe that today is the day I will finally see my twin again.

Father is already reading the *Journal* at the breakfast table when I come downstairs in my plainest charcoal dress. It's one I play the cello in, so it has a wide skirt, closer to the halan style, except much longer. One of the maids serves me tea and fresh biscuits drizzled with honey.

"Do you have a busy day today?" I ask innocently when Father sets down the paper to butter another biscuit.

"A luncheon in the suburbs with an expatriate," he says. "Followed by a tour of his gardens. There are so many tiresome things one must pretend to take an interest in when one is ambassador."

"I'm going to spend the afternoon with Hilah," I say. "My friend who visited last weekend."

Father nods absently. "Such a respectable girl. That's fine, Rivka."

I smile to myself in grateful relief.

Early in the afternoon, long after Father has left for his luncheon, I slip out of the embassy. Walking to Horiel alone is nerve-wracking. When the streets are crowded, I'm afraid someone I know will see me, and when they're empty, I feel exposed. I wish I could hide beneath the Veil, but Caleb's home is far from mine, and I don't dare use the spell for that long. Fortunately, I reach the Levis' apartment without incident.

Caleb lets me into the kitchen. Marah is at the table, brooding over a glass of tea, but she brightens at the sight of me. "I'm so happy for you, Rivka. Listen, can you give Samira another cello lesson on Ninthday?"

I say yes, though I'm really too distracted to think about Samira. Caleb glances at the roughly carved wall clock and writes on his slate. *You and Elisha can use my room to talk. Let me show you.*

He leads me down the corridor to a cramped bedroom.

The bed is carelessly made with plain white sheets and a gray wool blanket. Its foot almost touches the desk, which is covered with schoolbooks and homework assignments. On our right, a small dresser and a bookcase lean against each other. Caleb makes a sweeping gesture, as if to say, *Make yourself at home.*

I face him. "Thank you."

He signs something I take to mean, *You're welcome.*

Someone knocks on the apartment door, and I jump. Caleb goes to investigate. Voices murmur in the kitchen, Marah's and another I don't recognize. My first thought is that it's not Arik, that this has all been a mix-up of unimaginable proportions and my hopes are about to be dashed. My next thought is guilt. Have I forgotten my brother's voice so quickly? I sink onto Caleb's bed, the blanket creasing beneath me.

There are footsteps outside the door, then silence. As though Arik is hesitating. Then the door swings inward, and there he is. My twin. He's tall, taller than me now. His hair is longish, curling around his ears. But his face is exactly the same.

"Rivka," he whispers, as if afraid I'll vanish.

I rush to him and hug him with all my might. He holds me just as tightly.

"Arik," I say, my voice grinding as if I haven't used it in a hundred years. "I said I would find you again."

"You have no idea how good it feels to hear someone call me Arik," my brother says.

We step apart to look at each other properly. Arik's eyes are filled with tears.

"Why are you crying?" I ask.

"I don't know." He laughs, and his tears run over. "Happiness? I can't believe it! I tried so hard to persuade myself I wouldn't see you again. I was sure it was impossible. But I couldn't help daydreaming about you appearing in the schoolyard at Horiel Primary one day . . ." He speaks with an Ashari accent now, and his voice has lowered.

We sit on the edge of Caleb's bed, unable to look away from each other.

"When Caleb Levi appeared on my street the other day," says my brother, "*Caleb Levi*, who I hadn't seen in years . . . He said your—our—father's an ambassador again."

I nod. "When he told me he was going to Ashara, I knew I had to go with him."

Arik frowns. "So you knew I was here? Does *he* know?"

"He knows, but he doesn't know I know."

My brother looks confused. "Then how . . . ?"

"Father told Mother, and Mother told me. She wasn't supposed to, but she did anyway, right before she—" I break off in horror. Arik doesn't know. He doesn't know anything that's happened since the day the policeman caught us in the park.

"Before she what?" Arik asks me, a strange quality to his voice.

I don't know how to tell him. I don't want to spoil the joy of our reunion. He probably thinks Mother is at the embassy right now.

"Mother is dead, isn't she?" Arik says quietly. "I've known for a while."

I look at him, stricken. "How?"

"The intuition."

"The what?"

"The intuition. The other sense."

"Oh," I say, startled. The other sense was how Arik knew he wasn't a magician that night all those years ago. When he tried to tell me, I didn't believe him. But he was right.

"I was afraid of this," Arik murmurs. "She was always so frail."

Remembering Mother's death has resurrected my own worn grief. "It got worse once you were gone. It was Father's fault. He forbade us to talk about you. Mother was heartbroken. She acted like you were dead, and I hated that, but when someone dies you want to be able to talk about them. Since she couldn't, she withered away. Father should've just let her talk about you!"

"It couldn't have been only that," Arik says gently. "Mother was never strong."

"I know," I say. "But if Father hadn't been so cruel, she might still be alive."

I tell Arik how I came to find him. "I could hardly believe it when Caleb said you were his friend at Horiel Primary!"

He flinches. "I wasn't much of a friend to him. I didn't even figure out he was the famous Marah Levi's brother for almost a month. It's hard to believe how badly he was treated, considering who his sister is. I should've done more to stick up for him, but I . . . I didn't want to make things worse for myself."

I'm uncomfortably struck by how similarly I've behaved at Firem.

"I'm glad he got out of Horiel and went somewhere better," Arik says. "Things got better for me too, especially after a violinist quit the medsha and I got to join."

"Tell me about your . . . family," I say. It gives me a twinge to call them that. I don't want to think that Arik has any real family but me.

"It's just me and Mother and Father," Arik says. "We live in an apartment like this one, on the other side of Horiel."

"You call them Mother and Father?"

My brother looks at me cautiously. "Yes. It was hard at first, especially with Mother, but they were nothing but kind to me when I first arrived. Now I'm used to it."

"Does Elisha Natan feel like your name?"

"It does," Arik says slowly. "It's not as hard to get used to a new name as you might think."

"But who do you think of yourself as?" I press him. "Arik or Elisha?"

My brother shrugs helplessly. "Both. But Arik is . . . the boy I was before."

"I'm here to call you Arik now," I say.

He smiles. "Tell me what you've been doing for the last four years."

"I don't know," I say, sighing. "Mostly wondering when I would see you again. And proving to Father that I'd forgotten you." I look at Arik anxiously. "I'm sorry. I had to make him trust me again. I did it to find you."

"I'm not angry," he says.

"He doesn't know who I really am," I say. "Half the time, I don't even know."

My brother frowns. "Who does, then?"

I don't answer.

"Your friends?"

"I don't have a lot of friends."

"Well, you just moved here."

"No, I mean even in Atsan. You were my best friend, Arik. After you left, our old friends . . . Well, they couldn't understand. So I avoided them. And once I got here . . . I didn't come to Ashara to make friends, I came here to find you."

Arik's expression is troubled. "You shouldn't not have friends because of me."

"It's not that," I protest. "It's that nobody understands. You're part of who I am, and I can't tell anyone you exist."

"What about Caleb?" my brother asks. "He knows I exist. He's your friend, right?"

"Yes," I answer, a beat too late, but Arik doesn't seem to notice.

"I'm glad," he says.

We talk until the angle of the sunlight streaming in through Caleb's window prompts me to check the pendant watch in my purse. It's almost five.

"I have to go," I say. "I need to be back at the embassy before dinner and my magic lesson with Father."

Arik's eyes dim with disappointment.

"When can I see you again?" I say, at the same moment Arik asks, "Can we meet again soon?"

We both laugh. "Next week?" I say. "If the Levis don't mind . . ."

Somehow, we summon the will to rise from the bed and trudge into the kitchen. Marah is standing by the pantry, signing rapidly to Caleb, who's stirring something in a mixing bowl. He drops his whisk to reply, and then they notice us.

"Now that I see you side by side," Marah says, "it's obvious you're related."

Arik and I exchange glances. Only this morning, I couldn't picture how he would look as a fourteen-year-old boy, but now I can't imagine him looking any other way.

"Can we come back next weekend?" I ask Marah.

"Of course," she says. "Whenever you need a safe place to meet, you're welcome here."

19

Two days later, I follow Marah through the maze of the slum in my borrowed halan garb. The air is choked with wood smoke and the smell of rotting garbage. In a shack somewhere, a child is wailing.

When we reach the Haruns', Samira answers the door. Her face lights up at the sight of us.

"You're here!" Behind her, a bunch of children, more than there were last time, huddle around the plywood table.

"Where's your mother?" Marah asks.

"At the neighbors'," Samira says. "Aunt Aisha's going to have her baby."

Samira stokes the fire and fills the teakettle from a bucket. While waiting for the water to boil, she rejoins her siblings at the low table. I recognize the five-year-old girl and the two-year-old boy from last week, but now there's also a girl of about seven and a boy of eight. Each child has a bowl of boiled potatoes.

"Samira, I can't stay," Marah says. "I have other families to see this afternoon."

The younger children drift from the table, skirting me as

they gravitate toward Marah. She gives each of them a hug, then points at me.

"This is my friend Rivka. You don't need to be afraid of her. She's here to teach Samira how to play the cello I brought her, remember? Soon she'll be able to play music for you." Marah glances at me. "You'll be all right?"

I don't relish the idea of being left here with five desperately poor Xanite children I barely know, but I nod, hiding my reluctance as easily as I hide my feelings from Father. Marah smiles gratefully, and then she's gone.

When I turn around, Samira is looking solemnly up at me. "I practiced every day."

"That's good. Today we can—"

Samira lunges for the toddler, yanking him away from the woodstove a moment before he grabs the teakettle.

"No!" she says fiercely. "Don't touch that. It's hot, and you'll burn yourself."

The boy starts to howl. Samira drags him over to the next-oldest girl. "You weren't watching, Shaden. You have to mind Marwan while I have my lesson. Don't look away for even a second."

Shaden accepts her screeching brother, but she pouts. "I'm still hungry."

Samira hands her a chipped bowl, her own, which still has some potatoes left in it. Then the kettle whistles, and she rushes to the stove.

While the tea is steeping, Samira fidgets with something hidden beneath her shirt. A fine metal chain snakes around her neck, dipping below her collar. When she sees me watching, she pulls an oval pendant out from under her shirt. "Do you want to see?"

She lifts the necklace over her head, drags it down her braid, and spills it into my hand. It's a cheap trinket made of tin. The oval charm is the size of a robin's egg, but flat. It has a seam around the edge, and I realize it's a locket.

"Can I open it?" I ask.

Samira nods. I pry the two halves of the locket apart. There's nothing inside.

"Why don't you keep anything in it?" I say.

She shrugs. "I don't have anything to put in it. But I like that it opens. It's like a secret."

"It's pretty," I tell her, returning the necklace. It's a small lie, but it seems like the right thing to say.

"Mother and Father gave it to me for my eighth birthday," Samira says as she pulls the chain over her head again. "It was my last birthday present."

I catch myself before I ask why. A tin locket might cost hardly anything, but it's probably still worth at least some food.

I gulp down one glass of tea to be polite, and then we begin our lesson. Samira's siblings play quietly on the other side of the room while she draws her bow across the strings. I fix her grip and place my right hand over hers, helping her make fluid bow strokes. Whenever her tone turns scratchy, she changes the way she's pressing into the strings until the sound improves.

"Can I use my left hand yet?" she asks eventually.

"I was about to suggest it," I say.

Samira lifts her left arm, and I put every joint in its place, as though I'm sculpting a cellist. "Keep your elbow out, your wrist straight, and your fingers curved, like they're around a tea glass. And keep your thumb behind your second finger."

I have her play a D-major scale note by note, tuning each one. When she concentrates on her left hand, her bow strokes turn jerky. But Samira doesn't give up. We don't stop working until she can play the scale almost perfectly in tune, with a reasonably pleasant tone.

"That's excellent," I say. "You're really talented, Samira."

My praise makes her shy, and she drops her gaze.

"I think we should stop for now," I say.

"Can't we do some more?" she pleads. "Marah's not back yet."

I laugh. "I don't want you to tire yourself out."

She sets her cello delicately on its side but does not move from her crate. There is a kind of hunger in her eyes. "Rivka, will you show me a spell?"

I'm taken aback by her request. Casting a spell in order to teach a student isn't frivolous, but I'm still hesitant. "Atsani magic is . . . different. We do magic with music."

She looks astonished. "I want to see!"

I suppose it can't hurt even if she'll eventually learn Ashari magic. I reach for her instrument, and she jumps up from the crate. I sit down gingerly, expecting to hear wood snapping beneath me, but the slats hold. Samira's half-size cello feels like a toy. I play a scale to get my bearings, then slide my hand up the A string and begin a short spell called the Glimmer. It's one of the first we learned in school and is of little practical use on its own, though it's woven into more complex spells of illumination. I focus the magic on the piece of plywood that serves as the Haruns' table.

As I repeat the melody, the board begins to glow. A soft vibration sounds through the room. Samira watches in awe while her siblings eye the shining table fearfully.

I'm halfway through another repetition of the spell when Samira's mother and Marah duck into the house. I feel them watching me, but I can't stop before I complete the phrase. The plywood blazes brighter.

"Rivka!" Marah warns. Gadi Daud screams. She runs to her children, attempting to wrap them all in her arms at once. Samira rushes to her, speaking rapidly in Xanite.

I finish the spell and meet Marah's unsmiling gaze. My heart drops into my stomach.

On the other side of the room, Gadi Daud stares at the glowing table, murmuring the same words over and over. Now that I've stopped playing the Glimmer, the light drains quickly from the wood.

While Marah reassures Gadi Daud in Xanite, Samira and I pack up her cello. She whispers her thanks in my ear before I straighten and gather the courage to face my host.

"I'm sorry for doing magic in your house," I tell Gadi Daud.

She seems to understand, but her eyes remain wary. I'm relieved when Marah hustles me out, waving to the children as we leave.

We've only walked a few steps from the Haruns' home when Marah says sharply, "Please don't ever cast spells there again."

Sour guilt washes over me. I wanted to make Samira happy, but now Marah is angry with me. Maybe she won't let me meet Arik at her apartment anymore.

"I'm sorry. Samira asked to see a spell . . ." I brace myself, expecting Marah to retort that I shouldn't pin the blame on a child.

Instead, she says, "I know. She told her mother that. But, Rivka, you don't understand how frightened most halani are of magic. Especially people who live here and have absolutely no reason to trust kasiri and plenty of reason to fear them. Samira's magic unnerves her family enough. They don't need magicians casting full-fledged spells in their house. Gadi Daud was nervous about you, but I promised her you were all right."

"Have I ruined everything?" I say softly.

Marah sighs. "I don't think so. Gadi Daud is starting to get used to the fact that Samira is a magician. And luckily, you're not too intimidating, especially dressed like that. But *never* do that again."

"I won't." Then, before I can help myself, I blurt out, "Are *you* afraid of magic?" Instantly, I wonder what's wrong with me. I'm usually so good at guarding my tongue.

Marah isn't offended though. "Not exactly. Not anymore. I know magic isn't inherently bad. I've seen Azariah cast dozens of spells. But sometimes when I see sparks out of the corner of my eye, I still get the urge to run."

"But why are halani afraid of spells?" I ask. "Because they can't cast them themselves?"

Marah doesn't answer right away. I've probably said something idiotic.

"When I was fourteen," she says at last, "I saw the police kill a woman with a spell in the middle of the Ikhad."

I suck in my breath.

"It wasn't even her they were after. She was just in their way."

We reach the place where the cobblestones return. The only sound is that of our shoes on the pavement. Then Marah says, "Are you afraid of the intuition?"

"The what? Oh, you mean the other sense."

"Is that what you call it? Yes. Are you afraid of it?"

"I'm not *afraid* of it." I wish I could turn back the conversation. "It's just . . . unnatural."

Marah laughs. "And what's magic?"

"That's different."

"Fair enough. But think about how you feel about the intuition. Now imagine that it wasn't just strange but could cause you real and permanent physical harm."

I shudder.

"That," Marah says, "is how halani feel about magic."

20

On Firstday morning, as I walk to Firem under the bright spring sun, I imagine Arik hurrying through the streets of Horiel District, gripping his violin case as he makes his way to Kazeri. I feel close to him even though I can't see him.

Can Arik and I meet at your apartment again this Seventhday? I write on Caleb's slate in the library after first period.

It should be fine, he writes. *He asked me the same thing yesterday.*

I glance up sharply. "You saw Arik yesterday?"

Caleb seems startled by my reaction. *He came over in the afternoon. I wasn't expecting him, but I was glad he dropped by.*

The shock wears off quickly, leaving in its wake a kind of gnawing anger. For Caleb to see Arik without me feels like a betrayal. It isn't fair that they can spend time together so easily when I cannot meet my brother without the utmost caution and subterfuge.

Caleb is watching me with concern. He lifts his eyebrows in a question. I shake my head. I know I'm being ridiculous, even if I can't help feeling left out.

On Seventhday, I arrive at the Levis' in a drab cello skirt

and blouse. When I knock, Marah answers. Arik and Caleb are sitting at the kitchen table behind her, passing Caleb's slate between them. The sight sends a spasm of jealousy through me.

I pull myself together and force a smile. Somehow it brings me to my senses and becomes a real smile. I'm being silly. I'm with my brother again. All is well.

"Rivka!" Arik pops up from his chair and envelops me in a fierce hug. "It's so good to see you! How was your week?"

"Too long," I say, laughing. "Yours?"

"Good! We started rehearsing this new piece. . . . Come, you have to try this rhubarb crisp Caleb made."

He pulls me to the table, where Caleb serves me a huge portion of crisp. He and Arik both have sticky plates in front of them. The crisp is delicious, the oats and brown sugar tempering the puckery tartness of the rhubarb. After I've polished it off, Arik makes to help Caleb wash up, but he waves us away to his room.

"Our father doesn't suspect anything, does he?" Arik asks as he sinks onto Caleb's rumpled bedding.

I drop into the desk chair. "No."

"Where does he think you are?"

"At Firem, studying with a friend."

Arik perks up, as though happy to hear I have at least one friend. "What's their name?"

"Hilah Menachem," I say. "Her mother's the governor of Orev County."

"Does she know—?"

"No."

Arik looks reassured. "So where does she think you are?"

"Um . . . she thinks I'm seeing Caleb in secret."

At first, Arik looks confused. Then he bursts out laughing. "Well, you are, aren't you?" If he weren't all the way on the bed, I would shove him.

My brother sobers. "She thinks you're seeing a halan boy and is still willing to cover for you?"

I shrug. "Hilah's funny. She grew up in the country, and there weren't any kasir children for her to play with, so her friends were halani. She doesn't seem to consider kasiri and halani as different as most people do."

"If only there were more people like her," Arik says wistfully.

In the bedroom next door, Marah is playing the violin. The melancholy air conjures images of the emptiness I saw through the train windows on my journey to Ashara. "What are we going to do, Arik?"

"Do?" he says.

"We can't go on like this." I gesture around Caleb's bedroom. "I want us to be sister and brother again."

"We are," Arik says, frowning.

"You know what I mean. I want us to live together. When I pictured us reunited, I always thought we'd be the Kadmiel twins again."

"I . . . I wish we could live together too, Rivka, but my parents don't know about you," Arik says. "And what we're doing right now is illegal."

"Who cares about the law?" I burst out even as Father's words reverberate in me again. *If you do it again, you will be sent to prison.* I shiver and immediately feel angry with myself. "The law might change when Parliament reconsiders forced adoptions in three months. And maybe if Father were to see you now, see us together, he would realize—"

"He saw us together at the police station," Arik says, his voice hardening, "and then he chose not to see me anymore. I remember the moment it happened. It wouldn't be any different today."

"But you've gotten into music school and everything!"

"It was never the music that mattered to him," Arik says. "It was the magic. And besides, I don't want to go back."

A cold feeling settles over me. "You don't?"

My brother's eyes widen. "Oh, no, I didn't mean—Rivka, I'm still your brother. I want to be with you more than anything. I just don't want to be a Kadmiel again."

"But I thought . . ." I was sure once I found Arik the rest would be simple. I imagined us belonging to the same family again. I didn't really think about how Father would figure into the picture.

"You love your new family best now?" I say miserably.

"It's not that," he says, distressed. "It's . . . What old family do you want me to love? Now that Mother's gone, it's just you and . . . him. He doesn't want me, and last week you sounded like you hated him. What kind of family would that be?"

"I don't know what to do," I say. "I've found you, but it's like nothing's changed."

"Everything's changed!" my twin says, astonished. "We're together."

We may be together right now, but it's not enough. And

Arik's right that there's no way for us to live under the same roof in Ashara. "Maybe we have to go to another city-state. Somewhere no one knows us. We can make a new life for ourselves."

My brother stares at me. It seems to take a few seconds before he comprehends what I'm saying. After a long pause, he says, "Rivka . . . My life is here now. I have Mother and Father and my teachers and classmates at Kazeri. I can't leave Ashara."

But what about me? I want to say. Even in my head, the words sound pitiful. I don't understand how this happened. Arik's the wilding, the one who was ripped from his family and shipped across the north lands like a parcel. He should be the one who feels adrift, like he belongs nowhere, but instead I'm the one who has nothing to lose anymore, who's ready to leave everything behind. Arik has connections that can't be severed, people who love him, a home he won't give up. He's probably spent the last four years making friends, not pushing them away.

When I say nothing, Arik continues in a hesitant voice. "Even if we did go to another city-state, they all have family laws. I can't be your halan brother, and you can't be my kasir sister. So what would we be in our new life?"

The answer is obvious. Arik can't pretend he has magic, but I can pretend I don't. I allow myself one small moment to mourn everything it would mean giving up—my freedom to go wherever I pleased, the automatic respect of the upper classes, the eventual right to vote—and then I say, "I would live as a halan."

I expected Arik to be moved by my willingness to make this sacrifice, but he doesn't look happy at all. "You don't know what you're saying. You think it'd be easy, but you have no idea what it's like to be a halan."

Anger scalds the back of my throat. "Like you're such an expert. We were raised the same way, Arik. Don't pretend we weren't."

"I'm not," he says, sounding annoyed for the first time. "But I know what I've lost. Kasiri don't see me anymore. Or else they look at me like they expect me to pick their pocket."

"If I don't understand, then I'll learn," I say. "I'll do it, Arik. Let's escape to Kiriz or somewhere."

But my brother is shaking his head, his expression sorrowful. "Fleeing wouldn't solve anything anyway. If we ran away to Kiriz to be siblings, nothing would change, except for us. This isn't about us."

"What? Of course it's about us."

"I meant . . ." Arik struggles for words. "It's not *only* about us. If we get to live as siblings, shouldn't everyone like us be able to?"

"I just want us to be together," I say tremulously. "I didn't come to Ashara to change the way things are. I came to find you. If we can find a way, it's enough."

"But that's selfish!" my brother blurts out.

The word slashes me like a sword. *Selfish*. Tears prick my eyes.

"I don't want to be an exception," Arik says, his tone almost pleading. "And aren't you giving cello lessons to Samira Harun, that girl the moratorium was passed for?

What if Parliament decides to lift the moratorium and leave the Family Laws intact? Even if we've found a way, what will happen to her?"

I don't answer. It finally hits me how stuck we are. Arik can't move into the embassy as the long-lost Kadmiel son. And he won't leave behind everything he knows so we can strike out on our own in another city-state. We're trapped here, forbidden from having any contact, our guardians unaware of our reunion.

"What should we do?" I ask, sure that he will see a way forward where I can't.

But he just says, "I don't know."

It's too much. It's like the day of our magic examination, when he stood there, resigned to his fate, while I fought and screamed. I can't stand it. Eyes brimming, I start up from Caleb's chair.

"Rivka, wait!" Arik says, but I burst out of the bedroom.

In the kitchen, Caleb is chopping an onion. He looks up in surprise when I storm past, and makes a sound, but I don't stop. I run down flight after flight of stairs, half blinded by tears. I make it out of the building without turning my ankle, and the fresh air and sunlight shock me into stillness.

Standing in the street, I look up at the fourth-floor windows. Caleb's and Arik's faces are framed in one of them. Turning away, I start walking as fast as I can, away from the Levis' apartment, away from Horiel District, away from the twin brother who thinks I'm selfish and loves his Ashari parents more than me.

21

On Ninthday, I accompany Marah to the slum again. She doesn't ask why I left her apartment so abruptly the day before yesterday, though I'm sure she must've overheard Arik and me arguing. I'm grateful for her tact, because I can't think of that afternoon without feeling a sharp pain in my chest.

The march to the city outskirts no longer hurts my legs. When we reach the Haruns' ramshackle house, Samira nearly bowls Marah over with a hug and then treats me to the same greeting. Her joyful welcome eases my heartache a little.

We enter the house and step into pandemonium. The older boy is chasing Shaden around the room while she shrieks in terror and excitement. Little Marwan is sitting on the floor, bawling. Gadi Daud isn't here.

Samira scoops up the infant, whose crying abates. "Bashir, no running inside!"

Bashir skids to a halt and grins up at Marah. Shaden leans against the wall by the woodstove, panting and giggling.

"I'm having my cello lesson now," Samira announces, "so I need some quiet. Don't you have homework?"

"I lost my pencil," Bashir says even as Shaden says, "There's no paper."

Samira chews her lip. "Father's bringing home more paper tonight." She sounds more hopeful than certain.

"I can bring you some paper," Marah says. "Could the other children in the neighborhood use some too?"

Samira hesitates, then nods.

"I'll try to get you a supply," Marah says.

She leaves to visit her other families, and Samira shows me her D-major scale. Her bow strokes are jerky, and she presses too hard into the strings, but the scale is remarkably in tune.

"That was good, Samira. I'm impressed."

She glows.

"Try to loosen your bow arm a bit. It's not made of wood."

She plays the scale again, and the improvement is marked. I've never had a cello student before, but they can't all be such naturals.

"I taught myself a song," Samira says.

"Oh?" I say. "Show me."

She plays a melody using most of the notes of the scale I taught her last week. Her bow slides wildly between the fingerboard and the bridge, and her left arm sinks to her side as she concentrates on pressing down the right fingers, but what emerges is unmistakably a tune.

"I can't believe you taught yourself that," I say. "What is it?"

"A song Mother sings," Samira says.

"And you just worked it out by ear?"

She cocks her head. "What's 'by ear'?"

"It means you figured out how to play it by listening, without any music."

"I had music," she says, frowning. "I know the song."

"I mean written music."

Samira blinks. "You can write music down?"

I stare back at her. It takes me a second to understand she has no concept of notated music.

"Yes," I say, "just like words. But really it's better to know songs by heart."

I work with Samira on the tune for a while. Her siblings gather round, mesmerized by the sound of this familiar song being drawn out of their sister's bulky instrument. Eventually, they grow bored and drift away. That's when Samira leans forward and whispers, "Can I show you something?"

"Of course."

Samira lays her bow across her lap and makes a circle with the fingers of her right hand. A marble of bronzy light materializes in the shelter of her palm. Her fingers spring apart, and the sphere of light explodes in a shower of gold sparks. Across the room, Marwan gasps with delight and claps his fat baby hands.

I knew from the beginning that Samira was a magician, but now I realize I didn't actually believe it. Because magic doesn't belong in a place like this, where the houses have no floors and the breeze whistles in through cracks in the walls and children go without so their younger siblings can have more to eat. And yet here's the proof.

"That was lovely, Samira."

"Mother cried the first time I did something like that," she says matter-of-factly. "Rivka, what's going to happen to me?"

"What do you mean?" I say cautiously.

"They didn't take me away because Marah persuaded Parliament to do the moratorium," she says, pronouncing this last word carefully. "But at the District Hall, they wrote down that I was a magician. Am I ever going to learn magic?"

"Do you want to?"

She nods without meeting my eyes, as though admitting to something shameful. "But I don't think Mother and Father want me to. And how am I going to learn magic here?" She looks around her one-room home.

A terrible thought crosses my mind, one that I immediately try to banish but whose truth I can't deny. If Marah hadn't won the moratorium from Parliament, this bright, inquisitive girl would be living with a kasir family in a proper house in the city. She would have her own room, with a bed and a desk and shelves crammed with books. She would have dresses without darns and leather shoes. She would be well fed, and she would attend a good school with other children like her, where she could learn magic and study music too.

Even as I envision this alternate life for her, a voice in my head shouts that it would be wrong. Her adoptive parents might mistreat her. Her new classmates would shun her for being a wilding, for being Xanite, for coming from the slum. Worst of all, she would be cut off from her parents and the little brothers and sisters she loves.

Still, I can't help thinking that Samira deserves to be plucked from her life of crushing poverty. No matter how much I want to, I can't convince myself that her being adopted by kasiri would be all bad. If only there were some way for her to have those opportunities without severing ties with her birth family.

All at once, I realize what I'm imagining is the Ashara people like Marah and Parliamentarian Nitsan want to exist. An Ashara with mixed families. An Ashara where Arik and I, and everyone like us, could be brother and sister.

"Rivka?" Samira says. I've been silent a long time. "Could *you* teach me magic?"

I frown. "You need to learn Ashari magic, Samira."

"But I want to learn musical magic," she says, tugging on the pendant around her neck. "I'm not learning any magic right now. Wouldn't this be better than nothing?"

"You don't have the training," I say. "By the time I started casting spells, I'd been taking music lessons for six years."

"But you could do something like what I can do with the light when you were younger, couldn't you?" Samira says shrewdly.

It's true. I feel myself weakening. The fact that Samira taught herself a song by ear in a week proves she has an instinctive sense for rhythm and pitch. What if I taught her the first spell I learned? Did I really need six years of musical study under my belt to cast it?

Samira senses me wavering. "I'll be careful, I promise. I'll do exactly what you say."

I'm about to give in when I recall the incident with the Glimmer and my promise to Marah. "Samira, I can't do magic here. Remember last time?"

A rebellious light gleams in her eyes. "Mother's not here. She won't know."

"I told Marah I wouldn't," I say, thinking Samira might be more in awe of the social worker than of her own mother.

"Marah's not here either."

She's so desperate for the tiniest taste of what it means to be a magician that I can't refuse her. I hope Marah will forgive me.

I sigh. "Put down your cello."

"What?" Samira's expression is betrayed. "Don't I get to play?"

"You learn to cast spells by singing first."

She swallows her disappointment. "All right."

"The spell I'm going to teach you is called the Seal. I need something . . ." My gaze falls on a tear in Samira's sleeve. She hastily tucks her arms behind her.

"Let me see your sleeve again," I say gently. "I need something to seal, and I think that will do."

Curiosity piqued, she forgets her shame and rises from the crate, holding out her forearm. I quiet my mind, banishing thoughts of a terrified Gadi Daud and a disapproving Marah. The spell is simple: eight notes into the heart of it and eight notes to complete it in balance. I focus on the frayed edges of Samira's sleeve, which part to reveal a sliver of brown skin.

I begin to sing. As the eighth note rings through the room, the cotton melds into smooth cloth. I sing through to the end. A fresh smell, like green growing things after a rainfall, fills the room. Samira peers in wonder at the joined fabric.

"That's the Seal," I say. Normally, I would never cast a spell to accomplish a task as trivial as fixing a tear. The Seal's real usefulness is as a building block in architectural and healing spells.

"That's it?" says Samira.

"It's not as easy as it looks. The spell isn't the tune alone. That's just the scaffolding. The important part is your will. But first, you have to memorize the melody."

I sing the Seal for her again, but only the music, without the power. It's like skimming the surface of a lake instead of plunging deep into the water. She tries to repeat it back to me but stumbles in the second half. I sing it with her a few times until she can do it herself.

"All right," I say nervously. "Now, try to open your mind to the magic around us." I feel foolish repeating the words our primary school teachers told us so long ago. "If that doesn't make sense now, it will as you practice. It might help to close your eyes. Imagine your mind isn't stuck in the darkness of your skull but is out under the sky."

The Xanite girl's eyes are screwed up tight, her hands curled into fists.

"You have to relax too," I say. "Imagine falling back to rest on something, like floating on your back in water—"

"I can't swim," Samira says, her eyes flying open.

"Then pretend it's a cloud. Something behind and beneath everything else. That's the magic."

The seconds slip by in silence. Then Samira says, "I think I feel it."

If she can talk, she probably doesn't, but she might as well make her first attempt. Casting about for something for her to seal, I find a folded bit of paper in the pocket of Marah's skirt. It's blank, so I tear a notch in it.

"Here," I say, giving Samira the scrap of paper. She presses it between her fingers, waiting for my instructions.

"Open your mind to the magic like you were doing," I tell her. "Now concentrate very hard on the rip in the paper, and picture it sealing itself back together. Then sing the spell."

Samira stands there with her eyes shut for a long time. Then she begins to sing, her voice clear and in tune. She performs the musical part of the Seal flawlessly, and when she reaches the end, her eyes pop open, bright with expectation. The paper in her hands is still torn. Her shoulders slump.

"That was good!" I say. "No one ever gets a spell on the first try. But you sang it perfectly."

She nods, but her posture remains defeated.

"Don't give up," I say. "Practice like you've been practicing cello, and you'll get it."

"My thanks," Samira says quietly. She looks around the room, blinking as though roused from a trance. Her gaze slides past her siblings, who are playing in the corner, and over the walls of her family's house. The warped boards aren't flush with one another, and the dried grass stuffed into the gaps is falling out.

"If I learn the Seal," she says slowly, "I could seal up our house. I could bring the boards together so the wind wouldn't get in."

I hesitate before saying gently, "That's different, Samira.

The fabric of your shirt, that piece of paper, they were torn, and the edges *want* to come back together. Those boards don't. They were just nailed together. You'd need an instrument to cast the Seal on them, and it would take more magic, more strength. Probably a more complex spell, actually. I'm sorry, but you won't be ready for a long time."

Samira's gaze is still fixed on the cracks in the walls. I have a feeling my words won't be enough to stop her from trying to close them up, even if all she succeeds in doing is making herself queasy and faint.

"You have to teach me more magic," she says at last. "I need to learn it, Rivka. If I could cast spells, I could make things better."

I hear Marah ordering me not to do magic in the slum, but how can I say no?

"I'll keep teaching you," I say.

Samira turns abruptly to me and clasps me in a hug.

Every time I consider asking Caleb about seeing Arik again, I hear my brother saying, *But that's selfish!* and cannot bring myself to speak. I keep hoping Caleb will tell me Arik wants to see me, but he doesn't mention my twin all week. When we were little and we fought, Arik was always the first to want to make up. He could never hold a grudge. Has he changed? Or has he not asked to see me because he thinks I don't want to see him?

I meet Marah at the Ikhad again on Ninthday. We don't speak on the long walk through the modest halan neighborhoods and the rows of run-down tenements. Soon after the street crumbles into dirt, something begins to feel different. There are no children racing through the lanes that snake between the tumbledown dwellings, no boys foraging for scrap metal, no women doing the washing. It's unnaturally quiet.

Marah's pace quickens. "Something's wrong."

I jog after her, her apprehension rubbing off on me.

A crowd of women is gathered in front of Samira's house. Marah barges into the throng, and, recognizing her, the women make a path. Gadi Daud is standing in the doorway, holding the infant Marwan in her arms. Tears are streaming down her face. I stop dead.

Marah rushes up to Gadi Daud, and everyone starts speaking at once. I can't understand anything except Samira's name, repeated again and again.

My heartbeat thundering in my ears, I squeeze past Marah and Gadi Daud and slip into the now-familiar room. All the children but Samira are here.

"Rivka?" Shaden says.

"Where's Samira?" I demand.

"They took her," Bashir says, his voice choked.

I feel dizzy. "Who?" Surely not Parliament. The moratorium still stands.

"The men with smoke for faces," the boy says.

"*What?*"

"It was *them*," he says, as though I should know who he means. And suddenly, remembering my first night in Ashara, I do.

I turn as Marah and Gadi Daud, still holding Marwan, enter the house. Marah's brown eyes are huge, her skin pale.

"The Society kidnapped Samira," she says woodenly. "We're leaving."

"Already? Don't you have other visits to make?"

"Everything's changed." Her voice is brittle. "I need to get back to the city right away."

I follow Marah outside. The women assault her with pleas in Xanite, and she reassures them as best she can, though her voice sounds shaky. I stick close to her until she manages to get away. Then we're walking through the empty slum again.

This time, I know what the emptiness means. The people have barricaded themselves in their homes lest more kasiri from the city come to steal their children.

Not until we've reached the run-down boardinghouses on the outskirts of the city does Marah speak. "I'm such an idiot."

"No, you're not," I say, horrified.

"Yes, I am!" Her vehemence scares me. "I should never have named Samira and her parents in Parliament. It's not like I don't know some kasir parliamentarians are Society members."

"But you couldn't have gotten the moratorium passed without naming her," I say, anxious to ease her distress. "They asked for her records."

"I could have gotten around that. One parliamentarian even complained about my breaking the rules of anonymity. He was right. God of the Maitaf, what have I done?"

"It's not your fault."

"The kidnappers told Gadi Daud they were taking matters into their own hands because Parliament was a bunch of cowards. They said that they were taking Samira to live with kasiri, where she belonged, and that the Haruns should forget about her."

The words are like a punch in the stomach. *Forget about her.* It's what Father told me to do with Arik. I want to hurt Samira's kidnappers just for saying that to her family.

"Oh, Rivka, where is she?" Marah says, fear and sadness creeping into her voice. "She must be so frightened."

"Her parents summoned the police, didn't they?" I say.

"The police!" Marah snorts. "They won't find Samira."

"Why not?" I ask, bewildered.

"Because she's the daughter of Xanite immigrants who barely speak Ashari and she's from the slum."

Her reply leaves me speechless because I know she's right and I'm disturbed that this knowledge is so clear to me. But then something else occurs to me. "Even if the police don't care about her, they'll listen to you."

Marah lets out a harsh laugh. "It still won't be enough. The Society's smart. And wealthy. They can buy off the police."

Frustration rises up in me. The Society can't be allowed to make the moratorium meaningless by carrying out forced removals themselves. "What do we do?"

"I need to talk to Shaul," Marah says. "If anyone can learn anything, it's him."

The name Shaul is familiar. He's Marah's friend, the one who fixes up the donated instruments she collects.

"What if he can't uncover anything?" I ask.

Marah clenches her jaw. "Then we find another way. We have to find her, Rivka. I swore to Gadi Daud I would do whatever it takes to bring Samira home."

23

When I walk into the residence dining room on First-day morning, Father is sipping his coffee and reading the newspaper. "You remember that Xanite girl Marah Levi spoke for in Parliament?"

I will my heartbeat to slow down. "What about her?"

"She's gone. It seems someone decided she'd be better off with kasiri." He crunches into a slice of toast.

I reach for the mug of steamed milk at my place and lift it to my lips so the heat of the drink will mask the heat of my face. I must choose the right reaction. Confusion. "Her parents changed their minds?"

"No," Father says. "The Society took matters into their own hands and took the girl away."

If I didn't already know, I'm not sure I would be able to keep the horror from showing on my face. On the other hand, I'm still allowed to be startled. "She's been kidnapped?"

"*Kidnapped* is a strong word," Father says. "The girl is a magician. It made no sense for her to go on living with sparkers. It was creating a de facto mixed family, a dangerous precedent. The Society is simply trying to maintain the separation between kasiri and halani. Besides, I'm sure the girl is better off now. Given that Levi works for Social Welfare, she was probably living in a hovel in the slum."

I have to choke down my outrage. The worst part is that I too wondered if Samira wouldn't be better off living among kasiri.

"Isn't it illegal, though?" I say, struggling to talk normally. "As long as the moratorium stands, her parents aren't doing anything wrong by keeping her."

"If you insist on seeing it that way, yes," Father says. "But it will be interesting to see whether anyone lifts a finger to find the girl and return her to parents who are utterly unfit to raise a magician."

I have no appetite anymore, but I force down the milk and a roll so Father doesn't suspect anything is amiss. I feel sick to my stomach thinking about Samira being held somewhere by fanatic kasiri while her distraught parents and siblings wonder where she is.

*   *   *

Marah brought the Haruns to the police station yesterday, Caleb tells me in the library after History of the North Lands Novel.

What have they done so far?

Caleb shrugs. I remember Marah's scorn for the police, but then Caleb writes something even more chilling. *Some police officers are in the Society.*

I can't believe the Society would do this to Samira, I write in despair. *She's a kasir.*

Caleb stares at me in disbelief. *She's a HALAN*, he writes, the chalk scraping loudly. *She may have magic, but that doesn't automatically make her a kasir. Her parents are poor halani. Besides, she was kidnapped because she's a magician.*

If Samira's still a halan, then Arik's still a kasir, isn't he?

No, Caleb writes. *Because he's been rejected by kasiri. They decide who counts as a kasir and who doesn't. It doesn't have to make sense.*

I was about to say it didn't make sense. But Caleb beat me to it because somehow this is all clear to him and utterly incomprehensible to me.

I still think of Arik as a kasir, I write. *He's just not a magician. I don't think you should have to be a magician to be a kasir.*

So a magician can be a halan? Caleb asks.

I hesitate for a second before nodding. It doesn't seem quite right, but it's the logical conclusion of my argument.

So what makes kasiri and halani different, if not magic? Caleb writes.

I have to stop and think. There are so many differences between us. We go to different schools, we work different jobs, we live in different neighborhoods. We're different, aren't we? But if you ask why kasiri are richer and better educated and why we lead nations and enforce the law, the answer is because we have magic. If someone could be a kasir yet not a magician, what would entitle them to these advantages? And if someone could be a magician yet a halan, why shouldn't they be able to serve as a government official or go to an elite university?

How about money? Caleb suggests. The question comes

across as sarcastic, somehow, and I meet his eyes, wondering if he's angry with me. He doesn't seem to be. I shrug, admitting defeat. It's a mess. In Atsan, things seemed so much more straightforward.

Caleb erases his slate and writes something new. *Arik is sorry he upset you the other weekend.*

I feel a burst of indignation. *Let him tell me himself, if it's true.*

Caleb shakes his head vigorously. *He didn't ask me to tell you he was sorry. He just told me he was sorry. I thought you might want to know.* He's too kind to say outright that he noticed I was crying when I fled his apartment that afternoon.

You've seen Arik again?

Several times, Caleb writes.

I try to block the jealousy before I feel it, but I fail. At least I can hide it from Caleb.

I'd like to see him again, I write. *Can we come over this weekend?*

✳ ✳ ✳

When I arrive at the Levis', Marah is talking to two strangers at the kitchen table. They eye me warily, but Marah waves me on down the hall. I find Caleb alone in his room. Arik isn't here yet.

"Who are those people?" I ask Caleb, pointing back the way I came.

Shaul and Devorah. Marah's been fighting with them all week. She wants to turn the city upside down looking for Samira, but none of Shaul's connections have heard anything about where

she might be. If they just start breaking into Society members'
homes, somebody's going to get killed.

I look up at him in alarm, but Caleb shakes his head
wearily. *She knows it's too risky. She just hates not being able to*
do anything.

"Hello," comes a cheerful voice from the door. I spin
around to face my brother. His smile falters, but I rush to
hug him, and for a second it's like our fight never happened.

"I'm sorry, Arik," I say when I let go of him. All the words
I've wanted to say over the last two weeks come spilling out.
"You were right. I shouldn't have asked you to escape to Kiriz with me. I know you have a life here now. You were right
about everything else too. It's not enough if we make it. There
shouldn't be any more forced adoptions, for anyone."

My brother stares at me, open-mouthed, and Caleb
laughs at the sight.

"I'm sorry," I repeat, afraid my apology was lost in that
flood of words.

"*I'm* sorry," Arik says. "I don't think you're selfish, Rivka."

"But I was," I say, plopping down on Caleb's bed. "I
was thinking only of us. But now, with what's happened to
Samira . . . I think the Family Laws have to go."

"What?"

"Samira should have the right to be a magician and stay
with her family permanently. The moratorium won't last forever. The law has to change. And then there's us. I can give up
having the same last name or living in the same house, but I
want to be able to see you in public. I want to be able to tell
everyone you're my brother. For that, the other Family Laws

have to be repealed too. So you see, it's for all of us. Samira needs the Family Laws repealed so she'll never be adopted, and we need them repealed so we can be brother and sister."

My brother nods slowly. "That's all true. But Rivka, Samira's already been—"

"Marah will get her back!" I say fiercely. "But Samira needs the real law on her side, not just the moratorium. And so do all the other wildings, even the ones who aren't born yet. If we get the Family Laws repealed, we can help them all. What do you think?"

Arik is quiet a long moment before saying, "I want to be able to tell my friends that I have a sister too. I want to stop hiding my past. If you're going to try to get the Family Laws repealed, I'll help you."

"Thank you!" I say, bouncing on Caleb's mattress, a sunburst of joy warming my heart.

Arik gets the attention of Caleb, who's leafing through a book, looking slightly grumpy. "Rivka wants to repeal the Family Laws."

Caleb looks blank for a moment. Then he raises an eyebrow. He scrawls something on his slate. *What's your plan?*

I roll my eyes. *I've only just figured out that it all comes down to getting rid of the Family Laws.* I start to hand the slate back to Caleb, but then I think of something. *Parliament has to make a final decision about the moratorium in a couple of months. Maybe that could be our chance.*

My brother and Caleb both look thoughtful.

"How can we make sure Parliament considers *all* the Family Laws, though, not just forced adoptions?" Arik says.

"We can ask Marah and Azariah," I say.

But with Marah arguing with her friends, we aren't going to be strategizing about how to influence Parliament anytime soon. So the three of us sit on the floor, my brother and I opposite Caleb, and talk about ordinary things like school and the coming summer. It is a new feeling to have friends, friends I don't have to keep secrets from, and I can't remember when I last felt this happy. If only I didn't have to keep these friends secret from Father.

24

The following afternoon, I walk to Firem. I've been feeling guilty for asking Hilah to cover for me so much, so I made plans to see her for real today. I arrive at the girls' dormitory and step into a lobby with a mosaic floor. A student sitting behind a counter looks up from her book.

"May I help you?"

"I'm here to visit Hilah Menachem," I say.

I sign in on the visitors' log, and the girl gives me Hilah's room number. I walk up a stone staircase and down the hall to the last door on the left. Hilah answers as soon as I knock.

"Rivka!" A smile brightens her face. "I'm so glad you're here."

Hilah's room is about the same size as my embassy bedroom, but it contains two beds, two desks, two wardrobes, and two bookcases. Hilah's bed is neatly made with a lilac coverlet, and three black-haired dolls are nestled against the pillows. Her walls are covered with colored illustrations: golden haystacks set afire by the sunset, apple orchards in autumn, sheep grazing along a riverbank. The other side of the room is unoccupied.

"You don't have a roommate?" I say.

She shakes her head. "There's an odd number of first-year girls, so I'm by myself." She sounds wistful.

"You can't take over the whole room?"

"The matron said I was absolutely not to," Hilah says with mock solemnity. "A new student could transfer in at any time and require that bed."

I laugh. "So are we going to study?"

Hilah looks at me. "We did that yesterday."

I'm pretty sure she's making a joke, but her straight face unnerves me. I don't know whether to laugh or apologize.

"I just wanted to see you outside of school," she says, flopping down on her lilac bedspread.

"You could come back to the embassy sometime," I offer lamely, sitting beside her.

"So you can trot me out in front of your father again?"

I wince, though her tone wasn't spiteful. "I'm sorry, Hilah. I'm not a very good friend."

"No," she agrees, propping herself up on her elbows. "But you're my only friend in the city." She is silent a moment. "Why don't you become a boarder, Rivka? Wouldn't you rather live in the dormitory than at the embassy? Your father must be busy all the time. And they'd have to put you with me since I'm the only first year without a roommate."

We look at the bare furnishings on the opposite side of the room, and for a moment I allow myself to imagine my linens on the bed and my dresses hanging in the wardrobe.

Hilah looks embarrassed to have made her wish so obvious. "If your father likes having you at home—"

"I don't think he'd let me board," I say, relieved to have

someone to blame. The idea of being Hilah's roommate is actually appealing, but how would I keep seeing Arik if I lived at school?

"That's too bad," Hilah says softly.

I try to think of some other subject to talk about, but before I do, she asks, out of nowhere, "What do you think about the Xanite girl's kidnapping?"

She might as well have dumped a bucket of cold water over me. A vivid image of Samira holding out her tin locket to me splashes across my mind, and my heart aches.

Since my guard was down, my reflexes are slow. What is the correct response? This is Hilah, not Father, but she still can't suspect that I have any special connection to Samira.

"I think it's wrong," I say. It's a relief to be more honest, and I trust Hilah won't be shocked, since she called it kidnapping. "Stealing a little girl like that is horrible."

Hilah nods. "It's awful. I'm glad you think so too. Some of the other girls . . . they think Parliament is neglecting its duty and the Society is keeping families pure."

"*Pure?*" I say. "What's that supposed to mean? Is it Samira who's impure or the rest of her family?"

Hilah blinks at me, and I curse my carelessness. What's happening to me? This is why I shouldn't be trying to make friends at school. It only gives me more opportunities to betray myself.

"How much do you know about the Society?" I ask, hoping to steer Hilah's attention elsewhere.

"Not that much," she says. "They don't really exist in the country, at least not in Daresh. Last year Parliament appointed a halan, the first one ever, to be governor of Tarib County, and the Society became very active there."

"There's a halan governor in Ashara?" I say, surprised.

"Was. The Society in Tarib County burned down the governor's house."

"What?"

"Luckily, the whole family escaped. But the governor resigned the next day, and Parliament replaced him with a kasir. So that was the end of that."

"Was anyone arrested?"

"There was an investigation, but they never caught anyone." Hilah gives me a knowing look. Evidently when it comes to apprehending Society members, she has as little faith in the police as the Levis. I didn't expect that from the daughter of a county governor.

"I don't support the Society," she continues. "They're in denial. The United Parliament is here to stay, and the law is the law."

"Is that how your parents feel?" I ask, curious how my classmate came by her politics.

She shrugs. "Mother scoffed at the idea of a halan governing Tarib County, but she doesn't have anything good to say about the Society either."

I weigh my next question carefully, but in the end I can't resist asking. "What do *you* think about a halan being governor?"

Hilah's expression is guarded, as though she suspects a test. "If they're qualified, why not? I don't believe that nonsense about halani not being as smart as kasiri. I mean, isn't Caleb beating us all in History of the North Lands Novel?"

"So you aren't opposed to integrated schools?"

She hesitates. "I wouldn't have wanted to go to the halan primary school in Daresh, but I think kasiri and halani *could* go to school together. Maybe we'd hate each other less if we did." She sits up straighter. "Why are you asking me all these questions? Are you going to tell your father?"

I snort. "Do you think I tell him anything?"

"I don't know," she says crossly. "I have no idea how you get along with your father. You never talk about yourself."

"I won't tell him."

Hilah's shoulders relax. "Somehow he didn't strike me as a supporter of integrated schools."

"Definitely not," I say. "But I don't see what would be so bad about them."

"See, this is why I like you!" Hilah says, grinning. "You actually *think* about things long enough to realize they're not the end of the world. The other boarders are always going on about Caleb being a stain on Firem's honor or something. It's absurd. I don't think any of them have ever spoken to him."

"Have you?" I ask.

"Well, no," she admits. "I don't really know . . . I mean, he's deaf, and . . ."

"You just write. And he's pretty good at lip-reading."

"I guess," she says, embarrassed. After a moment, she adds, with studied casualness, "How is he anyway?"

I groan. "Hilah, for the hundredth time, I am not secretly seeing Caleb Levi."

"Right," she says, but her gaze is skeptical. I don't know how much longer my friend will put up with being kept in the dark.

25

"I hear you want to get the Family Laws repealed," Marah says by way of greeting when she lets me into her apartment the following afternoon. Since Ninthday was the day I taught Samira, Father is used to my being out, and I'm taking the opportunity to see Arik again. This time, I wore my halan clothes so as not to stick out so much in Horiel. I made myself invisible before I left the embassy and uncast the spell once I entered the halan district.

Arik and Caleb are at the kitchen table, Caleb slicing leeks while my brother watches. I join them and smell something heavenly baking in the oven.

"Rhubarb cake," Arik says without my having to say anything. He takes in my outfit, his expression half-surprised, half-amused.

Marah is still standing by the door, lost in thought, and I don't understand why she doesn't come to the table until the landing creaks again. She opens the apartment door for Azariah.

"Hello," he says to the room.

Caleb glances up from the cutting board and smiles. Azariah adds a signed greeting.

"Hello, Azariah," I say.

"God of the Maitaf," Arik mutters next to me.

"You must be Rivka's brother," Azariah says.

My twin looks deeply unsettled at being recognized by Azariah Rashid. "It's an honor to meet you," he says haltingly.

"What did the police say?" Marah asks abruptly.

Azariah sinks into a chair at the table. "They apologized profusely but insisted they still had no leads. To be honest, I believe them."

"They fear the Society more than us," Marah says.

"That's true," Azariah says, "but it's also possible the Society has simply covered its tracks too well."

"The police need to search every Society member's house," Marah says.

"But nobody knows exactly who's—"

"Oh, don't give me that. It's an open secret the deputy head of—"

"But there's no proof!" says Azariah. "These people can't be arrested."

Marah is silent, but I can feel the anger radiating from her. Caleb brings the chopped leeks to the counter and slips on a pair of quilted oven mitts to check the cake.

"Every day, it gets harder for me to look Gadi Daud in the eye," Marah says at last.

"It's not your fault," Azariah says in a weary tone that makes it clear this has been his constant refrain for some time. Marah doesn't reply, but she sits down beside him and rests her head on his shoulder. Azariah instinctively puts his arm around her and tucks a lock of hair behind her ear.

I feel like I should look away, but I can't. Azariah looks at me self-consciously over Marah's head. I think back on every gesture, every word I've observed between them. Their gazes never lingered on each other. They never so much as brushed hands. In retrospect, it seems like they were deliberately acting in a way to deflect suspicion. But now either Marah has forgotten I'm here or she's decided she doesn't care if I know.

Caleb brings five chipped plates to the table. He notices Marah and Azariah's closeness, and his eyes flick to Arik and me. But he just urges slices of cake upon everyone, and for a few minutes we let the summery taste of rhubarb blot out our troubles.

Then I say, to no one in particular, "What would it take for Parliament to consider repealing all the Family Laws when they discuss the moratorium again at the end of the summer?"

Azariah looks at Arik and gives me a knowing smile. "I see where this is going."

"It's the only way for us to really be siblings in Ashara," Arik says. I could hug him.

Azariah sighs. He looks at Marah, whose gaze is fixed on her cake.

"You think it's impossible," I say.

"Not at all!" he says. "I think it could happen, actually. I'm certain Ayelet Nitsan's committee will recommend ending forced adoptions. And Nitsan herself opposes all the Family Laws, so she might try to build on the momentum of her committee's recommendation and propose repealing more of them."

"Parliament still might not take up the Family Laws in their entirety," says Marah, quelling my rising hopes. "The only thing they *have* to make a decision about is the moratorium on forced adoptions."

Azariah grimaces. "That's true. If you repeal one of the Family Laws, the rest start to get messy, but I suppose they could keep the ban on intermarriage and say that children who've already been adopted, like Arik, still can't have any contact with their birth families."

"That wouldn't be fair," I protest.

"No," Azariah says. "But it's the sort of thing Parliament would do."

"It'll take public pressure to convince Parliament to repeal all the Family Laws," Marah says, scraping up cake crumbs with her fork. "The problem is most people don't feel personally affected by them. Wildings are rare. It's unusual to know one, let alone to have a wilding child or sibling. Most people can go their whole lives without even having to think about the Family Laws."

"*We* feel personally affected," I say. "We *are*."

"That's true." Marah looks thoughtfully at my brother and me. "If the two of you asked Parliament to repeal all the Family Laws the day they vote on the moratorium, it could make an impression."

"What?" I squeak.

"Marah," says Azariah in disbelief, "they'd arrest them on the spot."

"It'd be risky," Marah says, "but it might be moving enough to nudge Parliament."

My heart beats madly in protest. "We can't. Father would find out, and that would be the end of everything. He'd take me back to Atsan, or make sure we both went to prison . . ."

"He'd do that to his own children?" Azariah exclaims.

"I'm not Ambassador Kadmiel's son," Arik says sharply. "He decided that long ago."

Azariah winces.

"Never mind," Marah says. "It was a stupid idea."

Arik twirls his fork, his brow furrowed. Caleb is staring off into space, having retreated into his own world after finding the discussion impossible to follow. I feel a twinge of guilt for having shut him out.

Azariah glances at his watch and announces that he has to meet his parents for a service at the Xanite temple. There is a flurry of clearing dishes and saying goodbyes. Then, as Caleb and Marah settle into a signed conversation, Arik and I go to Caleb's room.

"Marah's right," my brother says when we're alone. "If we want all the laws to change, we have to demand it."

"How can we?" I say. "It's too dangerous."

"But what if there were more of us?"

"More of us?"

"More siblings like us," Arik says. "Wildings and their birth siblings. If it wasn't only you and me but a whole bunch of people like us . . . We'd have strength in numbers."

He's grinning with excitement, but I'm hesitant. "How will we find a whole bunch of people? And even if we do, how could we trust them? I don't want to depend on—"

"But, Rivka, we can't do this alone," Arik breaks in. When I remain silent, he adds, "You asked Caleb and Marah and Azariah Rashid for help finding me."

"I had to," I say.

"And now *we* have to."

I meet his warm brown eyes. My eyes. They make me feel more certain, and I know I trust Arik. "All right," I say. "We have to. So we will."

Curled up in bed, a light sheet over my knees, I idly practice braiding my hair. It's late, but I can't sleep. Arik and I talked for almost an hour about how to locate other siblings like us without coming up with anything resembling a plan.

"We have to look for wildings, because they're the ones who know where their birth siblings are," I pointed out.

"But some of them might be afraid to contact their birth siblings for fear of being rejected or turned in to the police," Arik said. "Especially wildings like me. To be born with magic in a halan family is unfortunate, but to be born without magic in a kasir family is shameful. Someone like Samira is more likely to be welcomed back than someone like me. And then there's the possibility that a wilding we approach will report *us* to the police."

I gripped the edge of Caleb's bed, rigid. "Then we only look for children. They're less likely to go straight to the police."

"There's someone at Kazeri," my brother said. "I think he might be a wilding too, though I'm not sure. I could try to find out, carefully."

It was something, but at this rate, it could take us the rest of the year to unearth even a handful of wildings. We only have a little over two months before Parliament's final vote on the moratorium.

I circle back to the problem again as I comb my fingers through my hair. Where would we be most likely to meet more wildings? Where can we find others like Arik? If only we could simply look them up in the changeling equivalent of a telephone directory . . . I sit up straight, the answer suddenly obvious.

The changeling archive. All the names are waiting there.

I can't believe I didn't think of this earlier. If I had, we could have asked Azariah to return to the archive and collect names for us. Now I'll have to wait two days before I can talk to Caleb at school and send Azariah a message through him. And who knows how many more days it will be before Azariah has time to visit the archive? I don't want to wait that long, not now that I've hit upon the clearest way forward.

I could go to the archive tomorrow. It's open. For a moment, I consider sneaking in under the Veil, but I quickly dismiss the idea. Even if I could somehow break into the building and get through the locked door to the records chamber under the archive keeper's nose, I would have to stay invisible for much longer than fifteen minutes. I would almost certainly get stuck.

Fortunately, I can go without concealing myself. All I have to do is pretend Azariah sent me for more information. Considering how dusty the archive was, it can't get many visitors. Surely the archive keeper will remember me.

My heart flutters in warning. This is not like me. My recklessness frightens me a little, but deep down I know I've decided.

※ ※ ※

The archive keeper recognizes me, as I'd hoped, but he doesn't look pleased. "Where is Banar Rashid?"

Standing on the doorstep, I keep myself from fidgeting and stand tall. I think of the way Hilah speaks and try to form my vowels like hers. "Banar Rashid is otherwise engaged. He sent me to check some information."

If the archive keeper detects my Atsani accent, he doesn't show it. I'm afraid he'll ask me for a signed letter or some other document, but the fact that I've come before seems to be enough. He lets me in.

Like last time, he escorts me into the record chamber and watches as I open the cabinet Azariah and I riffled through before. I pick out a file at random and jot down something nonsensical in my Epic Poetry notebook. The thick silence makes me sweat.

I need to get rid of the archive keeper, just long enough to create a diversion. The coughing trick can't possibly work again. The cabinets are still furred with dust, though, so perhaps . . .

I clear my throat, trying to make it sound as scratchy as possible. "May I have one of those throat lozenges, sir?"

The archive keeper grunts in annoyance, but he plods off. As he departs, I open my senses to the magic in the chamber. The wards I felt when I walked in crystallize into a crisscrossing web of enchantments. One small spell added to the mix shouldn't attract attention, and the one I intend to cast won't linger.

I check the location of the cabinet containing Arik's file, then hurry to the opposite end of the next aisle over. I only have a second to choose the cabinet that looks most ancient. There's no time to hesitate. I begin to sing as softly as I can, picturing the wood bulging, the drawers buckling under the weight of all that paper. I reach the last note. Nothing has happened.

My heart sinks. Was my weakening spell too weak? Was the variation I used for the wrong material? I thought I chose the melody for wood, but it's been two years since I studied this spell in school. I should've checked the spell books in Father's—

A loud crack splits the silence, and I jump back as the cabinet collapses on itself, vomiting mildewed files through splintered wood. I scream and retreat another few steps so it looks like I just arrived on the scene. The archive keeper comes rushing up the aisle and swears. Files are still tumbling out of the caved-in cabinet, scattering farther across the floor.

"It—it just fell apart." I'm trembling with the fear that the archive keeper will suspect my sabotage, but it helps make me look shaken. "The wood must've rotted . . ."

The archive keeper swears more colorfully, shoves the paper-wrapped lozenge in my hand, and kneels at the edge of the wreckage, snatching up files. I shuffle back to the aisle where I was working, listening to the official muttering about inconvenience and cheap building materials.

With a wall of cabinets between me and the archive keeper, I set to work. I leave our old cabinet open but kneel in front of the one with my brother's file. Notebook on my thigh, I start copying down names and addresses from records of the same era. With four drawerfuls before me, it's difficult not to be greedy, but the archive keeper could decide at any moment that watching me is more important than cleaning up. I force myself to stop, gather my belongings, and return to the site of destruction.

"I'm finished, sir." The archive keeper is still stacking old files. "I can show myself out, if you like."

He waves me away like a buzzing fly, and I dash from the chamber, triumphant.

⭑ ⭑ ⭑

The next day after school, I walk to an address not far from Firem. It's a large house, with window boxes overflowing with geraniums. I move partway up the block into the shadow of a stone gatepost and take a book out of my schoolbag. It's an odd place to be reading, but I can't think of any less suspicious way of passing the time.

I don't have long to wait before a girl in a school uniform stops at the gate of the house with the geraniums. She looks about twelve, the right age to be the changeling whose adoptive name is Dinah Tsadok. She unlatches the gate and goes into the house. I check the time on the pendant watch in my bag.

I return the next day. The girl comes home from school at the same time. On the third day, a few minutes before I expect her to appear, I slip my hand through the bars of the gate and leave a letter marked *Dinah* on the front walk where she won't be able to miss it. Then I flee.

When I arrive at the Levis' on Seventhday, Arik and Caleb are in the kitchen, and a familiar-sounding violin partita is drifting out from Marah's bedroom.

"Look, Rivka," my brother says, "I can spell my name in signs."

He moves his hand in a series of shapes while Caleb looks on, amused but also pleased. The string of signs seems too long, though.

"Is that Elisha?" I say.

"Oh. Yes. But I learned Arik too." He shows me. "And I guess Rivka would be . . ." He starts my name, using the signs from the middle of his own, but he quickly gets stuck and appeals to Caleb, who finishes it for him.

I'm embarrassed that it hadn't occurred to me to try to learn any sign language before. "Will you teach me to spell my name?" I ask Caleb shyly.

We lose track of time as Caleb teaches us some basic signs. I feel even more ashamed when I discover Arik already knows a handful. Then I remember the main reason I came and take out my notebook with the names and addresses from the changeling archive. I show the boys the list, telling them how I got it, and once they understand they are torn between horror and admiration.

"Promise you won't do something like that again," Arik says. "You could've—"

"Stop. It's done. We need to talk to as many wildings

as we can before Parliament votes once and for all on the moratorium." I tear a page out of my notebook. "These are the ones who are halani now. I'll take the kasiri. We have exactly two months."

⚓ ⚓ ⚓

On Tenthday morning, I walk to the Ikhad, my progress impeded by the thick crowds. My impatience only makes me more jittery. What if Dinah hasn't come? What if no one is waiting for me? Or what if someone is? What if Dinah showed the letter to her parents?

At last, I reach the covered market. I hurry to the southwest corner and slow in front of a glassmaker's stall. Two women in dark dresses are examining a vase with an undulating rim. A farmer lumbers by, pushing a cart filled with chard. And there is Dinah, standing in the shade of the thatched roof clutching a closed white parasol.

I walk up behind her. "Excuse me?"

Startled, she drops her parasol. We both bend to pick it up and almost bump heads.

"I'm sorry, I didn't mean to frighten you," I say quietly. "Did you lose a ribbon?"

The girl stares at me with light eyes. Does she remember the code? "Yes."

My heart pounds, and the sounds of the marketplace recede. "What color?"

"Blue," the girl says. It's the right answer. After a moment, she asks, "Who are you?"

"My name is Rivka," I say. "Let's go somewhere else."

She follows me obediently out of the square. "You're not from Ashara," she says.

"I'm Atsani," I say shortly, anxious to reach a place where we can talk without being overheard. I feel as though every eye is upon us.

"But then why—?"

"Wait." My skittishness is making me brusque. A few blocks south of the Ikhad, I find the park where I told Caleb I had a twin. To my relief, it is empty.

We plop onto a bench, and I take a good look at my companion. She has a round face and curly brown hair. She fidgets with her parasol and kicks at the gravel on the path with the toe of her shiny black boot. I would never have guessed she wasn't born a kasir if I hadn't already known she was a wilding.

"Are you a changeling too?" she asks.

"No. My brother is."

"And you're foreign?" she says, frowning.

I tell her the bare bones of Arik's and my story. Her eyes grow larger and larger, and I detect longing in her gaze.

"The letter," she says. "How did you know my name and . . . what I was?"

"I got into the archive of changeling records." I don't elaborate, and she seems too awed to question me. Taking a deep breath, I explain how when it comes time for Parliament to reconsider the moratorium on forced adoptions, we hope to persuade them to end all the Family Laws.

"Will I be able to go back?" Dinah asks when I finish. The desperate hope in her face makes my heart ache.

"Would you want to?" I ask.

"I . . . I don't know." She looks quickly at me, as though expecting a reproof. "Of course I want to! I think of my family every day. But my new parents love me too. Even if the Family Laws were changed, it would be ungrateful of me to . . ."

"You don't owe them gratitude," I say, irked. "They're only raising you because they cooperated with a government that takes children away from their families."

"I used to think that," Dinah says miserably, "but now I don't know. Mother lost her first daughter to the dark eyes. I'm all she has."

"To be honest, I don't think you'll be able to go back," I say. "But you could see your birth family again. Do you want that?"

"Yes!" Dinah says, clasping her hands. "And I want to join you. I want to help you repeal the Family Laws."

I'm elated, but outwardly I try to remain calm. "Do you have any birth siblings?"

"A sister and a brother. My sister is fifteen, and my brother is . . ." She pauses. "He's nine now."

That means he was seven when Dinah was taken away. How well does he remember her? Can we trust a child so young?

"Do you think they'd be happy to see you again?" I ask with utmost seriousness. "Can you be certain they won't go to the police or breathe a word to your parents if you were to make contact with them?"

Dinah gives me an odd look. "Halani don't go to the

police." For the first time, I'm reminded that she wasn't always a kasir, and I feel foolish.

"What about your parents?"

"Why can't we tell them?" Dinah asks.

"We can't risk it," I say firmly. "We're not sure all parents would welcome back their wilding children, so we're not involving any of them. And we don't want Parliament to think this is about parents wanting their children back. It's about us."

Dinah presses her lips together and looks at her lap. "I know my sister and brother would be happy to see me again. And I'm sure they can keep a secret."

"Even your brother?"

"The day the officials came for me, he begged me not to go," Dinah says, her mouth crumpling.

"If you're sure," I say, "then contact your siblings. Maybe only your sister first. She can decide whether your brother can be trusted with the secret. Ask them if they want the Family Laws gone and if they're willing to appear with you in Parliament. It'll be dangerous for all of you. Getting in touch with them is already breaking the law, and appearing together will be even riskier. But if there are enough of us, maybe we can make the law fit us instead of the other way around. Can you do that, Dinah?"

She lifts her chin. "Yes."

"If your brother and sister can't commit to the whole plan, they have to promise not to tell anyone about it," I say. "Don't tell them the whole truth until you're certain you can trust them. I know they're your siblings, but even in two years things can change."

"I know," she says impatiently. I can tell she's already confident of her siblings' willingness to join us. I fervently hope she's right.

"Once you have news for me," I say, "leave a message with the halan bookseller at the northeast corner of the Ikhad."

"The old woman?" Dinah says.

"Good, you know her." This part was Caleb's idea, and it took a while for him to convince me this would be the best way for us to exchange messages with the other children. He's good friends with the bookseller, but more importantly, he said Marah has known her for ten years and trusts her with her life.

"Tell her your name and whether you've found your siblings and whether their answer is yes or no," I continue. "Then tie a thread or a piece of string to the nail in the southwest roof post of the Ikhad. I'll show you where it is. You can hang something there whenever you need to get in touch with me. And if you see a black thread on the nail, that means the bookseller has a message for you from me. Can you remember all that?"

She nods eagerly.

"Good." I rise from the park bench. Dinah jumps up beside me, her brown curls bouncing on her shoulders.

"I'm so glad I met you, Rivka," she says.

I drop my severe demeanor and break into a smile. "So am I."

27

In the library on Firstday, I tell Caleb about Dinah. He looks delighted. Then he tells me about staking out a halan wilding's apartment building with Arik on the way to school this morning. Learning they walk to school together gives me a pang. Before I can think better of it, I write, *I wish I could see Arik as often as you do.*

Caleb's brow pinches in sympathy. *That's what this is all for, right? Someday the Family Laws will be gone.*

I try to smile, warmed by his attempt to comfort me.

Mother's really happy I've made friends with your brother, Caleb writes.

I cock my head, frowning.

She wants me to have halan friends.

Don't you? I write, startled. I know I'm Caleb's only friend at Firem, but I assumed he had friends in his neighborhood.

He studies me for a moment before shaking his head. *Until four years ago, I had no friends. I didn't make any at Horiel. And I've gone to kasir schools ever since.*

Abruptly, I remember the sight of Caleb standing in

a circle of students at the school for the deaf, signing and laughing.

You have friends at your other school, don't you?

He nods. *We're not that close though. They've never invited me over, and I'd never invite them to my apartment. So when I brought you, I think Mother was worried we would be another Marah and Azariah.*

I stiffen. *What's that supposed to mean?*

Just that Marah's best friend is a kasir, and Mother thought I was going to make a kasir my best friend too.

Gadi Levi's manner toward me the day we met takes on new meaning. She was polite, but also distant. I hesitate before asking, *Does she know about Marah and Azariah?*

Caleb's lips twitch in amusement. *Of course. Mother's not stupid. Azariah's parents know too.*

I know I'm wading into something that's none of my business, but I can't help asking, *If the Family Laws are repealed, will Marah marry Azariah?*

Caleb makes a face and then begins to laugh. I glance nervously around the stacks.

I don't think Marah wants to marry anyone right now, he writes. *They're only eighteen. Marah's obsessed with her job. And Azariah's still at university.*

I thought it was romantic, I write, disappointed.

Caleb rolls his eyes.

The next day, we're sitting in our usual alcove when I hear footsteps on the hardwood floor. The short-haired girl we sometimes see working here has risen from her table and is walking into the stacks.

I turn back to my biology text until the quiet scrape of a chair being pushed back makes me look up again. Caleb tiptoes to the next alcove and peers at the books and papers the girl left on the table. Shocked, I motion him back, but he beckons me instead. Glancing over my shoulder, I get up and join him. He points at the name written across the top of an essay: *Batyah Yachin.*

It takes me only a second to place it. It's one of the names I collected at the changeling archive. Not only that, but I spied on the Yachins' house twice last week and never saw anyone come home from school. I wondered if Batyah was a boarder somewhere. Now Caleb's found her.

I drag him back to our alcove and grab his slate. *How did you know?*

He looks up the nearest aisle of shelves, but Batyah hasn't reappeared. *I had a feeling.*

I look at him skeptically, and the faintest irritation flashes across his face. *The intuition*, he writes.

The word sends a ripple through my stomach. I try to quash my discomfort with the other sense. After all, Arik has it. And thanks to Caleb, another wilding has just fallen into our laps. Maybe the intuition isn't such an odd, useless ability.

✤ ✤ ✤

The following afternoon, I wait in the square after school until I spot the girl from the library coming down the front steps, a flute case in her hand. She starts walking toward the Ikhad. Gathering my resolve, I hasten after her.

"Excuse me!"

Batyah stops and glares at me, taking in my Firem jacket, which is identical to hers. "I don't know you," she says curtly. "And I'm late for my flute lesson." Without waiting for a reply, she marches off.

"Wait!" I call after her. "I want to talk to you."

Two ladies out for an afternoon stroll cast me disapproving glances from under their parasols. Batyah does not slow down, and I have to dash to reach her again.

"What do you want?" she says. "You're the Atsani girl, aren't you?"

She can tell by my accent. "My name's Rivka. You're Batyah, right?"

She glances at me as though I'm a fly on a slice of fruit. "Look, I'm a third year, you're a first year. Why are you bothering me?"

We aren't alone on the street, but it's not crowded, and if I lower my voice, no one will hear me. "Are you a changeling?"

Batyah stiffens. A flush darkens her face, whether from shame or rage I can't tell. "How do you know?" she says, her voice taut with fury.

"I just do," I stammer, not wanting to go into the archive or Caleb's intuition.

"Did someone at Firem tell you? *No one* at Firem knows."

"Really?" I say, astonished. She must not have gone to Firem Primary, but it seems like somebody would've figured it out eventually.

The anger in Batyah's eyes is making me more and more nervous. I've gone about this all wrong. The only thing that keeps me from fleeing now is my determination to recruit another wilding to our cause. Arik and Dinah aren't enough. We need Batyah.

"If you tell anyone at school, I swear I'll make your life miserable," she hisses.

"I won't tell anyone," I say at once, in the same undertone. "Batyah, please, I don't—I want to talk to you *because* you're a—because of that. I want Parliament to repeal the Family Laws, and I was wondering if you would help."

Batyah snorts. "You're a terrible liar. Your story doesn't even make sense. You're Atsani, for God's sake. What do you care what Parliament does?"

Her accusation worries me for a second, but then I dismiss it. I know I'm a good liar. Apparently I'm terrible at telling the truth.

"Next you're going to tell me *you're* a changeling," Batyah says scathingly.

"Not me," I whisper. "My brother. He's a halan wilding."

Instead of falling silent or expressing her sympathy, she laughs, and not kindly. "Must have been quite a shock, going from ambassador's son to sparker."

I'm so stunned all I can say is: "Father wasn't ambassador then."

We begin our second turn around the same block. In front of a furniture store, two apprentices are loading an ornate dresser into an old-fashioned black carriage.

Batyah's unfriendliness is discouraging, but I'm not going home until I've won her over. Recruiting Dinah was easy.

I hardly had to work for her goodwill. Batyah is different. How do you gain a person's trust? Being reluctant to trust anyone myself, I feel like I don't know.

Hoping to prove my sincerity, I tell her how I found Arik and describe our vague plan to sway Parliament. Batyah listens in silence until I'm through. Then she says, "Who put you up to this? Was it my parents?" She spits the last word.

"I'm not trying to trick you!" I protest.

"Right," Batyah says. "And the moment I go to the wretched old building where I used to live, the police will swoop down on me. I'll be expelled from Firem. You have no idea how hard I've worked to get to where I am. I did everything I was told. I put my past—my parents, my brother, everything—behind me. This is the year I graduate. I don't know who's trying to sabotage me, but it won't work." Batyah's voice trembles. "I'm not going to fail now."

She rounds on me. "So don't ever speak to me again. Understood?"

Before I can reply, she stalks up the street, and this time I don't follow. I don't know what else I could say to convince her I'm telling the truth. As Batyah vanishes around a corner, I realize there is now someone in Ashara who knows all the ways in which Arik and I have broken and plan to break the law. And I may have just made an enemy of her.

28

On Seventhday, I pour out the story of my disastrous attempt to recruit Batyah to Arik.

"We need her," I say. "We only have so many names."

"Are you sure it's worth it?" my brother says, sitting cross-legged on Caleb's bed. "We also only have so much time. How much of it can you afford to spend trying to make someone like her come around?"

"Arik, she knows about us. I told her almost everything before she made it clear she wanted nothing to do with me."

Arik picks up on my unspoken fear. "You think she might report us? But you said she's hidden that she's a wilding from everyone at Firem. Don't you think she'd be too afraid you'd expose her to try anything against you?"

"Maybe, but being a wilding isn't illegal. What we're doing is. I won't feel safe until Batyah's on our side. And I need your help to persuade her."

"My help?" says Arik. "I thought we agreed you talked to kasiri and I—"

"I want her to meet you." My brother straightens in alarm. "Not side by side with me," I add hastily. "That would be too risky. But I don't think she believes that you and I have actually managed to reunite. And she let slip that she has a brother. If I show her it's possible to see your brother again, she might reconsider."

Arik smiles uncertainly. "What do you need me to do?"

⚘ ⚘ ⚘

We wait until Thirdday, when I know Batyah will be walking toward the Ikhad after school for her flute lesson. I watch for her on the steps of Firem and tail her for a few blocks. If she notices me following her before I'm close enough to speak to her, she'll run away, and my opportunity will be lost.

I seize my chance to catch up to her when a street vendor's strawberry cart blocks me from view. On the other side, I find myself within ten paces of her.

"Batyah," I call, not too loudly.

She whirls around. I have never seen fury light up in someone's face so quickly.

"Which part of *don't ever speak to me again* was unclear?" she demands as I come nearer.

"I'm sorry," I say, my voice dropping low, "but I want you to know you could see your brother again and still graduate from Firem."

"Shut up," Batyah says, as though she can't bear to imagine things she's convinced herself are impossible.

"It's true. Everything I told you is true. And I . . . I want to show you my wilding brother."

Batyah does not storm away, as I feared she might. Her face is drawn, her cheekbones jutting out sharply. "You're making me late for my flute lesson," she says at last. "Again. Are you going to make a habit of this?"

"I can wait till it's over. Will you meet me at the Ikhad when you're done?"

The older girl hesitates a long moment and then says, "Fine."

I know how easy it would be for Batyah to pretend to agree and then never come find me at the market. I'm tempted to hint that I'll tell the whole school she's a wilding if she doesn't show up, but I don't want Batyah to join us because I've blackmailed her. I want her to join us because she wants to end the Family Laws too. And the truth is she can threaten me with worse than I can threaten her with. So I say nothing.

Half an hour later, I'm threading my way through the sea of shoppers at the Ikhad, searching the throngs for Batyah's head of short hair. What if she went straight back to Firem after all?

I've almost resigned myself to her having lied when a tall figure in a school uniform catches my eye. It's Batyah, slicing a path toward me through the crowd. When we meet, I give her what I hope is a winning smile.

"I don't see a brother," she says, her eyes darting every which way.

"Yes, well, the Family Laws haven't been repealed yet," I say in an undertone.

"Then where is he?" she demands.

"There's a stationery shop at the northwest corner of the square. My brother is standing outside. Go see him. He's the proof I'm telling the truth."

Batyah doesn't move. "Give me something to ask him. Something only he would know."

I hide my irritation and plumb my memory. "Ask him what kind of tree we sat under the first time we were reunited in Atsan. It was an oak."

Satisfied, Batyah turns on her heel.

I fish a coin out of my purse and buy a skewer of grilled beets from a street vendor. I eat them while waiting under the edge of the Ikhad roof near a stall festooned with silk scarves.

"He looks just like you."

I jump, dropping my last chunk of beet on the ground. Batyah is standing behind me, her expression utterly different from before. All the distrust and pessimism are gone, leaving her looking much younger. She stares at my face so intently I wonder if there's beet juice on my chin.

"Did you talk to him?" I ask.

"He knew it was an oak," she says in a husky voice. "But it didn't matter. The moment I saw him, I knew he was your brother."

"So are you willing to—?"

"Not here," Batyah says. "Let's talk somewhere more private."

Ten minutes later, she signs me into the Firem girls' dormitory. I follow her up the stairs, afraid we'll encounter Hilah. How will I explain my sudden acquaintance with a third year? Luckily, we reach the senior girls' hall on the top floor without running into my friend.

Batyah's room is larger than Hilah's, and her roommate is

absent. She crosses to the plainer side of the room and sits on her bed, gesturing for me to take her desk chair.

"He's your older brother?" she asks, as though we never stopped talking about Arik.

"We're twins."

"God of the Maitaf." Batyah's voice is thick with anger and disgust, but neither seems directed at me.

"How old is your brother?" I ask cautiously.

"Eighteen," she says, turning away. "We were—are—two years apart."

That's Marah's age. Practically grown up. But he and Batyah may have been close. And he's a halan, so he probably wouldn't go to the police.

"Could you get in touch with him? Are you willing to stand with us when we ask Parliament to repeal the Family Laws?"

To my surprise, Batyah replies almost right away. "I can find him. I'll talk to him. I think he'll say yes."

"You haven't seen him in six years?" I ask gently. Batyah and her brother are the oldest siblings we've approached.

"No. But he won't have forgotten me."

The yearning in her voice constricts my heart.

"Can he really be my brother again, though?" she continues. "Can I really be his sister?"

"If the Family Laws are repealed, it won't be illegal for us to see our halan siblings anymore," I say. "We could go out in public together. We could even—"

Batyah's laughter gives me goose bumps. "Do you really think changing the law will make such a difference? Look at school integration."

"This is different," I say, painfully conscious of the utter failure of school integration. "Nobody's trying to force halani and kasiri together. It's just allowing us to be family if we want to be."

Batyah shakes her head. "Rivka, there wasn't a single day in primary school that someone didn't remind me that I would never amount to much because I was born a halan. By the time I was twelve, I was staying up past midnight every night making sure my homework was perfect, trying to prove them wrong. When I made it to the top of my class, I thought they would realize I was as clever as them, but it only made them hate me more. I was the only student in my Final class to be accepted to Firem. I decided I'd start over here and not let anyone find out I was a wilding. It worked."

"I'm sorry about—"

"The point is," Batyah says impatiently, "if I do well this year, I could get into a good university and have a chance at a successful career. What do you think will happen if I start spending time with a halan boy and telling everyone he's my brother? It's not only that everyone will know I'm a wilding. My prospects will be gone. Kasiri will call me ungrateful for embracing my birth family when my adoptive parents gave me a better life. If I associate with halani, they'll say I have no ambition, or worse, that I'm a halan sympathizer who will cause trouble wherever I work."

"I—I hope it won't be like that," I say, faltering at her grim vision of the future.

"You're naïve if you think it won't be," Batyah says.

"Look, if you don't want to help us, I'll go," I say, rising from Batyah's chair.

"No! I want to join you."

"So you aren't worried about throwing away your career?" I ask, confused.

"All this," Batyah says, waving a hand vaguely as if to indicate the dormitory, or Firem, or even the years she spent proving herself, "is just to have something to live for. If I could have my brother back, why should I care about a fancy university and a plush government job anymore?"

It takes a moment for her meaning to sink in. I have her at last. I conceal my relief, not wanting Batyah to know how badly I needed her.

"Thank you," I say. "I'm so glad—"

"You sound *so* Atsani," she says, laughing with actual mirth. It's the first time I've seen her so much as crack a smile.

⚜ ⚜ ⚜

The weeks slip past, and summer reaches its height. The corridors of Firem are stuffy, and Arik complains about sweating through medsha rehearsals every day in Kazeri's sweltering music room. I squeeze in rendezvous with wildings every spare moment I have. Several children I leave letters for never show up to meet me at the Ikhad. Two others promise to try to reach out to their siblings, but I never hear from them again. It's frustrating—and worrisome—to lose them. I can only hope they weren't caught. Luckily, some of our other recruits know of more wildings, so word has been spreading faster.

What with all these meetings, cello practice, and my schoolwork, I'm not sleeping enough. The nightmares in which Samira is calling for help from behind a granite cliff or from the bottom of a well don't help. When I wake up, distressed, I cling to the fact that it's only a dream, until I remember with a horrible, heavy feeling that Samira really is a captive somewhere.

By midsummer, we've made more progress finding wildings and their siblings than we ever imagined possible. Caleb, Arik, and I gather at the Levis' to take stock of our numbers.

"I met another wilding yesterday," says Arik. "A Xanite boy named Yusuf. He's thirteen, and he has an eleven-year-old sister he's going to try to contact. Counting him, we've recruited twelve wildings."

"And how many siblings?" I count on my fingers. "Dinah has two. Batyah has one."

Arik scribbles sums in a notebook. Two of his wildings have no siblings, and another hasn't tried to find her sisters because she's certain they wouldn't be glad to see her. Still, the tally grows steadily.

"Nineteen siblings," he says at last. "With the wildings, that's thirty-one. Plus you and me . . ." He writes *33* and underlines it. Caleb raises his eyebrows, impressed.

"This is good," I say, heartened. "But we could still use more. And there's something else we should discuss. Batyah's been—"

"Asking if this is all an elaborate plot to get her arrested?" my brother asks wearily.

I laugh. "No. But she's wondering how big we really are."

At Firem, Batyah has made a point of ignoring me whenever our paths cross, for which I'm grateful. It's easier to keep secrets that way. So when she found me in the library at the end of the week and beckoned me into the stacks, I was alarmed.

"How many of us are there, really?" she hissed when I joined her between the shelves.

"What?" I'd been expecting some terrible news.

"You say there are others like us and our brothers," Batyah whispered, "but I have no proof they exist. If it's just four of us making demands in Parliament the day they vote on the moratorium, they'll have no trouble trundling us all off to prison."

I sighed. The eternally suspicious Batyah.

"I told her how many we were," I say to the boys. "But I don't think she'll believe me until she sees the others with her own eyes."

"I thought she trusted you," says Arik.

"I understand why she's afraid," I say. "If I were her, would I believe me?"

"So you're going to introduce her to others?" my brother says doubtfully.

"Actually, I think we should have a meeting. With everyone."

The boys are both looking at me uncertainly.

Thirty-three people? Caleb signs. *Halani and kasiri? Where will you meet?*

I'm so thrilled to have understood everything Caleb signed that the problem he's raising barely sinks in. "I think it's important for everyone to see that they're not alone. We need to feel like we have a common cause before we appear in Parliament. The siblings should meet Arik and me since they only have the wildings' word that we actually exist. And I think we should decide on an exact plan and share it. It's one month until the vote."

"It's a good idea," Arik says, "but Caleb's right that finding a place to meet will be hard."

If anyone knows of a place, Caleb writes on his slate, *it's Marah's friend Shaul.*

As it turns out, Shaul's many skills include engineering secret meetings for bands of suspicious-looking children. The next time I see him at school, Caleb reports that Shaul has found us a place.

It's a pharmacy, he writes.

"A pharmacy?" That's not what I was expecting.

Before the Assembly fell, it was a meeting place for halan students.

Radicals? I write, astonished.

Caleb raises an eyebrow. *What do you think you are?*

His question knocks me off balance. I'm not a radical. Radicals are people who hate the government and want to shake up society. Do Arik and I fit that definition now? Putting the question out of my mind, I take the chalk. *Let's call the meeting.*

29

With Caleb acting as go-between, we arrange for the meeting to take place on Seventhday afternoon. When the day comes, I walk to the pharmacy after lunch. A wooden sign with a painted mortar and pestle hangs over the door. Through the window, a white-haired man behind a counter is handing a packet wrapped in brown paper to an elderly halan woman. I hurry on around the corner.

The alley's cool shadows are a welcome relief from the heat. I pick my way through garbage bins and puddles of uncertain origin, looking for the sign Caleb told me would mark the pharmacy's back entrance. At last, I spot a braided rug flung over the iron railing of a stairwell. I descend the concrete steps and knock on the door at the bottom.

The door opens a crack, and my brother's eye appears in the slit.

"Password," comes his muffled voice. I almost laugh because of course he recognizes me. It feels like we're playing at spies. But then I remember that more than half the people invited to today's meeting are children we haven't met.

"Feverfew," I say. Caleb chose the password and insisted on a medicinal herb to match the location.

Arik lets me into the pharmacy basement. As my eyes adjust to the dimness, I make out a square underground chamber. The walls are lined with shelves of brown glass jars, and the room has a bitter herbal scent. Caleb is standing nearby, a flickering lamp at his feet. A wooden staircase rises at the opposite end of the room, and I can see a line of light under the door at the top.

"That opens behind the pharmacist's counter," Arik says. "He'll be letting people down, but only when the coast is clear."

The three of us settle onto the cold floor. Following Shaul's advice, we instructed our contacts to stagger their arrivals. It wouldn't do for a whole pack of children to pile into the pharmacy at once.

After a while, someone knocks on the alley door. It must be a kasir. They're arriving through the alley, while the halani are coming from upstairs. I jump up to answer it.

"Rivka?" It's Dinah, her voice high with fear.

"I'm here," I say at once, letting her in without bothering with the password. "Would you like to meet my brother?"

Arik stands beside me in the semidarkness, and Dinah gasps. The hope in her eyes shines brighter than any lamp.

"Are you a wilding too?" she asks Caleb.

He doesn't respond. I suspect it's too dark for him to lip-read.

"Caleb is our friend," I tell Dinah.

"My sister should be coming with my brother," she says,

sounding fretful. "I told them I'd come early so they should come late, like the bookseller said . . ."

"That's good," I say. "Come sit down."

"Would you like some pistachios?" Dinah says, opening her purse.

Pistachios are a rare treat for Caleb and Arik, and they eagerly accept her offer. We sit around shelling nuts until another knock comes at the alley door. A moment later, the door to the pharmacy swings open. The wildings are coming.

By two o'clock, we're all gathered in the basement. A few wildings tell us their siblings couldn't make it, but excluding Caleb, I count twenty-eight children, so most of us are here. The storeroom is certainly crowded enough. Caleb takes up his post outside the alley door, ready to rap a warning should anyone suspicious-looking come along.

"Hello," I say over the hum of voices. Everyone quiets.

I clear my throat. "Thank you all for coming. I'm Rivka. I know the kasir changelings, but the halan changelings have only met my brother, Arik. Or Elisha." I raise a lamp to illuminate our faces, and a murmur ripples to the edges of the room.

"If everyone could introduce—"

"You're not from here!" a young voice pipes up.

"Hush!"

I glance around in confusion, and my gaze lights on Dinah, who is gripping a nine-year-old boy by the shoulders, her expression mortified. I smile at the boy, but before I can say anything, someone else says, "He's right. You're a foreigner."

I look around nervously, trying to see who spoke. The meeting has hardly begun, and already I'm skating on thin ice. The children stand in clusters, keeping close to their siblings but edging away from the others around them. Because they're gathered in families, kasiri and halani are mixed together, but more than a few people look like they wish there were a kasir side or a halan side of the basement for them to move to. The truce feels like it might shatter at any moment. I must choose my words carefully, but this, at least, is something I'm accustomed to.

"It's true," I say. "I'm Atsani. My brother was Atsani too, but now we're both in Ashara, and Ashara is where I want to live. Ashara has the United Parliament, and if we have anything to say about it, it will soon have no Family Laws."

A rumble of approval and excitement fills the basement. The danger is past, for now. One by one, the wildings introduce themselves and their siblings. Dinah's brother lights up when she introduces him, and his joy at being held by her again is almost too much to bear. A boy with unruly hair introduces himself as Yusuf. His sister, Yasmin, is a solemn-looking girl whose glossy brown hair brushes the shoulders of her gown. Batyah's older brother, Maayan, shares her intense eyes. She catches my eye as she introduces him, and I know part of her didn't believe any of what I'd told her until now.

I understand how she feels. For weeks, it's really been only Arik and me. Now we're not alone. We may be kasiri and halani, rich and poor, Atsani, Ashari, and Xanite, but down in this dark basement that smells of medicine, it almost feels like we're an odd sort of family. We may not be standing arm in arm, but at least the kasiri aren't sniffing at the halani's mended clothes and the halani aren't scowling at the kasiri behind their backs.

"So what's the plan?" Batyah's brother asks. He has the deep voice of a grown man, and it carries through the storeroom.

"Parliament must make a final decision on the moratorium on forced adoptions in four weeks," I say. "On the day of the vote, we'll all attend the session in the chamber of Parliament. We'll sit by ourselves, on our own sides of the room. The parliamentarians will probably argue about whether or not to make the moratorium permanent. When the time is right, I'll give a signal." I hope Batyah's brother doesn't ask me precisely when the time will be right. I won't know the best moment to act until it comes.

"Watch for me to stand up," I continue. "That will be the signal. Then we'll walk to the front of the chamber and ask Parliament to repeal *all* the Family Laws."

The silence in the pharmacy basement is hard to interpret. I lift my chin, trying to look more confident than I feel.

"Hmm." Maayan sounds more pensive than doubtful, but I still want to shrink under his gaze. "Kasiri won't give up forced adoptions, let alone the rest of the Family Laws, without a fight. They won't even respect the moratorium that was passed legally. Look what happened to that Xanite girl."

"Samira," I say automatically.

"Yes, her," Maayan says. "The Society kidnapped her. They said they'd give her the kasir upbringing she deserved, but for all we know, they're keeping her locked up somewhere until Parliament lifts the moratorium and things go back to the way they were. Or maybe they just tied her in a sack and dumped her in the Davgir."

Blood pounds in my ears, and I have a sudden urge to paste my hand over his mouth.

"They haven't dumped her anywhere," a new voice objects. "She's being well cared for."

I search for the speaker among the disembodied faces hovering in the gloom. "Who said that?"

"Me." A girl my age timidly raises a hand. Her loose hair and long, elegant dress mark her as a kasir, but she's pressed against a simply dressed halan girl a year or two older than her. I can't remember their names, but the halan is the wilding and the kasir the sister who was left behind.

"What do you know about Samira Harun?" I demand. Arik lays a hand on my arm, but I have to know. "Do you know where she is?"

"No," the girl replies. "But I heard my father say she was safe and being treated well. Fed and clothed as befits her station, he said."

"Your father's in the Society," I say. It's not a question. Several people gasp. The halani standing near her recoil. Somebody stumbles against a shelf, and glass clinks.

"Careful!" my brother warns. "Don't break anything."

The girl who brought up Samira's well-being says nothing. Only her sister remains by her side.

"He talks about Society affairs in front of you?" I say, torn between scorn and the hope that she knows something that could lead to Samira's rescue. Arik gives my arm a squeeze that is more reproving than comforting. I know what he's thinking: if he were Ashari, our own father would probably be an eager and active Society member.

"He doesn't," the kasir girl says nervously. "I . . . overhear things."

"This is crazy," Maayan says. "What are we doing here with children of Society members?" More exclamations erupt throughout the storeroom.

Batyah's brother glares at the kasir girl. "You 'overhear' things? Are you sure about that? You aren't, oh, *reporting* things?"

The girl shakes her head, trembling, but Maayan has already turned away. "I can't do this. We can't work together if we can't even trust there aren't Society informants among us."

He starts up the wooden stairs and is halfway to the top before I realize he intends to leave. Batyah watches him go without a word. And then other halani are following him: Dinah's sister, Arik's wilding recruit Yusuf. The steps groan as they march upward toward the door, abandoning us.

30

"Stop!" I say, just as Arik says, "Wait!"

I'm surprised how quickly the children on the stairs obey us. Even Maayan pauses on the third-to-last step and turns back.

My brother clasps my hand, and I understand that it is better that he, a halan, speak first. It is Maayan we must stop from walking out. If he stays, the others will follow his lead.

"Your sister is a kasir," Arik tells him. "Like mine is. Just because they're kasiri doesn't mean we can't trust them. You trusted your sister enough to come here today."

"She's not practically Society," Maayan retorts from the darkness above us.

"Are you sure?" I say, looking not at him but at Batyah, whose lips are pursed.

I hold my breath, afraid I've insulted one or both siblings. But Maayan descends a few steps, until lamplight flickers across his face again. He looks questioningly at Batyah.

The whole basement waits for her to speak.

"For all I know, my parents are Society," she says, her tone prickly. "I talk to them as little as possible."

I can't tell what Maayan is thinking. Does he hear a confession or a protestation of innocence?

Batyah moves toward the stairs. "Maayan, please stay," she says, so quietly the other children on the steps bend closer to hear. "We need you."

Her brother hovers on the stairs a moment longer, then cuts a path through the children crowded below him to join Batyah again. His expression remains stormy, but at least his work boots are firmly planted on the concrete again. The other would-be deserters drift back down the stairs almost sheepishly now that their leader has changed his mind.

I hide my relief and instead say, "We cannot judge each other by who our parents are. We are not our parents. My father disowned Arik, but here I am, working with my brother to end the Family Laws."

I catch some grumbling in the corners, but nobody questions me.

I turn back to the daughter of the Society member, who is standing stiffly next to her sister. "I'm sorry if I was harsh before, but I know people who care a lot about bringing Samira home. Do you have any idea where she might be?"

Her tenseness eases a little, and she shakes her head. "From what I've heard, somebody in the Society has her in their home, but nobody ever says who."

"How many Society members do you know?" I ask.

The kasir girl recites names, none of which are familiar. Then one rings a bell.

"Wait, repeat that one."

"Asaf Zevulun?"

I turn to Arik. "That's a parliamentarian. He's on Nitsan's committee."

My brother shrugs. "Everyone knows some parliamentarians are in the Society."

Someone makes a disgusted noise in his throat.

"And then there's Shimshon Omri," the girl finishes.

"Omri?" I say, my heartbeat jerking. Merav's surname is Omri. What was the first name of the man from the embassy party? "Does he work for the government? Foreign Affairs?"

"Yes."

Shimshon Omri. Merav's father is in the Society.

"I'll pass on what you've told me," I tell the girl. "Thank you."

"I hate the Society," she blurts out. She's talking to me, but her words are intended for the whole room. "I hate what my father does. I wouldn't—I'm not like him."

"Prove it," someone mutters.

I go rigid, but resist the urge to snap. Our alliance is fragile, and I will only weaken it further if I appear to favor kasiri.

"We need unity," I say quietly. I look around the basement, meeting Batyah's eyes, and Maayan's. For the first time, he regards me with grudging respect. "We're all here because we believe the Family Laws are wrong. Remember that. And when you catch yourself making assumptions about all halani or all kasiri, think of your brother or sister."

A solemn silence follows my words. I can feel each person's gaze on me. I can still feel them after everyone has dispersed, trickling out in ones and twos; after Batyah abruptly embraces me before slipping out the alley door; after my brother and Caleb leave. Standing alone in the darkness, surrounded by jars of herbal tablets and powdered remedies, I can still feel the presence of the children who will stand up to the world with Arik and me.

⤙ ⤙ ⤙

Two days after the meeting, I walk to Horiel. I'm surprised to be greeted by Marah.

"It's good to see you," I say. "You're not around much anymore."

"I worked twelve hours yesterday," she says, stifling a yawn, "so Mother made me sleep in today. I should really be going out, I've got to find bedding for five families, but I'm so tired . . ."

"One day off won't hurt anyone." I want to comfort Marah somehow. Since Samira was kidnapped, she's been pushing herself to the bone. As though she needs to atone for failing the Haruns.

"That's one more day these children are sleeping on dirt floors," she mutters.

"I have something to tell you," I say. I rattle off the names of Society members the wilding's sister gave me.

Marah listens attentively. "I don't think any of those will come as a surprise to Shaul, or Azariah. But I'll let them know."

I find the boys on the floor of Caleb's bedroom amid a sea of homework. They both have their sleeves rolled up past their elbows. Caleb looks up and signs me a question. I don't understand, but Arik is able to translate. "Do you want to go to the bakery?"

"Is that a good idea?" We've been bolder of late, venturing out of the Levis' stuffy apartment to get some air. In Marah's skirt, with my hair braided, I look enough like a halan to fool the average passerby. It's risky, but it feels so good to walk through Horiel with Arik and Caleb that I can't give it up. Still, we've never gone into a shop.

"They have the best cherry scones this time of year," Arik says hopefully.

I roll my eyes. "Caleb, you could *make* cherry scones."

He shakes his head, taking his slate from the desk. *Not like these. Besides, Mother told me I'm going through the sugar too fast.*

The bakery is five blocks away. When we enter, Caleb greets the flour-dusted woman behind the counter. Arik also says hello, but I hang back, inspecting a basket of rolls giving off a warm, yeasty smell.

Caleb asks the baker for three cherry scones. Arik tries to pay for them, but Caleb pushes his hand away. I'm tempted to just slap a silver coin on the counter, but that might attract unwanted attention.

As Arik hands me my scone, a young woman charges into the bakery, the morning's *Journal* flapping in her hands. "Mother, Gadi Nitsan's told Parliament to end forced adoptions for good!"

Arik and I exchange jubilant glances. As the baker's daughter spreads the newspaper over the counter, Caleb tugs my sleeve and asks me something. The only signs I recognize are what I think are the letters of Samira's name. I shake my head. "It's the committee's report."

We dash out of the bakery, intent on buying our own newspaper, but there isn't a paperboy in sight. So we run home to the Levis', where we find Marah and Azariah bent over a copy of the *Journal* on the kitchen table. The boys and I crowd around.

Parliamentary Committee Recommends Ending Forced Adoptions of Changelings

Even though this is what Azariah predicted, seeing the words printed in ink stops my breath for a second. I read on hungrily.

> On Eighthday, the parliamentary committee appointed to study the impact of forced adoptions submitted to the United Parliament its final report, which recommends ending the practice of relocating changeling children and turning the current moratorium on forced adoptions into permanent law. The thirty-seven-page report describes the numerous ways in which changelings, both kasir and halan, perform poorly on various measures of success and claims their problems are due to their adoptions at age ten.

The article lists some of the committee's findings. Changelings are less likely to attend university or get married than ordinary people. They earn less money than average, whether they're halani or kasiri. They're more likely to be unemployed or to commit suicide.

All four halan committee members signed the report. The two kasiri, including Asaf Zevulun, the parliamentarian who said mixed families would mean Ashara's ruin, refused to.

> "To end forced adoptions is to destroy part of the foundation of our society," Zevulun said. "This report is a disgrace." Nitsan hinted that legislation proposed in the wake of her committee's recommendation might not limit itself to making the moratorium permanent but could set its sights on the Family Laws as a whole. "We are not excluding any possibilities," she said.

I read that paragraph again. It sounds like Nitsan might propose repealing all the Family Laws, not just the law on forced adoptions, on the day of the vote. I'm almost too excited to keep reading, but Caleb nudges me, pointing out the name of our school further on.

> Yakov Peleg, a professor of history at Firem University, questioned the committee's methods and cast doubt on their conclusions. "To have any validity, Nitsan's study ought to have compared changelings who were adopted into appropriate families with changelings raised by their birth parents. Of course, given the law, that is impossible. Who's to say these poor wretches wouldn't have committed suicide at even higher rates had they not been adopted?"

The professor's quote infuriates me. How dare he call

Arik a *poor wretch*? Marah looks equally repulsed.

"Do you know that professor?" I ask Azariah flatly.

"I've never spoken to him." Azariah hesitates, as though gauging the depth of my rage. "He's right, in a way. I don't deny the statistics about wildings, but it's impossible to say that being adopted led to all that. The problems could've been even worse if they'd stayed with their birth families."

"You're wrong," I say. "Of course children might have a hard time if they were different from the rest of their family, but it still wouldn't be as bad as forced adoptions." I turn to Arik. "Wouldn't you have been happier if you'd never been taken away?"

My brother wavers. It feels like a blow.

"I would've given anything to stay with you, Rivka," he says quickly, no doubt glimpsing the betrayal in my eyes. "But I wasn't happy our last year together."

"Because of Father," I spit.

Arik nods. "Letting wildings grow up in their birth families isn't enough. Their families have to accept them too. And that means kasiri have to stop believing halani are inferior."

The kitchen is uncomfortably quiet. I can sense Marah's silent agreement with my brother, Azariah's guilt and despair, and my twin's sadness.

"Look," Marah says, "I don't care if Nitsan's methods weren't perfect. Frankly, the whole investigation was unnecessary. We don't need a study to tell us it's wrong to take children away from their parents. But if a scientific-sounding report convinces more Ashari that forced adoptions are bad, so much the better."

An admiring smile plays on Azariah's lips. His love for Marah shines so brightly I can't believe I didn't see it the first day I met them.

❧ ❧ ❧

Within days, Ayelet Nitsan has introduced a bill to repeal the Family Laws in their entirety. At dinner on Thirdday, Father won't stop going on about Nitsan's mission to wreck Ashara. I pretend I'm too full for dessert and escape to the music room. Father won't bother me if he hears me working on my spells.

Nitsan's proposal creates a minor stir at Firem. Our classmates and the Epic Poetry teacher make a point of being extra awful to Caleb, as though he is personally to blame for the fact that the Family Laws might be abolished. In the corridors, I overhear Merav and her friends calling Parliamentarian Nitsan all manner of names, the politest of which is "sparker radical."

At lunchtime, Hilah rakes her lentils into patterns with her fork and casts nervous glances at nearby tables even though no one ever pays any attention to us in the dining hall.

Finally, she leans toward me, her eyes wide and frank. "Can I tell you something?"

I nod, slightly on my guard.

"It's just . . . I'm not sure I'm completely against changing the Family Laws," she says in an undertone. "Intermarriage is probably a bad idea, but I don't know about forced adoptions anymore . . ."

My friend looks at me fearfully, as though she expects me to be scandalized. I'm trying to work out whether I should pretend to be. Hilah thinks Samira's kidnapping was a crime and isn't opposed to integrated schools. She knows I feel the same way. Would her latest confession really shock the Rivka she knows?

Suddenly, a strong temptation to tell Hilah the truth comes over me. I'm weary of deceiving her, of being someone who is almost but not completely me around her. She's come so close to saying she thinks Arik and I have the right to be brother and sister. But when I open my mouth to speak, my heart clenches into a cold fist of fear, and I can't get the words out.

⤙ ⤙ ⤙

Arriving in Horiel on Seventhday is a relief after a difficult week. I can finally celebrate Nitsan's proposal to repeal the Family Laws with Arik.

"This is exactly what we'd hoped!" my brother says, stuffing mint leaves into a teapot at Caleb's instruction. "Now *we* don't need to ask Parliament to consider all the Family Laws. Nitsan will make sure they do."

"You know, if she can get this bill passed herself," I say, "we might not even need to reveal ourselves in Parliament on the day of the vote." If we could get what we wanted without risking arrest and imprisonment . . .

Caleb quickly gathers why Arik and I are so delighted. *I don't mean to be pessimistic*, he writes, *but Marah says it won't be easy for Nitsan to get the repeal through. She needs fourteen votes out of twenty-one. Assuming all seven kasiri vote against repeal, she'll need every single halan to vote for it. But Marah thinks some halan parliamentarians support the Family Laws.*

"Why would they?" I say, dismayed. Arik and Caleb trade helpless glances and shrug.

"Well, if Nitsan can't persuade Parliament to repeal the Family Laws," I say, "then we will."

31

Another week passes. Since the meeting of the wildings, Arik and I have been busier than ever. Our underground movement now includes twenty-four wildings and more than thirty siblings.

On Seventhday, I set out for the Levis' again. Soon after crossing into Horiel District and uncasting the Veil, I smell smoke on the breeze. I keep walking toward Caleb's, and the scent grows stronger.

Now there are shouts ahead, and a crackling sound that makes me shudder. I would turn back, but this is the only way I know to the Levis', and somehow the fire I know is ahead pulls me inexorably toward it.

I round the corner, and suddenly the street is crowded. Farther down the block, a building is burning. Smoke billows from the upper two floors, all but concealing a malevolent orange glow at the heart of the fire. The gathered onlookers are whispering, "Nitsan, Nitsan." An icy sensation trails down my spine.

Numb, I press forward until I can see the fire brigade passing buckets, trying to fight a blaze that is too high. Men shout at me to move back. The summer air around me grows even hotter, like the breath of an oven. The air snaps and wood groans as the smoke keeps pouring out. Something black and delicate dances slowly down from above, past my shoulder. The notes of a cooling spell, the one I offered to cast on Caleb's burned hand, rises in my throat, but it's not right for a fire, and the heat, the heat is incredible, baking my face.

"Rivka!"

A hand closes painfully around my arm, and someone yanks me back, hauls me halfway up the street. It's Azariah.

"What are you doing?" he shouts, his face red.

The air on my skin has cooled, but smoke is darkening the street, and I start to cough.

"Does Nitsan live there?" I try to point, but my whole body is shaking.

"It's her law offices, I think." Azariah looks over his shoulder at the bucket brigade and curses. "That won't do any good. It's magical fire."

"Do people live upstairs?" I hear myself say.

"I don't know."

Is he lying? What could be up there but apartments?

"Stay here. Don't move." Azariah dashes toward Nitsan's law offices, as if to join the halan firefighters, but then he throws up his hands toward the blaze. Blue sparks spiral from his outstretched fingers.

A distant wail grows into an ear-splitting siren that slices through the roar of fire and voices. The throngs part as a black fire truck barrels onto the scene. No sooner have the first firefighters alighted—kasiri, by the way their hands are already forming shapes—than Azariah is at my side, swearing in my ear as he drags me toward the Levis'.

"They'll put it out, right?" I say.

"Yes, though it's kind of late, don't you think?" He's still shouting even though the street is quiet here.

Marah lets us in. She takes one look at our faces and says, "What happened?"

"Nitsan's law offices are burning," Azariah says roughly.

I hear Marah's gasp, but I stumble toward the table where my brother and Caleb are sitting, staring at me. Arik was showing Caleb a medsha score. I look down at the music, latching onto the normalcy of it, shutting out the smoke and the crack of breaking beams.

Flustered, my brother gathers the pages into a sheaf. "I—it's just something my teacher lent me."

"Are you learning to conduct?"

"No, to compose," he says sheepishly.

To compose. If Arik had magic, he would be Father's pride and joy. It hurts that Arik would so readily show his score to Caleb yet act so shy about it around me, but I push this thought aside as behind me Marah says, "It was a warning from the Society."

"It was more than a warning!" Azariah says. "If Parliament wasn't in session today, I'd call it an assassination attempt."

"Assassination attempt?" I say faintly, dropping into a chair. "Could that happen?"

Azariah's expression hardens. "A few years ago—"

"Don't tell her that," Marah says, touching his arm.

"What?" I say. "Tell me."

"You'd never have let anyone keep it from you," Azariah tells Marah. To me, he says, "The kasir parliamentarian who voted with the halani for integrated schools was murdered three weeks after the law was passed. Everyone knew the Society was responsible."

My breath hitches in my throat.

Caleb brews a pot of mint tea, and we all gather at the table. It's really too hot for tea, but I drink it in the hopes that it will calm me. So far, it's not working. Only two weeks remain until the vote. But what if Nitsan doesn't survive until then?

⚵ ⚵ ⚵

I wake up each morning in the grip of dread. It doesn't ease until I've found Father bent over the day's *Journal*, coffee cup pinched between his fingers. As long as he doesn't tell me Nitsan has been assassinated, I can relax. Miraculously, no one died in the fire, but the building was destroyed. I wonder how Nitsan will keep practicing law.

Arik and I send our last message to the wildings and their siblings. The instructions are the same as those I gave in the pharmacy basement. Be in the chamber of Parliament on the day of the vote. Watch for the signal.

When Seventhday comes again, I wait until Father leaves for some Atsani expatriate's country mansion before stealing away in my halan garb. I'm astonished how much easier I breathe in Horiel than at the embassy. It's not just the absence of the thick webs of spells that blanket kasir districts.

When Arik opens the Levis' door, music floods out. Marah is playing a particularly anguished-sounding violin sonata in her bedroom.

"I've heard from a couple of people," Arik says, raising his voice. "They'll be there next Seventhday."

"Good," I say, disappointed that I haven't heard from anyone. Caleb emerges from the hallway, and I ask, "Is Marah all right?"

He shrugs and motions toward the door, asking if we want to go out.

"Cherry scones?" I suggest.

Caleb brightens.

"My treat," I say, cutting off the boys' objections with a look. Unlike me, neither of them has an allowance.

After buying our scones, we walk to the park and settle on a bench warmed by the sun. We sit without talking much, watching children play in the hollows beneath the spruces. Too soon, I must bid the boys farewell. I still have to prepare for my magic lesson tonight.

As we leave through the gate, a motor rumbles in the distance. I think nothing of it, but my brother stiffens. He pulls Caleb back against the rusted fence. Moments later, a black automobile rounds the corner, sunlight catching on its silver bumper.

"That's odd," Arik says. He and Caleb are wearing identical wary expressions. It strikes me that I've never seen an auto on the streets of Horiel before.

The driver slows at the sight of us, though we're well

out of the auto's path. I think I glimpse the silhouette of a woman behind the wheel, but the tinted windows make it difficult to be sure, and after a moment the auto rolls past.

"Who do you suppose that was?" I ask the boys.

Caleb shakes his head darkly.

"It's probably just somebody taking a shortcut back to the city center," Arik says, but he sounds uneasy.

The auto disappears up the street, leaving a coil of black exhaust floating near the ground.

32

Back at the embassy, I uncast the invisibility spell and change into a light summer dress. I dip my comb into the pitcher on my dresser and run the dripping teeth through my hair to flatten away all traces of my braid. Then I sit down at my desk to finish composing a spell for my evening lesson.

Shortly before dinnertime, I hear Father in the hallway. His footsteps are quick and loud, not deliberate like usual. And they're headed straight for my bedroom. I straighten in my chair as my door flies open.

Father is standing on the threshold, crushing the doorknob in his fist. His eyes are like two embers, glowing with fury. An icy hand scoops out my insides. He knows something, something big. But what? My secret life now encompasses so many big things.

"Father?" I croak.

"You were in Horiel District this afternoon." It isn't a question. Father must have evidence not even the most convincing lie could sweep away, and right now my well of lies seems to have run dry.

He strides into my bedroom. Panicking, I rise from my

chair before he can loom over me. I still have to look up to meet his terrible gaze.

"What do you have to say for yourself?"

I keep quiet, afraid to speak until Father reveals how much he knows.

"Gadi Yoram said you told her you would be with Hilah today. You lied to her."

I nod hesitantly, thinking the confession might soften him, but his anger doesn't flicker.

"Aren't you the least bit curious how you were found out?" he says acidly.

I say nothing.

"Deputy Liron was driving through Horiel and saw you in the street in some ridiculous getup, with two sparker boys."

Deputy Liron. I can't believe my bad luck. "Why was she driving through Horiel District?"

"Deputy Liron is a grown woman! She has the right to drive wherever she pleases!"

"You never said I couldn't go to Horiel." I know it will fan Father's rage, but I need to keep him talking. As far as he knows, I have no idea Arik even lives in Ashara. But what if he suspects I've found out?

Father's face darkens. "You were seen in a halan neighborhood dressed as a halan. Deputy Liron said you seemed to know the sparker boys well. It's obvious you've been sneaking off to Horiel for a long time. All those days you said you were studying with Hilah, that's really where you were, wasn't it?"

"N-no," I stammer. "I *do* study with—"

"If I hadn't met her, I would think you had made her up,"

Father says. "What is all this running about behind my back? Lying to my face and mixing with sparkers?"

I stare up at him, speechless.

"Are you in love with one of those boys?"

"*No*," I say reflexively.

Father slaps me so suddenly I don't even see the blow coming. "Don't lie to me!"

"I'm not!" Tears of shock and pain spring to my eyes, and I blink furiously. "They're just friends!"

"You are a kasir, Rivka. You are the daughter of the Atsani ambassador to Ashara. You do not have sparker friends!" Father doesn't look at all remorseful for striking me. "Who are they?"

"Caleb Levi, from school." His name tumbles out of me since I'm on firmer ground now. "And his friend Elisha."

To my intense relief, he doesn't ask for Elisha's surname. "If Deputy Liron hadn't seen you today, how long would this deception have gone on? You have destroyed my trust in you."

Even as Father continues to shout at me, my heartbeat slows. He doesn't know the truth. Deputy Liron's telling on me is going to make things very difficult now, but they could be much worse. I brace myself against my desk, waiting for Father to announce my punishment but feeling safe knowing he hasn't discovered my most crucial secrets.

Then Father says, "It was a mistake to bring you here."

My head snaps up. "What?"

"You've been running wild without my knowledge. Your consorting with halani is a disgrace, but even worse is your lying."

Father's charges roll right off me. I'm not the least bit

sorry for anything I've done in Ashara. Part of me knows I should hang my head, try to look contrite, but I can't.

"I haven't time to deal with this childish rebellion of yours. You need more supervision than I can provide."

I realize the decision he has made the second before he announces it.

"You are going back to Atsan immediately."

"No!" I don't have to feign anything now. "Father, please. I'm sorry. Do anything you want to me, but don't send me home."

"Why are you so desperate to stay in Ashara?" Father demands.

Fear plucks my breath away. I'm on springtime ice again. "I don't want to be so far away from you," I say, but the lie sounds hollow. I can see Father's skepticism in the set of his mouth.

"On the contrary, you seem eager to escape the embassy as often as possible. It's obvious you hold my parental authority in utter contempt. No, you will pack tonight."

"What?" I say, aghast.

Father's gaze is pitiless. "You will be on tomorrow's train to Atsan. I'll wire my sister in the morning. She should receive the message in time to meet you at the station when you arrive."

It wouldn't be very hard for me to burst into tears right now. I'd do it if I thought it would do any good, but I doubt Father would be moved. Still, I have to try to stop this.

"Please give me another chance, Father. I'll never go to Horiel again. I'll—"

"Your word is worthless, Rivka," Father says. "My decision is final."

33

At two in the morning, hidden under the Veil, I tiptoe down the carpeted embassy staircase. My schoolbag, containing a nightgown and the halan clothes Marah lent me, is slung over my shoulder. I unlock the front door and ease it open, holding my breath. It makes no sound. Then I'm out in the summer night, my pounding heart and the crickets' strident chirps warring in my ears.

The familiar walk to Firem is transformed at night. The moon sheds its eerie light on the worn cobblestones, and shadows writhe between the gas streetlights. Here and there, a figure lies slumped along the gutter. When I reach the girls' dormitory, I try the door, but it's locked. I peer up instead at the windows gleaming in the moonlight and work out which one is Hilah's.

Taking a deep breath, I uncast the Veil, trying to forget the menacing night around me. I recall how to adapt the Glimmer, the first spell I showed Samira, for glass. Then I start to sing again. I keep my gaze fixed on Hilah's window as magic begins to stir. After a couple of rounds through the tune, the glass begins to shine. The glow intensifies, a hum rising with it. When no one comes to the window, my hopes begin to flag. How much brighter and louder can I let the window get before I risk being caught by another boarder?

Finally a light flicks on behind the window, visible even through the radiance of the windowpane. I stop singing. My magical light fades, but the electric light is steady. A silhouette appears in the window. I wave my arms wildly. The window opens with a crack, and I wince.

"Hilah!" I call softly. "It's me!"

"Rivka?" She rubs her eyes and leans out the window, her hair tumbling down her right shoulder. "God of the Maitaf, what time is it?"

"Around two thirty, I think. Hilah, I need you to let me in."

"What?"

"I . . . I've run away from the embassy."

"*What?* Why?"

"Can I tell you upstairs?"

"No," Hilah says. Why is she choosing now of all times to be stubborn? "Do you have any idea how much trouble I'll be in if I get caught letting—"

"My father was going to put me on the train to Atsan in the morning."

There is silence overhead. Then Hilah says, "What's going on, Rivka?"

"This isn't the best place to talk."

There's another pause, and I can tell she isn't happy.

"If I let you in, you have to tell me everything. *Everything.* What you're doing on the weekends when you say you're studying with me, why you're about to be sent home . . ."

I can't believe we're having this conversation in the dead of night with me standing in the street and her hanging out a window.

"Well?" she says.

There's so much I've kept hidden from her. Arik, Samira, my friendship with the Levis, and now, our imminent plan to appear in Parliament. I'm ashamed to have lied so much to my only kasir friend, but I'm still afraid to tell her the truth.

Hilah ducks inside and raises her arms to slam the window down.

"Wait! I'll tell you everything."

Two minutes later, Hilah is pulling me into the dark entryway of the dormitory.

"Thank you so much," I say, sagging with relief. "I owe—"

"You owe me an answer to every single question I ask you."

In her room, she dumps her extra set of sheets in my arms. I spread them haphazardly on the empty bed, not really experienced with making beds and too exhausted to care. I flop onto the mattress, fully clothed.

"No falling asleep," Hilah says, perched on her bed with her arms around her knees. "Start talking or I swear I'll go wake the matron right now."

"My father's deputy saw me in Horiel yesterday with my brother and Caleb Levi," I say dully. "She told on me, and my father said I was going straight back to Atsan."

"In Horiel?" Hilah says. "With Caleb? I *knew* it!"

"Hilah. I'm not in love with Caleb."

"Wait a second. Your brother? You don't have any siblings."

"I do," I say, and I explain.

"So," I finish, my voice hoarse, "when Father said he was putting me on tomorrow's—today's—train to Atsan, I had to run away. I need to be here for the vote on the Family Laws next Seventhday."

Hilah sits on her coverlet, not quite looking me in the face. The silence wears on until she finally says, "Why didn't you trust me? You *used* me."

"I'm sorry."

"How many times did I tell you you could trust me?" She takes a shuddering breath, and I expect her to tell me to leave, but instead she says, "Let me help you."

"What?" I wonder if I've misheard.

She meets my gaze, and there's an intensity in her eyes I've never seen before. "I want to help you repeal the Family Laws. People make so much of the difference between kasiri and halani, but I've never been able to see it. And what happened to you and your brother was wrong."

I'm too stunned to speak. I've known for a while that Hilah doesn't agree with a lot of our classmates' views, but I never imagined she'd want to join us like this, all at once, after learning all my secrets at four in the morning.

"You don't have a wilding sibling, do you?" I ask at last.

She shakes her head, her expression solemn. "And I'm not a changeling. So I guess I can't help you make a big impression on Parliament, but I'm going to be there next Seventhday."

"You don't have to—"

"I *want* to," she says.

I twist my hands in my lap. "Hilah, I don't deserve a friend like you."

She waits long enough before responding that I know part of her agrees. But then she says, "Yes, you do. You're the only person in our class who still talked to me after I said all my friends at home were halani."

"I'm sorry for keeping so much from you."

"You could have told me. But . . . I can sort of understand why you didn't. I can't believe you managed to hide all this from your *father* for so long."

I sit up straight. "Father. In a few hours, he'll discover I've run away. I can't stay here. This is the first place he'll look for me."

"Where else can you go?"

"I don't know," I say, fighting a rising tide of panic. I have so few connections in Ashara. "You're my only friend. Except for Caleb, but I can't stay with the Levis. Father knows Caleb was one of the boys I was with in Horiel."

"What about your brother?" Hilah asks.

"My brother? But he has parents."

"I mean you could stay with him with their knowledge. If Arik told them about you, do you think they'd turn you in?"

"I have no idea." My options are dwindling though.

"It looks like the only way to me," Hilah says.

"I'd have to go to Caleb's first," I say. "I don't know my way to Arik's apartment." I try to estimate how much time I have. "I should leave by six thirty. When I'm not up at seven, Father will discover I'm missing, and this is the first place he'll look for me." And when he doesn't find me here, he'll start trying to figure out where Caleb lives. I have to beat him to Horiel.

Hilah glances at the clock on her desk. It's just past four. "No point going back to sleep, I guess. Dawn's not far off."

Right then, I yawn.

"Well, *you* should rest," Hilah says. "I'll wake you at six."

I don't have it in me to protest. I burrow into the nest of sheets on the bare mattress and fall asleep at once.

34

At quarter past seven, Caleb and I are standing in front of a grimy brick building on Dogwood Street in Horiel District. I arrived at the Levis' apartment twenty-five minutes ago to find Marah already up and brewing a pot of tea in the kitchen. She had to rouse Caleb, but as soon as he understood the situation, he agreed to take me to Arik's. Now we're here.

Caleb points at a third-story window. Before I can decide whether it would be a bad idea to cast the Glimmer in a halan neighborhood while dressed in Marah's clothes, Caleb picks up a pebble from the gutter and lobs it at the glass. I guess that's another way to do it. The pebble strikes the pane with a crack and drops to the street, where Caleb scoops it back up. I watch the window anxiously. I can't believe it was only yesterday that we were eating scones in the park.

As Caleb is raising his arm to throw the stone again, Arik appears, squinting down at us. Caleb tosses the pebble aside and signs, *Come down*. Then he jerks his thumb at me. My brother's eyes widen, and he vanishes from the window.

When Arik emerges from the building, his hair sticking

up in back and his expression worried, I fill him in on all that's happened. I don't even have to ask him for help.

"You have to stay with us," he says without hesitating. "There's no other way. Let me just talk to my parents first. They're eating breakfast. I'll try to . . . prepare them. I'll come back down for you."

Caleb waits with me while Arik is gone. I clench my fists to keep my hands from shaking. Has Father gone to Firem yet? Could he be on his way to Horiel already? I reassure myself that he doesn't know about the Natans, but much good that will do me if Arik's parents refuse to take me in.

Finally, at quarter to eight, Arik returns to fetch me. Caleb gives us an encouraging smile and goes on his way. Wavering between relief and dread, I follow my solemn brother up to his apartment.

A man and a woman are standing in the cramped entryway, framed by the doorway to the kitchen. Ezra Natan is a slight man with dark hair and gray eyebrows. There's a gentleness in his gaze that eases my trepidation slightly. Hadassah Maor is even smaller than her husband. Her hands are buried in the folds of her apron, and her expression is fearful.

Arik clears his throat. "Mother, Father . . ." It's jarring to hear him call these strangers that. "This is my twin sister, Rivka."

They are silent. It must be my duty to speak, but I don't know what to say. Do I thank them? Apologize for imposing on them?

"It's an honor to meet you," I say, as if I'm at an embassy dinner. Immediately, I wish I hadn't sounded so stiff.

"She is so like him," Gadi Maor murmurs, her eyes drinking in my face.

"I've wanted to introduce her to you for a while," Arik stammers. He has trouble meeting his parents' gazes, and I realize he's ashamed of having deceived them over these last months.

"Why is your father intent on sending you back to Atsan today?" Banar Natan asks me. It seems he's the kind of person who likes to get straight to the point.

"Because he found out I was spending time with halani," I say. It's an odd feeling, being honest with two people I only just met.

"But he doesn't know about this?" Gadi Maor says, pointing between my brother and me.

"No. He doesn't realize I've found Arik."

My brother stiffens, and Gadi Maor looks confused. "Who's Arik?" Then her eyes widen. I've just broken the law again.

"Arik is my birth name, Mother," my twin says calmly. "Rivka still calls me that."

"Is it really wise to defy your father in this way?" Banar Natan asks me, his tone kind but unyielding.

"I . . . I can't go back to Atsan now. If I do, I don't know when I'll see Ar—Elisha again." Gadi Maor looks visibly relieved to hear me call my brother by his new name.

"You cannot stay out of your father's reach forever," Banar Natan says.

"He's an ambassador," his wife says. "He'll have us arrested if he learns we're hiding you."

"Mother!" Arik says, a note of fear entering his voice.

"Ambassador Kadmiel has no idea who you are or what my name is now or where we live."

"And I won't stay for too long," I say, hoping their idea of what "too long" means isn't radically different from mine. "Only until next Seventhday."

"Next Seventhday?" Banar Natan says. "Ah. The day Parliament votes on the Family Laws. But do you have some hope the repeal will pass? The outlook isn't very good."

Now isn't the time to tell him and Gadi Maor about our coalition of siblings. They've had enough shocks this morning. Instead, I say, "Whatever happens, I promise I won't stay past next Seventhday." By then, either we'll have succeeded or we'll all be under arrest.

"So can she stay with us?" says Arik.

His adoptive parents exchange a long look. Then Banar Natan says, "Of course you can stay, Rivka. We are glad to be able to help our son's sister."

Gadi Maor turns around abruptly and disappears into the kitchen. Is she upset? I glance at my brother, hoping for some reassurance, but he looks equally uncertain.

He leads me down a narrow hallway to his room. His bed is unmade, his wardrobe open, and the desk under the window heaped with notebooks, papers, and a couple of dishes. A wooden music stand straddles a whirlpool of sheet music.

"Goodness," I say, "our room never looked like this."

"Sorry," Arik says sheepishly. "But we did have maids."

Chastened, I look away.

We improvise a pallet for me by stuffing a fitted sheet with winter blankets. After we spread another sheet on top, my eyes fall on the worn violin case next to the desk, and I think of my own cello, abandoned at the embassy. I turn to Arik. "Play for me?"

He smiles and opens his case.

✦ ✦ ✦

Lunch is an awkward affair. Gadi Maor treats me like a guest, passing me the sausages and cabbage so I can serve myself first and giving me the bread from the center of the loaf.

"It's not the sort of food you're used to, I'm sure," she says.

"Everything's delicious," I say honestly. The food is plainer than what's served at the embassy, but Gadi Maor is an excellent cook, and I'm ravenous.

Silence reigns for most of the meal. Arik's parents seem hesitant to ask me about myself lest they violate the contract they signed when they adopted my brother. They aren't supposed to know anything about his past, and I'm more or less the embodiment of that past.

Later, in his room, I ask my brother if his parents really want me here.

He sighs. "They're not going to turn you out, Rivka."

"That doesn't mean they want me here." I whisper because there's not much privacy in small Horiel apartments.

"Of course they want to know their son's sister," says Arik. "But?"

"But, well . . . You have to understand how it is for Mother. She couldn't have children, but she always wanted them. I think she's afraid of losing me."

"I'm not going to steal you away," I protest.

"I know, but you're a reminder I wasn't always her son."

We contemplate this in silence. Then Arik says, "Sorry, but I really have to do some homework."

"Of course," I say. "Don't let me disturb you." It's a very guest-like, un-sisterly thing to say. I hate this sense of distance between us.

"I left all my homework at the embassy," I add.

"I could share," Arik says mischievously.

I roll my eyes. "No, thank you." I start to say I'll practice cello and then remember with a pang that my cello isn't here. I feel a longing to play music, though, so I ask, "Can I play your violin?"

Azariah looks taken aback, but then he grins. "You still can?"

"I guess we'll find out. It won't bother you?"

"No, go ahead."

So while Arik clears a space to write at his desk, I unpack his violin. The instrument is chestnut brown with orangey flames. I tuck it under my chin and pluck the strings. Then I lift the bow and begin a scale. The first couple of notes are painfully out of tune, but my fingers quickly get the hang of it again. I go up one octave and come down again.

"Not bad," Arik says.

I smile against the chin rest and think back to the sorts of things I used to play on his violin when we were little. I begin my favorite waltz. Arik hums along as I play the tune by ear, making only a couple of mistakes.

"You're pretty good for not having played a violin in four years," he says.

"We'd switch instruments at school on examination days while we were waiting to demonstrate spells for the Magic teacher," I say.

"Still."

I play for a little longer, just for the pleasure of making music. It's not the same as playing the cello, but it loosens the knots of anxiety in my stomach.

After an equally awkward supper, Arik and I return to his room, and I listen to him practice his medsha music. When it's time for bed, he extinguishes the gaslight and leaves the window open to let in the night breeze. We lie awake talking until late.

Then I'm floating in the dim haze between wakefulness and dreaming and thinking of a different life I could lead. Arik and I will never be the Kadmiel twins again, but could we be the Natan twins? Father must hate me now. If somehow Banar Natan and Gadi Maor were to become my parents, I could be Arik's sister again, living under the same roof as him.

It is a tantalizing vision, but as I drift off, I know deep down it will never be. Father is my legal guardian. Arik's parents cannot afford to adopt a fourteen-year-old girl who requires food and clothes and secondary-school tuition. And above all, no matter how I disguise myself or who my friends and siblings are, I am a kasir. The way I see the world is shaped by fourteen years of wealth and ease, and even if I wanted to, I couldn't erase that. My place will never be in Horiel.

35

Gadi Maor makes cinnamon rolls and oatmeal with dried cherries and honey for breakfast, and I know by Arik's surprise that she's made special food on my account. I try to do her lavish meal justice, but I feel slightly ill. I want Arik's mother to like me, not treat me like some foreign dignitary.

After breakfast, Arik shows me the medsha music he's been trying to write, and I look over the cello part. We wonder if Caleb will come over, but he doesn't appear. Late in the afternoon, when I hear a pot clang in the kitchen, I ask Gadi Maor if I can help her make supper, but she politely refuses. I hide my disappointment. After the meal, I help Arik wash the dishes and then clumsily play his violin while he finishes his homework.

On Firstday, I get up with my brother even though of course I can't go to school. Banar Natan has already left for his watchmaking shop, but his copy of the *Journal* is still at the table. Arik takes a gigantic bite of bread and jam and pulls the newspaper toward him. He turns the pages slowly, as though searching for something.

I set down my glass of tea, suddenly fearful. "Has anything happened to Parliamentarian Nitsan?"

"No, thank God. But look." Arik hands me the paper. "You've been reported missing."

Sure enough, there's a brief article stating that Rivka Kadmiel, the daughter of the Atsani ambassador to Ashara, has been unaccounted for since the early hours of Eighthday. It doesn't call me a runaway, but it does say I may be staying with halani. Worse, there's a reward offered to anyone who can provide information about my whereabouts.

"That money would mean a lot to somebody," my brother says, voicing my thoughts.

Somebody like one of the Natans' neighbors. I guess I won't be leaving the apartment until Seventhday.

After Arik leaves, I offer to help Gadi Maor wash up, but she again turns me down. I mope in my brother's bedroom all day, wondering what rumors are flying about me at Firem. By the time Arik returns from school, I'm so restless I could almost run away again.

"It's so good to come home knowing you're here," he says when he bursts into his bedroom. My spirits lift a little. I want to tell him how his mother called me Gadin Rivka at lunch, as though she were my servant, but it feels petty to complain.

Secondday promises to be as excruciating as Firstday. In the morning, I idle in the sitting room with one of Arik's books, pretending to read while Gadi Maor stitches a sleeve to a shirt. When the sleeve is attached, she starts to dust the furniture. It reminds me of when one of the maids comes into the parlor while I'm reading, and suddenly I can't stand it.

"Gadi Maor?"

"Yes?" she says, continuing to dust.

"I . . . I'd really like to help you. With chores, cooking, anything. Since I can't go to school, I have nothing to do, and it seems only right that I . . ."

Gadi Maor straightens and squints at me. For a moment, I'm afraid I've offended her by refusing to be treated as a guest. Heat is creeping into my face when she says, "All right. I'm sure I can find something for you to do."

The day wears on, and I wonder if she only said that to get me to stop bothering her. But late in the afternoon, she comes to find me in Arik's room. "I'm going to start supper, if you'd like to help."

I follow her eagerly into the kitchen. She sets a wooden cutting board and a knife on the table and takes an onion out of the pantry. "Chop this."

I stare at the knife and the brown-skinned onion. Doesn't slicing onions make you cry?

"Cut it in half first," Arik's mother says, her back to me as she rummages in a cupboard.

I brace the onion with my left hand, pressing the blade into the bulb.

"Not that way!" Gadi Maor says. "From top to bottom. And you want to cut the ends off first."

She corrects my grip on the knife, then shows me how to cut each half of the onion into slices and then into little squares, like mosaic pieces. She doesn't laugh at my incompetence or mention the glaringly obvious fact that I've never worked in a kitchen in my life. By the time I've diced the onion, she's thrown together an entire crust for a savory tart.

"I'm sorry I'm so slow," I can't help saying when she whisks away the cutting board. My eyes sting from the fumes.

Gadi Maor brushes my apology aside. "Your brother couldn't have done any better."

It gives me a thrill to hear her call Arik my brother. "He can't cook?"

She snorts. "All I can say is he could learn a lot from Caleb Levi."

Next she shows me how to peel a cucumber.

"Does Ar—Elisha like cucumbers now?" I ask as I curl off strips of green rind.

"He's never complained about them." There's something expectant about her tone. For once, she doesn't sound like she's trying to end our conversation. So I keep talking.

"He used to hate cucumbers. Once when we were seven, after a recital, his teacher was so pleased with him he kept offering him these crackers with cucumber slices. With our parents watching, he couldn't refuse. I watched him choke down five or six of them."

I look up at Gadi Maor. She's beating a bowl of eggs, a wistful smile on her face.

✢ ✢ ✢

The day of the vote in Parliament, I wake up at dawn and sit bolt upright on my pallet. "It's today."

Arik grunts and squints at the window. "It's ridiculously early."

"I have to be at Parliament early." We all do, to make sure

we get seats in the chamber. And no siblings are to arrive at the same time, so I must leave Horiel before Arik.

"The doors won't even be . . ." A giant yawn swallows the rest of Arik's sentence.

I scramble out of bed, electricity coursing in my veins. I pick up my dress from the back of Arik's desk chair, where I hung it last night so it wouldn't be wrinkled today. It's the dress I ran away from the embassy in.

In less than twenty minutes, I'm ready to leave, but Arik forces me to eat two slices of bread loaded with butter and jam.

"I'm going to be sick before I even get to Parliament," I say as I struggle with the first piece.

"You can't faint of hunger," he says.

"Arik, what if the others don't come?"

"They'll come. Don't you trust them, Rivka?"

I realize I do. What terrifies me is that they trust me too. I haven't prepared what I'm going to say if it becomes clear Nitsan's repeal bill won't pass and we have to reveal ourselves. I've sat down half a dozen times over the past few days to draft a speech, but I haven't been able to write a word. Right now I would give anything for us not to have to come forward in Parliament, but I'm afraid that's too much to hope for.

"I'm not ready, Arik."

"Yes, you are. Or you will be once you eat your other slice of bread."

"When did you become my mother?" I ask. But I eat. And then I lace up my walking boots and leave the Natans' apartment for the first time in nine days.

36

A crowd is already gathered on the steps of Parliament, standing in two distinct clusters. One of kasiri, the men still wearing their black jackets in the early morning cool, and one of halani, a flower bed of colors compared to the magicians. As I begin to cross the square, the doors of Parliament open, and the crowd seeps in. I start to run.

In the atrium, I dart through gaps in the throng, almost slipping on the green floor. Outside the chamber of Parliament, I hesitate. What if one of the parliamentarians who met me at the embassy dinner party recognizes me? They must have read about my disappearance in the newspaper. It'll all be over before the session even begins. I have no choice but to risk it, though.

I step into the chamber to find only a few people scattered among the benches for the public. Mercifully, the parliamentarians' tiered desks are still empty. Pushing down my bubbling trepidation, I walk down the gold-carpeted aisle and choose a seat near the front of the room, where I'll be easily seen if I stand up. Assuming an acquaintance of Father's doesn't spot me first.

Spectators start to pour into the chamber, and the hum of voices builds. The more packed the room grows, the safer I feel. Soon I am hemmed in between a frowning woman in a black silk dress and a silver-haired man who is staring fixedly at his pocket watch. The benches fill to overflowing, and people crowd against the walls. A magically amplified voice announces that the chamber has reached its capacity and no more members of the public will be allowed in. I look over my shoulder, searching the sea of faces for our wildings, for my brother. Did everyone get in?

I catch sight of Batyah farther back in the kasir section and feel a wave of relief. Then I notice who's sitting next to her. It's Hilah. She sees me and breaks into a grin. I smile back, realizing I'm grateful she's here. I find Marah sitting between Gadi Daud and a man I assume is Samira's father. My cello student's face flashes through my mind. I notice Dinah too, wedged between two grown men. Once I've located a few more familiar faces from the pharmacy, I relax by a hair. I am far from alone.

The chamber doors close with a bang, and the first parliamentarians file into the room.

"Finally," the woman next to me mutters. I make myself small between her and my other neighbor.

The legislators wear sober expressions as they make their way to their desks. When I pick out Parliamentarian Nitsan's long gray braid, I let out my breath. She's made it to this day unharmed. Soon all twenty-one representatives have found their places, and a hush falls over the chamber. It is as quiet as a snowfall.

The presider calls Parliament to order. "Today we consider a bill to repeal Statute Sixty-Seven of the civil code, commonly known as the Family Laws. The bill is sponsored by Parliamentarian Nitsan of Horiel District."

The halan representative with the long gray braid stands up and says, "I bring Bill One Thirty-Three to the floor."

In the middle tier, Asaf Zevulun, the kasir who argued so vehemently against the moratorium in the spring, stares murderously at Nitsan.

"We will begin with a period of public testimony," the presider says. "Then we will proceed to a floor debate. At the conclusion of the debate, the final vote will be taken."

The public testimony passes in a predictable blur. Three or four kasiri urge Parliament to hold firm and preserve the Family Laws, and a couple of halani encourage the legislators to take the enlightened position and vote for repeal. I could have written the testifiers' lines for them.

The presider declares public testimony to be closed and opens the floor debate. Now comes the tricky part. I must gauge the mood among the parliamentarians and decide when, if ever, to give the wildings the signal. If only I could read how the legislators planned to vote in their expressions.

One by one, the parliamentarians make speeches. They all seem to want to say their piece, as though they hope to be immortalized in history books someday, whether as a hero who staved off an attack on the Family Laws or a visionary who led the way for progress. I count representatives on my fingers as they announce their intentions. The kasiri are more eager to state their views, and soon six of them have promised to uphold the Family Laws. In between, two halan parliamentarians argued in favor of repeal. The only kasir who has yet to speak is Zevulun, and his feelings are no secret. He will never vote for repeal.

Which means I'm up to seven no votes. All fourteen remaining parliamentarians have to be yeses, or Nitsan's bill will not pass.

Another parliamentarian stands up, a halan with a black beard.

"Since the moratorium on forced adoptions was instituted in the spring," he begins, "I have reflected upon the Family Laws many times. Each time, I have reluctantly come to the conclusion that they are necessary. Changelings will grow up ostracized if they remain with their birth families, and any mixed family will face intolerance from all sides. Parliamentarian Nitsan, I have great respect for your tireless efforts to make our country more just, but Ashara is not ready for this. I must follow my conscience and vote to keep the Family Laws."

I feel numb. He's going to vote no. Six kasir parliamentarians, plus Zevulun, plus this halan. The vote is lost.

I must give the signal.

My heart is threatening to fill my whole chest, but I push myself to my feet. My bench mates grumble as I excuse my way to the aisle. They seem to think I want to slip out to the ladies' room. As I walk down toward the parliamentarians instead of up toward the doors, the presider pauses in giving the floor to another legislator and glances at me.

I was sitting so close to the front that it takes me only

a few seconds to reach the testifier's desk. I turn around. I know they're here, but it feels like an eternity before a figure rises in the kasir section. It's Batyah, and for once, she doesn't look angry at the world. Her expression is serene. More children stand up in every corner of the room, and a rush of whispers spreads through the chamber.

Out of the corner of my eye, I see Arik moving toward the parliamentarians' desks, but he doesn't approach me yet. The wildings and their siblings keep coming until we are a band of over sixty children, kasiri on the kasir side and halani on the halan side, but holding hands to make a human chain across the front of the chamber. Murmurs pile thickly upon murmurs.

Then the presider's voice slices through the rumble of voices. "What is the meaning of this?"

I look up at him. "I am Rivka Kadmiel, sir."

"Rivka Kadmiel?" the presider says in disbelief. "Gadin Kadmiel, is your father aware you are here?"

I don't dare say no, but neither can I stay silent. "Do I need my father's permission to come to Parliament?"

I meant it earnestly, but as soon as it's out I know everyone will hear it as defiant.

"No," the presider says. "I was alluding to the fact that you are currently considered a missing person."

I have no reply to that. Prickling with perspiration, I turn to all the parliamentarians and say, "We're here to ask you to vote for Bill One Thirty-Three. To repeal the Family Laws."

There is a collective gasp from the audience.

"I'm an Atsani citizen," I continue when nobody rushes to drag me from the front of the room, "but in my city-state, we have the same laws. Forced adoption. No contact between changelings and their birth families. No intermarriage. No mixed families."

"Excuse me, but this is preposterous!" cries Zevulun. "This girl is a foreigner, and speaking out of turn. What are you going to do about this mob?"

To my amazement, the presider does not answer Zevulun. He appears gripped by indecision. Maybe because half of us are kasiri, some of us the children of important officials. We may be disrupting the session, but he probably doesn't want to risk any of us being injured in a confrontation.

It still takes me a moment to regain my nerve. "I am a kasir. But in Atsan, I had a brother. A twin brother. When we were nine, we were examined for magic. I was a magician. My brother wasn't. He was a changeling. I was never supposed to see him again."

The parliamentarians' faces are frozen in shock. The chamber doors slam. Dimly, I understand someone must have entered or left the chamber, but it seems unimportant.

"The law told me to forget my brother," I say, "but my memory of him couldn't be erased. My love for him couldn't be erased. So I swore I would find him again, even though he was now a halan."

Parliamentarian Zevulun's eyes are bulging so much they look in danger of popping out. I forge on.

"This spring, my father was appointed ambassador to Ashara. I moved here with him. This city is my home for now. It's also the place where I was finally reunited with my brother."

I need to hurry. Any minute, someone could march over to shut me up. Maybe the police are being summoned even now.

"I found my brother again," I say. "We're still siblings, no matter what the law may say. We should have the right to claim each other as such, even if I live with my father on Embassy Row and he lives with his halan parents. What's more, my brother and I should never have been torn apart. My brother should have had the right to grow up a Kadmiel even though he had no magic. Samira Harun has the right to be raised by the parents who love her, in the same house as the siblings she grew up with. Why shouldn't we have mixed families in our cities? Why shouldn't kasiri and halani be brother and sister? The truth is, we already are."

I turn to face the public, and the others imitate me. Every eye is on us, and I can see the expressions of shock, horror, awe.

"I want to ask my brother to join me," I say.

37

Arik steps out of the line on the halan end. He walks across the golden carpet, his gaze never leaving me. When he's close enough, I grab his hand, and we turn to face Parliament. The legislators' eyes widen as they see the resemblance between us.

"Say something," I breathe.

Arik clears his throat. "My name is Elisha Natan," he says. "I live in Horiel District. I'm a halan. And this is my twin sister, Rivka Kadmiel."

My heart swells.

"In Atsan, my name was Arik Kadmiel."

I hear gasps. Arik was meant to have buried his birth name forever.

Together, we turn around so the public can see our faces. I can tell by the hush that everyone sees the likeness.

Parliamentarian Zevulun's voice explodes in the silence. "They are in flagrant violation of Statute Sixty-Seven! Arrest them!"

I clutch Arik's hand and scan the back of the chamber for police uniforms.

"They're hardly going to escape this room, Zevulun," the presider says dryly. "Gadin Kadmiel, I assume this concludes your little spectacle?"

"No, sir," I say, giving Arik's hand a squeeze.

He draws himself up and speaks in a clear voice. "I'm not the only changeling who came to Parliament with his birth sibling today. My fellow wildings and their siblings are here with my sister and me."

Several parliamentarians exclaim. The public is riveted. I pick Samira's mother out in the crowd; she's covering her mouth with her hand.

Our orderly chain splinters into a chaotic dance of siblings seeking out siblings. We are like two galaxies colliding and forming new constellations. Batyah takes her brother Maayan's hand and pulls him to stand next to Arik and me. Yusuf is already on my other side, his arm wrapped around his sister's shoulders. Some siblings look less alike than others, but from their faces, it is clear the people in the audience have no doubt what they are seeing.

When we have settled into our families and all the shuffling has quieted, the presider sniffs. "Well. You have made your point. You may all return to your—"

"With respect, sir, we wish to remain here until the vote is taken," I say.

"Out of the question," snaps the presider. "Step down, all of you."

None of us moves.

"If you do not disperse, you will be forced to do so." The presider's voice is testy, but I detect an undercurrent of fear.

Something tells me he won't summon the guards to drive us away. I stand firm, and no one breaks rank.

Suddenly, the chamber doors swing open.

"Out of my way, I'm an ambassador!"

My blood turns to ice. There are shouts of outrage and some aggressive jostling around the door until the crowd parts for Father.

"Where is my daughter?" he thunders.

I let go of Yusuf's hand and step forward, pulling my brother with me.

"I'm here, Father," I call over the intense muttering.

Father starts.

"Rivka!" he shouts, relief and rage compressed in his voice. "What are you—?" He breaks off, his eyes going wide with shock. He's finally realized who is standing next to me. Arik's palm is damp against mine.

It's like that afternoon at the police station. I feel ten years old again. Any second now, Father's anger will come crashing down on me in front of Parliament and hundreds of spectators.

But it doesn't. Father's face is ashen. He stares at his son. Then he stares at me. For the first time in my life, I see my father at a loss for words. Then the crowd closes around him.

"Some order, please!" bellows the presider. "We must continue with the floor debate."

Arik and I slip back into place, shoulder to shoulder with our allies. We all turn to face the parliamentarians. They hold our fate in their hands now, and I want them to have to look us in the eye.

"Aren't you going to clear out these brats?" Zevulun demands of the presider. "Or don't you have the spine?"

Setting his jaw, the presider ignores Zevulun. He notices Ayelet Nitsan standing and grants her the floor.

"I stand in awe of your bravery," she says to us. "You are the future of Ashara."

My hopes lift seeing the passionate determination in her face.

She turns to address her colleagues. "This morning, I came to Parliament filled with doubt. I feared there were not enough among us ready to vote in favor of repeal. But now . . ." She gestures at us. "Now I have hope. Look at these young people. They are not asking you to make their love for each other lawful. They are showing you that no law can quench that love. They are risking everything to show you that the Family Laws are already irrelevant. They are wiser than us. I hope you will listen to them and join me in voting to repeal the Family Laws."

She sits down with great dignity, and applause erupts behind me, the wave of sound almost pushing me forward. I glance over my shoulder. Everyone on the halan side of the chamber is clapping, in stark contrast to the stiff kasiri on the other side of the aisle. Here and there, though, a few Ashari magicians are applauding, among them Azariah and, I think, his parents. I don't see Father anywhere.

The bearded halan parliamentarian who spoke before requests another chance to be heard. The presider nods.

"A short while ago, I explained why I felt I had to vote against repeal," he says. "These children have changed all that. If they are willing to accept their siblings whatever their magical ability, who are we to tell them their brother or sister must be taken from them forever?"

He turns from his fellow parliamentarians to face us. "I will vote with Ayelet Nitsan to repeal the Family Laws."

Thunderous applause, punctuated by shouts of joy. Arik and I look at each other, silently exulting in this hard-won victory. We might have our fourteen votes now.

A few more halan parliamentarians make speeches, each one declaring their intention to vote for repeal. Then a page brings Parliamentarian Zevulun a note. Upon reading it, he springs to his feet, and the presider acknowledges him.

"I am appalled that my colleagues are giving in to the demands of a band of manipulative children who have made a mockery of Ashari law in front of hundreds of witnesses in this hallowed hall of government." The whole sentence comes out in one breath, and he gasps before going on. "I beg you to remember that their ringleader is a foreigner. Will we let an Atsani girl dictate the laws of our city?"

There is a swell of approval from the kasir side of the chamber.

Zevulun blusters on about how foolish it would be to permit mixed families: how envious halan children would be of their magician siblings, how ashamed a child without magic would feel in a kasir household, how important pure bloodlines are for preserving a strong vein of magic in the Ashari population. After insisting forced adoptions are what's best for changelings, he starts to lecture us all on the fundamental differences between kasiri and halani.

Arik and I exchange glances as Zevulun drones on well past the time given to the halan parliamentarians. Surely it's the presider's job to force him to conclude. But whenever the presider looks ready to speak up, Zevulun loudly brings up a new point. An angry murmur builds behind us, and I know the public is also losing patience with Zevulun.

Suddenly, the chamber doors open with a whoosh. Shouts of surprise rise from the back of the room. Still clutching Arik's and Yusuf's hands, I twist around as someone screams.

The chamber doors are flung wide, and the nearest members of the crowd are stumbling back in a frenzy to get away from the people who have just entered the room. There are three of them, two men and a woman in elegant dark clothes. Their heads are shrouded in writhing tendrils of darkness.

38

A man's voice booms through the chamber. "Members of the United Parliament, we bring a warning!"

"God of the Maitaf, it's the Society," Arik breathes. Fear compresses my lungs.

The parliamentarians are all frozen at their desks. Ayelet Nitsan is glaring daggers up the aisle.

"We speak for the Society," the man at the point of the triangle formed by the three intruders says. "As you know, we currently have in our care the changeling girl Samira Harun. If Parliament repeals the Family Laws, Samira dies. We are watching. The moment Bill One Thirty-Three passes, the order will be sent to the place where the girl is. If you want Samira to live, do not repeal the Family Laws."

His last words echo beneath the ceiling.

No. Not Samira.

"God of the Maitaf," my brother repeats.

"Maybe he's bluffing," I say. "They won't kill her, she's a magician!"

Arik looks incredulously at me. "A wilding from the Xanite slum? Yes, they will!"

Amid the rising din, a wrenching cry goes up from the halan section, and I see Gadi Daud practically climbing over people in order to reach the aisle. When the throngs realize who she is, they make a path for her. Gadi Daud stops a few yards short of the Society members, afraid to go any nearer. Samira's father and Marah catch up to her.

A phalanx of Parliament guards appears in the doorway behind the Society members, but before they can lay hands on the man and the woman in back, the two faceless magicians whirl around and let loose simultaneous spells. Orange sparks snap in the air.

Several guards in front twitch but do not fall. Instead, they stagger aside as the men behind them throw up their hands and roar an incantation in unison, unleashing a volley of green sparks at the intruders.

The masked kasiri respond with an even denser cloud of fiery sparks. Despite their greater numbers, the guards attempt only two more halfhearted attacks before retreating into the corridor.

"Cowards!" Batyah says.

"Accomplices, more like," her brother says contemptuously. "They barely even tried."

The center Society member laughs, and a shudder racks my body.

"We are not lying." He's talking to Marah and the Haruns. "I assure you, Samira is in our custody. But if you require further proof . . ." He digs in the breast pocket of his waistcoat.

"Marah thinks they're bluffing too?" Arik says in disbelief. "How can she risk it?"

"Marah wouldn't gamble with Samira's life," I say. "Maybe she's buying time . . ."

"Time for *what*?"

The wildings and their siblings are looking to Arik and me, their faces full of uncertainty. We're still standing in our long chain, but the bond that felt so strong only minutes ago now feels brittle.

Out of the corner of my eye, a streak of white and black catches my attention. A young kasir is racing up the outer aisle. As he approaches the sinister headless figures from the side, I recognize him. It's Azariah.

He stops short of the woman and lifts both hands in a complicated arrangement. Absurdly, it reminds me of making shadow puppets. Azariah's lips move in a long incantation, and for a moment, the smoke around the woman's face begins to clear, like mist burning off the river. Before she can be unmasked, though, she aims a spell at Azariah. Turquoise sparks crackle. Azariah crumples to the carpet.

Somebody screams. When Arik clasps my hand, I realize it was me.

"They wouldn't kill him," Batyah's brother says. "He's a kasir."

"You're *not helping*," Batyah hisses. To me, she says, "Maayan's right. It was only a stunning spell."

In their section, the halani hunch low. Some look tempted to seek shelter under the benches. Two or three kasiri drag Azariah's inert form away from the Society members. Their unearthly veils swirl ever darker around their faces.

"Here!" the man in front cries, raising his right fist. "This is the girl's pendant. It hung around her neck not half an hour ago."

He's waving Samira's tin chain. The sight of it feels like a blow to my stomach. Gadi Daud, forgetting her fear of the magician, lunges for her daughter's necklace and rips it from him. She and Banar Harun bend over it, desperate to see if the pendant is really Samira's.

"We need that," Arik says.

"What?" I say, confused.

"We need to see her pendant. Now." He looks at me with such urgency that I understand. The intuition. Dropping his hand, I bolt up the aisle.

"Rivka!" Batyah shouts.

I ignore her, pounding up the golden carpet until I almost collide with Gadi Daud.

"Can I see it?" I gasp.

Samira's parents don't hear me. Gadi Daud cups the tin chain in her hands, swaying. Banar Harun stares woodenly at the necklace he last saw around his daughter's neck. I look for Marah, but she's kneeling beside Azariah, talking to another kasir.

"Remember!" the Society leader calls, his amplified voice ringing. "If you repeal the Family Laws, Samira Harun will not live past tonight!"

With that, he and his two companions sprint out through the open doors. I glimpse the landing lighting up with colored flashes as they meet the guards, but I don't see what happens next because Marah finally notices me. The chamber is in an uproar, and she has to shout to be heard.

"Rivka, I'm so sorry!" she says, her expression bleak. "We can't go through with the vote. Parliament's on your side, I'm sure of it, but Samira . . ."

"The necklace!" I burst out, quivering with impatience. I turn to Gadi Daud and reach for the chain, but she jerks away. It occurs to me that she might not recognize me dressed in a black gown with my hair loose.

Marah yells something to her in Xanite and then tells me, "It's Samira's! She'd recognize it anywhere."

"I *know*! I just need to see it!"

Finally, Samira's mother tips the necklace into my hand. It looks the same as before, but something about the charm catches my eye. It's a metal oval, smooth and seamless. Except when Samira showed it to me, it was a locket.

I push away my awareness of the countless traces of magic layered over Parliament and focus on the cheap bit of tin in my hand. There it is. The faintest presence of a spell, like the tickle of a feather. The Seal.

"What is it?" Arik's voice in my ear makes me jump. I glance up as Caleb and Hilah come rushing up the aisle.

"One second." Between the parliamentarians arguing and the audience chattering, the noise is almost unbearable. I can't concentrate. The hallway outside looks empty now, so I stumble out of the chamber. The Haruns, Marah, my brother, Caleb, and Hilah troop after me.

There is no one on the marble landing. The Society members are gone. I hope the Parliament guards are giving chase.

Focusing on Samira's necklace again, I sing the counterspell to the Seal. The locket's seam returns. I pry it open, bracing myself for disappointment, but tucked inside is a bit of paper.

"What's that?" Marah says as I unfold it.

"A message from Samira, I hope." I glance at my brother. "Arik knew it was there."

I flatten the scrap of paper on my palm. Scratched upon it in tiny letters are the words *I'm in Shimshon Omri's house.*

"God of the Maitaf," says Hilah, reading over my shoulder. "That's Merav's father."

A chill shoots up my spine. I show the note to Arik, Caleb, and Marah. Marah swears under her breath, chokes out a translation to Samira's parents, and then says, "I'm going to kill Omri."

"Hilah," I ask, "do you know where Merav lives?"

"Twenty-nine Pilshan Street," Hilah says without hesitation. "I heard her giving out the address when she had that party in the spring."

"Wait a minute," Marah says. "What are you—?"

"I'm getting her out," I say. "Now."

"No," Marah says. "That's madness. We have to plan—"

"There's no time. We have to rescue Samira now. Without her, the Society has nothing to threaten Parliament with, and the repeal can pass."

"Rivka, the repeal can wait," says Marah.

"No, it can't. It's not just about Arik and me. It's about them." I jerk my head toward the chamber doors. "If the Family Laws aren't repealed today, they could be arrested. The wildings could be exiled to other city-states like Arik was. Parliament has to repeal the Family Laws today, and they won't do it unless they know Samira won't be killed."

Fury surges through me. How dare the Society hold a ten-year-old girl hostage to force Parliament to bend to its will?

Marah is obviously torn. "It's too dangerous. Banar Omri is an adult magician." She notices Caleb watching us all with a frown and begins to sign.

"But he's not at home," Hilah says as Marah talks to Caleb. "All the Omris are here. I saw them."

"Perfect," I say. "I'm leaving."

"I'm going with you," Arik says, moving to stand by my side.

"So am I," says Hilah, joining him.

Catching on, Caleb signs, *Me too.*

No, Marah signs at once. Out loud, she says, "None of you are going. I guarantee you the house hasn't been left unguarded. We can alert the police—"

"You told me yourself the police are useless," I say.

"What if Azariah came with us?" Arik suggests. "He's a grown-up magician."

"He's still unconscious," Marah says, worry veiling her eyes.

"Let's go," I say. There's no more time to debate who might come with us. "We'll break Samira out and bring her here so Parliament can repeal the Family Laws."

Marah tries to catch Caleb by the hand, but he steps out of reach. *Let me do this*, he signs.

For a second, it seems like she's going to keep fighting, but then she nods once. She signs something I don't understand and kisses Caleb on the forehead.

"Make sure they don't vote until we return," I say.

Marah meets my gaze. "I'll buy you all the time I can."

39

Arik, Caleb, Hilah, and I huddle under a shop awning on a lane off Pilshan Street.

"Now would be a good time to decide on a plan," Arik says.

"How are we going to get into the house?" Hilah asks, still panting from our run from Parliament. She forgets to face Caleb, but he seems to grasp the problem.

The servants' entrance? he scrawls on his slate.

"Surely it won't be unlocked," I say.

Caleb shakes his head. *But if one of us could lure whoever answers the door far enough away, the rest of us could sneak in.*

"If they don't lock the door behind them," Arik says.

We're already losing precious minutes. Then it hits me. "They wouldn't have to be lured very far away if the rest of us were invisible," I say.

Hilah looks blankly at me, but Arik, who knows how I sneak out of the embassy, asks, "Can you make us all invisible?"

The thought makes me queasy, but I push the sick feeling down. We can't afford to make a single mistake, and that includes getting caught before we even make it inside.

"I can do it long enough to get us through the door," I say, hoping I'm not wrong. I don't mention the possibility of becoming stuck under the Veil.

"Wait, you can actually make people invisible?" Hilah says, impressed.

"Who will knock at the servants' entrance?" asks my brother.

Caleb, who has been watching our lips closely, points to himself. *Only a halan would go to that door, and you should stay with Rivka*, he scribbles.

With that, he darts into Pilshan Street, and the rest of us follow.

The deserted street is lined with stately town houses. We pass by number twenty-nine, and I feel as if eyes are watching me through its many windows. We turn the corner and slip into the alley. Caleb counts the houses and points to a door a third of the way down.

We crowd into a stairwell opposite the servants' entrance of the Omris' house. While Caleb perches on a middle step, I quietly cast the Veil over Hilah, my brother, and me. The complete trust in their eyes almost makes me falter, but I sing true, and the three of us disappear. Caleb shudders, gripping the step beneath him.

"God of the Maitaf," Arik says.

"Give me your hand," I tell him. "And take Hilah's." After some fumbling, we form a chain, and I turn to Caleb. Since he can't see us anymore, all I can think to do is touch him lightly on the shoulder. He jumps and then scrambles out of the stairwell. I lead Arik and Hilah after him.

We flatten ourselves against the wall of the house on one side of the servants' entrance while Caleb tries the door. It's bolted, so he knocks. As the seconds crawl by, I try not to think about the Veil settling more permanently over us.

A woman in a blue dress and a white apron answers the door. I catch my breath.

Caleb signs something and points down the alley.

"Who are you?" the housekeeper says, puzzled.

Caleb gestures more urgently toward the street and motions for the woman to come out.

She doesn't move. "What's the matter? Can't you speak?"

He shakes his head, tapping his ear and his lips. Then he takes one step the way he was pointing, hoping to draw the housekeeper with him. She frowns, irritation and suspicion clouding her face, and my heart sinks. But Caleb makes his expression pleading and beckons her again.

At last, she crosses the threshold. Now she's standing on the doorstep, but there's not enough space behind her for Arik, Hilah, and me to squeeze through. I keep still, every muscle taut, Samira's locket digging into my palm

"Is someone hurt?" the housekeeper asks, looking down the alley. "I don't see anything."

Caleb takes a few more steps toward the street, begging with his eyes. Finally, the Omris' housekeeper joins Caleb on the cobblestones, leaving the door open behind her. I don't hesitate. Pulling Arik along behind me, I leap soundlessly up the step and dart into the entryway.

There is only one way to go. When a staircase rises on our right, I take it. We reach a corridor with a polished hardwood floor. Framed watercolors punctuate the stenciled wallpaper. The house is eerily silent.

"Where do you think they're keeping Samira?" Arik whispers.

"I don't know," I say, on edge.

"I don't think Merav knows Samira is here," comes Hilah's disembodied voice. "She doesn't seem smug enough."

I nod, though they can't see me. Most likely Banar Omri wouldn't have trusted Merav with the secret.

"That means Samira must be well hidden," Hilah continues.

"Let's start looking," my brother says.

We tiptoe past the closed doors on this hallway. "I think these are bedrooms," I murmur.

"Do we dare check?" Arik says.

I steel myself and push open a door. I catch a glimpse of a canopied bed and a tasseled rug before I ease it shut. "Bedroom. If Merav sleeps on this floor, Samira can't be here. Hilah, tell me if you feel any spells."

"Nothing out of the ordinary right now," she says. The Omri townhouse has that familiar tautness that comes from strengthening spells on the foundations, fire-resistance spells in the walls, perhaps protective wards on the windows to alert the household to break-ins. It's no different from the tension I feel at the embassy. If the Society has Samira guarded with additional spells, which I'm sure they must, we aren't anywhere near her yet.

In a fit of panic, I open the bedroom door again and drag Arik and Hilah inside. "It's too risky to go on like this."

"What are you talking about?" says Arik.

"If I leave the invisibility spell in place too long, I won't be able to uncast it. I'm going to undo it on you."

I'm glad I can't see the expressions on their faces. Their shocked silence makes me feel guilty enough. I reach for Hilah's hand. When I have both her and my brother in my grasp, I still my thoughts and pour all my concentration into singing the Veil's counterspell. They rematerialize before me, and I melt with relief.

"What about you?" Arik demands, not releasing my still-invisible hand.

"I'm staying hidden so I can scout upstairs. You two wait—"

"No," says my brother. "If we were in danger of getting stuck invisible, aren't you too?"

"I can't risk walking into someone's arms," I say. "Besides, I know I can stay invisible for at least fifteen minutes with no trouble."

"Fifteen minutes?" Hilah says. "It's already been at least five! Who knows how long it will take to find—"

"I'll be fine," I say, grateful I only have to sound confident, not look it. "I'll be back soon."

As I slip out of the bedroom, I hear my brother saying, "Don't try anything alone."

I climb a carpeted staircase to the third floor. I'm nervous, but I remind myself that everyone who can possibly manage it is at Parliament. Whoever was unlucky enough to be left behind on guard duty is probably near the bottom of the Society's hierarchy.

I conduct a quick survey of the rooms. Behind one

door is a nursery, complete with sun-bleached curtains and a dusty rocking horse, behind another a cozy library with honey-colored shelves and leather armchairs. I still sense nothing.

Dread coiling around my heart, I climb the last flight of stairs. Midway up, something in the atmosphere changes. I feel a faint but insistent pull upward and to my left. I reach the landing and hold my breath. There is no sound on the fourth floor but a clock ticking somewhere. It's coming through the open doorway ahead. I'm about to gulp in air when somebody coughs.

For a second, I'm petrified. Then I steal down the corridor and peek around the doorjamb.

It's a music room, paneled in dark wood. There is a harpsichord, a concert harp, lion-footed chairs upholstered in yellow silk. And in one of the chairs sits a gangly man in a black suit, contemplating his pocket watch. He is alone.

I retreat downstairs.

"I think Samira's in a music room on the fourth floor," I tell Arik and Hilah. "I felt spells. And there's a guard."

"Only one?" Hilah says. "That's good. It'd be harder for me to lure more than one person out of the house."

"For *you*?" I say.

Hilah nods. "It has to be me. Arik's a halan, and you have to be the one to find Samira. She doesn't know me."

"How are you going to lure the guard away?" I ask.

Hilah shrugs. "Tell him they want him at Parliament after all? If he's been left behind, he's probably eager to go."

"But he won't know you. Why would he believe you?"

"Do you have a better idea?" Hilah asks. "Because otherwise we're wasting time."

Our nerves are making us short with each other, but Hilah is right. We don't have many choices. Suddenly, I realize I'm still clutching Samira's locket. I press it into Hilah's hand.

"Take this. It'll be a token of your trustworthiness."

My touch startles her, but then she grins. "Brilliant. All right. You two hide until you hear us come down. I'll try to say something so you know it's safe."

With that, she leaves the bedroom, Samira's necklace swinging from her fist. I press my ear to the door. Arik tugs at a lock of hair near his temple. I wonder where Caleb is.

I have no idea how much time has passed when I finally hear footfalls on the staircase.

"You're certain Banar Omri wanted me to leave the girl?" a man says, his tone wary.

"He said not to worry about her," Hilah says in a clear voice, with the same deference she used with Father when she visited the embassy.

"Well, it's not as though she can escape," the stranger grumbles. "If having someone on guard duty wasn't important, why have I been stuck here for hours while everyone else gets to watch the spectacle at Parliament?"

"I don't know, sir," Hilah says, her voice fainter.

Arik and I wait until all is quiet. Then he says, "Uncast the spell on yourself before we go upstairs."

"But what if a servant stumbles upon us?" I argue. "If she only sees you, I'll still be able to rescue Samira."

"You need to be visible to rescue Samira anyway," Arik

says. "She won't know she's being rescued till she sees you."

"Fine." I know the real reason for his insistence is his fear for me. I try to settle my mind even though I'm itching to return to the music room. Then I sing the notes of the counterspell. Nothing happens.

Arik swears.

"I'm just distracted," I say, though my stomach gives an anxious twist. "Uncasting the Veil can wait. We need to find Samira *now*."

Before Arik can object, I yank open the bedroom door. I almost pull him off his feet in my haste to reach the fourth floor. We proceed more cautiously through the open doorway.

The music room is empty now, and I take in new details. The harpsichord's spindly legs. The brass pedals of the harp. And on a decorative shelf in the corner, more instruments: a violin, a flute, a tambourine.

The tug of magic is stronger here. I follow it past the harpsichord to a bookcase built into the wall. "She's here. There must be a hiding place behind these shelves."

"Why would Banar Omri hide Samira in the music room?" Arik says. "Doesn't the rest of his family use it?"

"Maybe not. The harp's missing strings, and those instruments on the shelf look like knickknacks."

I face the bookshelves, standing in the spot where the currents of magic feel strongest. "Samira, can you hear me?"

There is no sound but the ticking of the clock on the wall. It taunts me, reminding me we don't have much time before Hilah and the guard she tricked arrive at Parliament, where the truth will come to light.

"I think there's a secret door," I say, prodding the book-case in search of a hidden mechanism.

Arik hurries over to help me, pulling armloads of music off the shelves. "It can't just be a matter of opening it, though, can it?"

He's right, of course. By the feel of it, freeing Samira from her concealed prison will mean breaking at least half a dozen spells cast by adult Ashari magicians.

After a long pause, my brother asks the crucial question. "Can you do it?"

Fragments of spell melodies rise in my throat, but none of them feel right. I feel like I'm facing a fortress I'm meant to destroy with a butter knife.

I swallow. "No."

Arik wets his lips. "Well . . ."

Despair threatens to engulf me. The notes of the coun-terspell I cast on Samira's locket at Parliament float to my lips, and I sing them softly. My brother listens hopefully, not knowing this bit of magic will do nothing.

Then the tight web of spells shivers ever so faintly. I break off. Instantly, I recall my first day at Firem when I acciden-tally broke Merav's levitation spell.

"What is it?" Arik asks.

"I *have* broken a spell before," I say. "Without knowing how it was cast. It was because it was Ashari magic, and I used Atsani magic to sort of . . . throw the currents off."

"Can you do it again?"

I close my eyes and sink into my awareness of the spells in the music room. There it is: the slightest tremor in the weave of spells. I sing an entire phrase, tweaking a spell of unraveling. The web of magic judders, but it's not enough. Sung spells are only good for guiding magic in trickles and rivulets.

"I need an amplifier."

Arik looks around the music room. "All this and no cello?" Then his gaze falls on the violin displayed on the shelf in the corner. "What about that?"

"I don't play the violin."

"You played mine all week."

"Is that thing even playable?"

Arik dusts off the instrument and plucks the strings. The intervals that ring out are far from perfect fifths, but Arik sticks the violin under his jaw, draws the bow across the strings, and twists the pegs until the instrument is in tune.

"It's a nice violin," he says. "It's a shame they leave it on a shelf." He holds out the instrument.

I take it by the neck and tuck it between my chin and my shoulder. I pull the bow across the D string. The horsehair is slick and needs rosin, but there isn't any in sight.

"This is so strange," my brother says, transfixed by the sight of a floating violin playing itself. Then he rouses himself. "Can I do anything?"

"I have to break the spells," I say, facing the bookshelf. "Not break them so much as . . . dislodge them." Knowing that Arik can't sense the ropes of magic makes me feel alone and helpless even though he's right beside me. I play the beginning of the unraveling spell I sang a few minutes ago, but my ice-cold fingers slide on the strings. "I can't do this. I need my cello. *You're* the violinist, Arik, you should be the one—"

"I'm not a magician," he says. "You are. And we don't have a cello. Don't panic, Rivka. What's the first thing you have to do?"

It's clear he has little understanding of the magic I'm attempting, but his quiet words reassure me. We could be back in our house in Atsan, practicing in front of each other. I remember Arik talking me through tricky passages, his confidence in me never wavering, until I succeeded in playing the music that had eluded me.

"I need to find a good key." I lift the violin again and play a D-major scale. It feels wrong almost immediately, somehow irrelevant in its cheerfulness. I experiment with other keys to no avail.

"Try something minor," my brother says at the same moment the thought occurs to me.

I choose A minor, no sharps or flats, and the effect is instant. The net of spells trembles. Emboldened, I play the unraveling spell in this key. The music disturbs the invisible streams of magic in their courses. It's still not enough.

"That's it," Arik says, though he can't have sensed any difference in the spells. "Keep playing. Keep your bow perpendicular to the strings."

It's ridiculous to correct my position at a time like this, but it calms me. If I pretend Arik is just helping me prepare for a recital, I can believe everything will be all right.

I have dozens of spells memorized, spells I could easily transpose to the violin, but the time I destroyed Merav's spell it was by improvising. I don't want to cast new spells of my own; I want to undermine the existing ones. Though I was always terrible at improvising when my cello teacher demanded it of me, this is different. I don't have to come up with anything melodically coherent. Instead, I feel my way around the Ashari spells, choosing notes that press into the gaps. I know I'm on the right track when the whole collection of spells shakes and begins to collapse.

As the cracks multiply and widen, I play faster, struggling to keep up with every note that demands to be played. My tone grows rougher as I saw away at the strings.

"Good. Don't rush." Arik keeps encouraging me, though he's only talking for the sake of it. "I like that arpeggio motif. Try it again."

I pretend I have his fingers, which know the violin so well. His hands, my magic. A low hum builds around us, rumbling up through the soles of my feet. I close my eyes, my tune climbing to the high-pitched E string. The spells are crumbling. I duck, as though plaster were falling in chunks from the ceiling, but it's not the physical world that's disintegrating. The magical hum intensifies, and Arik breaks off, looking uneasily around him.

One by one, the Ashari spells wink out, and the freed magic surges toward me before dissipating through the music room.

"Help me!" a child cries. "I'm in here!"

40

The voice startles me so badly I almost drop the violin. "Samira! Can you hear me? It's Rivka!"

There is a pause. Then: "Rivka? It's me! I'm in here!" Knocking comes from the other side of the wall.

My brother scrabbles for a hidden spring in the bookcase. I fling the violin and bow on a chair and join him while Samira's frantic thumping continues on the other side.

Suddenly, a plug of wood gives way under my thumb. I cry out in surprise as the bookcase shudders and swings toward Arik and me. We jump back as Samira comes shooting out of the opening like a runaway train. She runs headlong into my brother, who grunts and stumbles. Samira recoils in fright.

"Samira, it's me," I say. "I'm invisible, but I'm here."

She turns toward my voice. There is no recognition on her face, only terror.

"It's me," I repeat. "I'm under a spell, but you can touch me. This is my hand." I reach out and take hers.

"Rivka," she chokes. She throws herself at me, nearly knocking me over. I hold her, feeling her relief and her lingering fear in the strength of her grip. She's wearing an ankle-length black dress and stiff new shoes, and her hair, like mine, is down, but tangled and mussed.

"I want to go home," she says over and over into my stomach.

"I've got you," I say. "You're going home."

Arik catches his breath and jerks his head toward the hallway. "Someone's coming."

Rapid footsteps sound in the corridor. There is no time to hide. The gangly guard strides into the room and stares through me at the yawning gap between the bookcase and the wall.

His gaze snaps to Arik. In the blink of an eye, his hands are contorted in front of his chest. Foolishly, I lunge for the violin, as if I could play a spell in time. There is a high-pitched cry, and ice-blue sparks explode in front of the Society member's face. Instead of shouting an incantation, he yells, shielding his eyes with his arm.

"Run!" Arik screams.

I seize Samira by the hand and dash around the blinded and lurching kasir. My brother is already in the hallway. We thunder down the stairs, heedless of the racket we're making. Halfway to the ground floor, with Samira lagging behind, Arik crouches and tells her, "Get on my back."

She obeys without hesitation. We pound down the remaining flights of stairs and burst out the servants' entrance into the alley, panting.

"You made those sparks," I say to Samira.

She nods, sliding down Arik's back. "I've been learning magic."

"If you hadn't hidden that note in your locket, we would never have found you."

"I tore the paper out of a book," she says. "I wrote the message as soon as I found out the name of the man who brought me food. They were always talking about me like I wasn't there. Then today they came and asked me if I thought the sparkers in Parliament cared enough about me to save my life instead of voting for some law. I told them Parliament wouldn't believe they had me, and I put my hand over my locket like this . . ." She reaches for her throat and finds nothing.

"You clever girl," I say.

"We have to get Samira to Parliament now," my brother breaks in. He bends, and she climbs on his back again. "Hold on tight."

When we reach the chamber, we find four guards idling by the entrance. Through the cracked door drifts the sound of an amplified voice I don't recognize.

"Has Parliament voted?" Arik asks the nearest guard.

He shakes his head, and wild joy billows through me. We're in time. I pull Samira and my brother into the chamber and shout, "Here is Samira Harun!"

The parliamentarian who was speaking breaks off. All heads turn toward us, like wheat stalks swept by the wind. The wildings and their siblings are still standing in a wall below the legislators' desks, and the sight makes my heart ache with pride.

"Samira!" Gadi Daud and Banar Harun burst through the crush of people in the back of the chamber. Samira reaches out her arms, and her mother catches her up. She clutches Gadi Daud's neck and bursts into tears, but when she turns her face toward her father, it is lit by a smile as brilliant as the sun.

A cheer rings out somewhere, and within moments, the entire halan section is on their feet, clapping. A few kasiri are applauding too.

"There you are!" Arik exclaims, and I spin around to see Caleb squeezing out from the crowd. He's safe. A knot unwinds in my chest.

Caleb smiles and hugs Arik tightly. Then he looks about for me.

"Listen," my brother says, "Rivka's—"

Someone calls his name, and then Hilah is with us, looking in wonder from Arik to the overjoyed Haruns.

"You got her out!" she says jubilantly. "Where's Rivka?"

"Right here," I say. "Are you all right? The guard came back, and I thought—"

"Oh no!" Hilah says, looking past my shoulder. "Did he hurt you?"

"No, we're fine."

"I'm so sorry. He started asking me questions, wanting to know who I took orders from and so on. I couldn't answer. I waved Samira's locket around, but he accused me of being some kind of decoy and rushed back to the Omris'. But, Rivka, why are you still invisible?" As soon as she asks, a look of horror spreads across her face. "You aren't—"

"She's stuck," says Arik. He looks at Caleb. "Rivka's stuck invisible."

41

At first, I protest that I'm not, but a few failed counterspells later, the truth is horribly clear. I have never stayed under the Veil this long, and with each passing minute, it's getting harder to uncast.

My brother and my friends surround me, shielding me from the throngs jostling for a glimpse of Samira. I sing the counterspell once more, but it feels like scrabbling for a handhold on a smooth glass dome. I keep sliding off.

"Quiet, please!" The beleaguered presider's voice booms through the chamber. Nobody pays him the slightest attention.

"How can I help?" Arik asks over and over. I can't bring myself to tell him there's nothing he can do for me. Hilah starts twisting her fingers and muttering bits of incantations, and I sense she's trying to do to the Veil what she saw me do to Merav's levitation spell in the Firem dining hall months ago. Judging by her fumbling movements and halting words, though, Ashari magic doesn't lend itself as easily to improvisation as Atsani magic.

I interrupt her efforts. "Is Azariah around? He must know the Ashari counterspell for invisibility. Maybe that will—"

Hilah shakes her head miserably. "They took him to his apartment to recover."

Her gaze searches for me, but she can't meet my eyes when she can't see them. A future in which no one ever looks me in the eye again stretches out before me, and I feel unmoored. My brother, whom I came all this way to find, will never see me again. How can I live like a ghost?

I know what I need to do, though every part of me hates the idea. I have to go crawling back to Father, so he can free me from this trap of my own making. It will be humiliating, but he won't deny me the counterspell. I'm already scanning the chamber of Parliament, wondering if he's still here, when a terrible thought comes to me. What if he refuses to uncast the Veil until he's personally delivered me to his sister in Atsan? And what if so much time has passed by then that even he, a highly skilled magician, can no longer bring my body back?

Just then, I catch sight of him standing in the back of the kasir section. He's staring vacantly into space, oblivious to the chaos in the chamber. A jumble of feelings surges up in me: anger at the way he treated me the night I ran away, sadness that he will not love Arik, fear that he will still try to take me away from Ashara. I hear his voice in my head, fragments of things he's told me since we moved here. *Your word is worthless, Rivka. You've grown into a mature and sensible young woman. You do not have sparker friends! I believe you can cast it successfully.*

Startled, I grasp at that last memory. Father had faith in my ability to learn the Veil all those weeks ago. I have to believe he'd have faith in my ability to uncast it now. I've been so busy panicking I've forgotten the advice he gave me that evening as I struggled to make the chair in his study visible again.

I close my eyes against my friends' distressed faces. My heart thumps solidly in my chest; a loose thread in my dress tickles my skin. I am here. Eyes still shut, I return to Father's study. What did he say about casting the counterspell?

Your mind must be solid, like rock.

I make my thoughts thick and opaque, then hard as stone. I sing the counterspell once more, picturing myself standing in the ring formed by Arik, Caleb, and Hilah.

I hear a joyful cry, and someone hugs me. I open my eyes to find myself trembling in my brother's arms. I can see my fists scrunching the black fabric of my dress. If Arik wasn't practically holding me up, I would sink to the carpet. For one awful moment, I think I'm going to throw up, but the feeling passes. Caleb and Hilah are laughing with relief.

I look through the crowd for Father again, but the sea of heads has blocked him from view.

Through my ordeal, the clapping and gleeful shouts have not abated. Now the cries are coalescing into words: "Samira!" and "Repeal!" I step out of Arik's embrace, keeping one hand on his steadying arm. The Haruns are standing nearby, Samira now in her father's arms.

A thunderclap crashes overhead, inside the chamber. Gadi Daud shrieks, and Banar Harun ducks, clutching Samira. A stunned silence follows the shock of the noise.

"My apologies," the presider says. "This session has been interrupted quite enough. We will gladly conduct a vote if everyone returns to their seats and allows us to proceed."

"That idiot!" Hilah says. "I thought the roof was coming down!"

"He's just trying to get on with the vote," I say, still shaken. I slip my hand into Arik's and approach Samira. "Will you come to the front with us?"

She smiles at the sight of me and nods, still clinging to her father's neck. I motion for Banar Harun and Gadi Daud to follow my twin and me down the aisle, raising my eyebrows in a silent question. They pad behind us down the long golden carpet.

As we walk, the parliamentarian who was speaking when Arik and I marched in with Samira resumes his speech. "I think the happiness of Samira Harun's reunion with her parents speaks for itself. I hope my colleagues will join me in voting to repeal the Family Laws."

A new wave of applause spreads behind us. All the wildings and their siblings are beaming at Arik and me. The Harun family hovers uncertainly near the testifier's desk, Samira hiding her face in her father's shoulder.

I brush her hair away from her ear and say softly, "Will you look up at the parliamentarians, just for a moment, so they can see you?"

She slowly lifts her head to gaze at the ranks of legislators. The intense fire I saw in her eyes during our lessons has returned, and more than one parliamentarian looks taken aback by the force of her stare.

"There have been no amendments to the bill," says the presider. "Unless anyone else wishes to speak, we will proceed to a vote on Bill One Thirty-Three, whose passage would repeal Statute Sixty-Seven, known as the Family Laws. A minimum of fourteen yes votes is required for passage. Members may of course abstain."

The pages pass out blank cards to each legislator. As the parliamentarians vote, I glance nervously around the chamber. My eyes fall on Father, still standing at the back of the room. His gaze is fixed on Arik and me, but his face is empty. The last time he looked like that was the day of Mother's funeral.

The voting concludes. My palm is slick against Arik's as we wait for the count to begin. A page gathers the cards and holds up the first one for another page to read.

"Yes." Her voice is crisp, and the word rings in the air.

"One," I whisper.

"What's happening?" Samira wriggles out of her father's arms to stand by me.

"They're counting the votes," I say quietly. "Fourteen yeses, and there will be no more Family Laws."

The page announces the second vote. "Abstention."

My heart pounds.

"No."

"Don't worry." Arik squeezes my hand. "Eighteen yet to go."

"Yes."

That's two.

The yeses keep adding up. Three. Four. Seven. Ten. When the fourteenth "yes" echoes through the chamber, my heart leaps. The audience stirs but keeps quiet while the pages tally the remaining votes. Three noes. Two abstentions. And sixteen yeses.

The presider announces the counts, as if there was a single person in the room who couldn't recite them already. "Bill One Thirty-Three passes. The Family Laws are hereby repealed."

The chamber erupts with cheers. I hug Arik. My brother, my twin, whom I will never have to hide again.

Arik can't stop talking. "Sixteen yeses! That's every single halan, and two kasiri too!"

Around us, the other wildings are also embracing their siblings.

"Session adjourned!" the presider declares, but nobody is listening.

"The Family Laws are gone?" Samira says, looking up at me in disbelief.

"Yes!" I kneel in front of her so we're face-to-face. "Nobody will ever take you away from your family again."

Samira clasps my neck, pressing her cheek against mine. Then she rushes to her parents, speaking excitedly in Xanite. Her father swoops her up toward the ceiling, laughing.

Yusuf and Batyah and Dinah and their siblings swarm Arik and me, calling our names, squeezing our hands, smiling like they're going to burst. Their giddiness is contagious. Everything has changed, and we can feel it.

It won't be easy. One legislative victory won't fix all our problems overnight. The Society won't give up just because Parliament repealed the Family Laws. But I came to Ashara to find my brother, and I have. And with our new friends, we've changed the city I now call home.

42

On Firstday, Arik has an evening chamber-music rehearsal, and on Secondday, Caleb has to work on a project with some classmates from the school for the deaf, but on Thirdday, Hilah and I meet my brother and Caleb after school. It's the first time the four of us have been together since the day we rescued Samira from the Omris' house.

We walk to the river and onto a stone arch bridge like the one in Atsan. Caleb perches on the wall, his back to the water below, while the rest of us face him.

"How are you?" Arik asks me. "How's the embassy?"

I sigh. "I don't think Father's said ten words to me since I came home."

"Well, he hasn't sent you back to Atsan," Arik says brightly.

There is a pause. It's time to tell them. I look at Caleb and say, "Father has resigned his post as ambassador to Ashara."

For one beat, everyone is frozen.

Then Caleb signs, *Why?*

A shadow has fallen over Arik's face. He doesn't need to ask why.

"It's so sudden," Hilah says. "You only arrived in the spring."

"It's because of me," I say. "And Arik. And what we did. I don't think he can bear to stay."

My brother finally speaks. "Are you leaving?" There's something funny about his voice. It doesn't sound like him at all.

"Father wants to return to Atsan by the end of the month." Caleb and Hilah look stricken, but Arik's face is wooden. "I don't want to go with him."

"Of course you don't," Hilah says, glancing at my brother.

But how can you stay? Caleb writes on his slate.

"You don't have to do this," Arik says thickly.

"I came to Ashara for you," I say. "What was it all for, everything we've done, if I have to leave you?"

"So you're staying," Hilah says, brightening.

I swallow. "I haven't talked to Father yet."

Arik looks abruptly away, forgetting that Caleb can't see his lips. "I don't want you to give up so much because of me."

"What I'm giving up is worth less than what I'm holding fast to," I say. "You're my brother."

"He's your father."

"Between my brother and my father, I choose you."

"This is what I mean," Arik says, his face pinched. "It's horrible that you have to choose."

"It's my decision to make. And really, I chose you long ago."

"Do you want someone to go with you?" Hilah asks. "When you speak to your father?" She means herself. Caleb wouldn't be welcome at the embassy, let alone Arik.

"Yes," I say gratefully. "I would like that."

So the following afternoon, Hilah accompanies me home from school. Instead of going up to the residence, we venture down the corridor toward the embassy offices. I feel as though I'm wading through deep water. To my relief, Deputy Liron's office is dark. I've avoided her since the day she betrayed me to Father.

There are two green leather chairs outside the ambassador's office.

"You can wait here," I tell Hilah, dropping my schoolbag.

"I'll come in with you, if you want."

"Thank you," I say, my throat suddenly tight, "but I should talk to him alone."

As Hilah settles in one of the chairs, I knock on Father's door.

"Come in."

I step inside. Father and I have been so stiff with each other since the weekend that the formality of the setting feels almost right. I feel less like Father's daughter than an Atsani expatriate come with some petition. Maybe that's exactly what I am.

Father glances up from a document he's studying at his desk. "Oh, it's you," he says coldly.

"Good afternoon, Father." My voice does not shake.

"Is something the matter?" Father asks. "I'm very busy. There is much to put in order before we leave."

I've thought about the right words for this moment since Father told me he was resigning. The difficulty is not remembering what I want to say but summoning the courage to say it.

"I don't want to go back to Atsan."

Father fiddles with some papers and examines a cardboard file.

"I want to stay in Ashara."

He looks up from the bureaucratic detritus smothering his desk. "That's a pity, Rivka, because you are my daughter, and you go where I go. You can hardly expect to go on living in the embassy when I am no longer ambassador."

"I don't expect that," I say. "I want to become a boarder at Firem."

Father is still, but he's listening.

"When you were first appointed ambassador, you thought I would go to boarding school in Atsan. This would be much the same."

"On that occasion," Father says in a low voice, "you told me that you did not want to stay in Atsan without me, that you would rather be with me."

An unexpected rush of tears threatens, and I have to fight them back. I pretend I didn't hear and flounder into an explanation of my plan. "Hilah doesn't have a roommate right now. There's room for another first-year boarder in the girls' dormitory . . ."

"You expect me to pay for room and board in addition to Firem's tuition?" says Father.

I'm starting to fear he will never give his consent, but still I say, "It's what you would have done if I'd stayed behind in Atsan in the first place."

"It has become abundantly clear that you should have," Father says, gripping the armrest of his chair. "Tell me, Rivka, why do you wish to remain in Ashara?"

I could give an evasive answer about not wanting to switch schools mid-year, about being attached to my new friends, but we'd both know I was lying. I'm finished lying.

"I want to stay in Ashara with my brother."

"You have no brother."

"I have a brother, Father. His name is Arik, and Elisha. He's Ashari. And I love him."

The silence is like that after the toll of a great bell.

"It was all pretense, wasn't it?" says Father. "All these years. You never changed from the pig-headed ten-year-old you were."

I don't deny it.

"You and I are what remain of the Kadmiels. You would abandon the family for a wilding? For a sparker?"

"He's my brother!" I cry.

"I am your father!"

"It doesn't have to be you or him. I'm still Rivka Kadmiel. But I want to live in Ashara. A city-state without family laws."

"You would live in this degenerate city, unsupervised, keeping company with halani, heaping shame upon the Kadmiel name . . ."

I'm surprised our conversation has lasted this long. Surely if his final answer was no he would have dismissed me by now.

"I expected great things from you, Rivka," Father says. "You were an impetuous child, but you grew into a level-headed young woman. I pinned the hopes of the Kadmiel family on you. In the past two weeks, I have watched you throw away everything you should stand for."

A bucketful of guilt drips down the walls of my stomach. If I stay in Ashara, Father will have lost everyone: son, wife, and daughter. I don't even think he's trying to shame me into relenting. His disappointment is genuine. I can feel it radiating from him, along with a simmering anger. But my mind is made up.

"I want to stay in Ashara."

"Fine!" The word pops like a firecracker. Father leans forward in his chair. "Remain here if you like it so much. I will pay your tuition, room, and board until you graduate from Firem. But as soon as you graduate, if you do not move back to Atsan, you will not receive another penny from me. You'll be on your own."

On my own. I let it sink in. When I finish at Firem, I'll have nowhere to live. Father won't pay for me to go to Ashari university. I might have to work. The thought of fending for myself is dizzying, but it's still three years off. Plenty of time to figure something out.

"All right," I say. "I understand."

Father's eyes widen in shock. Then he scoffs, "No, you don't. You're still a child. But so be it."

Looking into his eyes, I can almost see an iron gate slamming shut between us. I used to be on the inside, but now I'm on the outside, with Arik.

When I don't leave, Father says in a voice as hard as ice, "What more do you want?"

"Nothing," I say quickly. "I just . . ." The air in his office is suddenly pressing down on me. "Thank you."

Father's harsh gaze doesn't soften. I feel like I haven't said enough, but I don't know what else to say. Part of me wants to tell him I love him, but I've spent so many years telling myself I hate him that I don't know if I do love him.

"Thank you," I repeat, and I turn around abruptly as the tears prickling my eyes overflow. Blinded, I fumble for the doorknob and make a clumsy exit from the office.

Hilah is a blurry figure in an ivory dress. I wipe my eyes and glimpse for a moment her sad, kind expression. Then I have to press a hand to my mouth because I'm crying and I don't want Father to hear.

My friend guides me up to my room and holds me on my bed.

"I heard every word," she says. "Don't worry, I won't let you starve after we graduate."

"Thank you, Hilah." I sniffle. "I'm sorry. I don't know what's wrong with me. I got what I asked for."

"But you lost something too." Hilah pushes away a few strands of hair stuck to my wet cheek.

"I'm happy," I say, laughing a little because here I am sobbing on her shoulder. "It's just that we were a family once, Mother, Father, Arik, and me, and now it's all broken."

"You have Arik," Hilah reminds me.

"Yes," I say, "and that's why it's worth it." But for now I can't help mourning what is lost.

✦ ✦ ✦

On a Sixthday afternoon, Hilah and I walk down the front steps of Firem and around the block to the girls' dormitory.

Father isn't leaving for Atsan for another two weeks, but within days of our conversation in his office, I moved into the empty side of Hilah's room with a trunk of clothes, my schoolbooks, and my cello. I haven't seen Father since, and I'm not sure he'll come say goodbye before he leaves.

Hilah and I change out of our uniforms into lighter dresses and walk from Firem to the Kazeri School of Music. Caleb is waiting for us on the steps. A few other people arriving at the school cast sidelong glances at Hilah and me, but no one says a word.

In the auditorium, Caleb spots the Natans, but they are already hemmed in by other parents, so the three of us find seats close to the front. The gaslights dim, and chattering voices subside. Twelve wooden chairs gleam on the shining stage. The musicians file out from behind the dark curtains. Arik cradles his instrument and steals glances at the audience. He is the first violinist.

The medsha begins to play, and the music lifts me above my troubles. I forget about Ashara and Atsan, magic and schoolwork, Father's coldness and his vow to cut me off when I graduate. There are only fields of sound, strings like sunshine, flutes like cool rain, the notes of the lyre like stars. I look over at Caleb, wondering if he's bored by the concert he can't hear, but he's smiling slightly, his bare arms pressed against the wooden armrests of his seat.

The last piece begins softly with brooding chords in the violas and cellos. The horn breaks through, solemn and clear, and begins a duet with the first cello. Then it's Arik's turn. While the low strings provide a carpet of sound, he plays a poignant solo that climbs higher and higher. Maybe it's self-centered of me, but it's easy to imagine that the melody unspooling from his violin is for me alone.

Arik reaches a high, precarious note, and his fellow violinists join him in a sudden crescendo. Then the whole medsha is playing, the sound pressing to the farthest nooks of the auditorium.

When the concert is over, after we have greeted the Natans and Arik has accepted a dozen compliments on his solo, the four of us walk to a park near the school. We sit in a circle in the shade of a maple whose leaves are turning fiery orange. Hilah produces a tin of currant biscuits from her purse and passes them around.

A ball comes sailing over our heads, bouncing on the grass between Arik and Caleb. A little boy dashes over, stammering apologies. Caleb tosses him the ball. The boy catches it and starts to smile, but his expression freezes. His eyes dart from Arik and Caleb to Hilah and me, sitting in our long dresses with our legs tucked under us. Then he turns tail and bolts.

Hilah laughs nervously. "Well."

"We can expect a lot more of that if we keep doing this," my brother says.

"They're the ones who have to change," I say. "Not us. Anyway, he was just startled. He meant no harm."

We munch on Hilah's biscuits, dropping crumbs in the grass. The sun slants through the scarlet maple leaves shushing in the breeze. Then Caleb writes on his slate.

Aradi Noach invited me to take his class on comedy and tragedy next year.

"Oh, Caleb!" I say. "Congratulations!" Arik and Hilah echo me, and Caleb glows.

So I need you to take Comedy and Tragedy too, he writes to me.

All right, I sign. I pause to think of the right signs and then add, *If Aradi Noach wants me.*

Caleb waves away my doubts.

"You know," Hilah says wistfully to Arik, "going to your concert makes me wish I hadn't quit piano."

"You could take it up again," I say. "You're still good."

"With you on piano, Rivka on cello, and me on violin, we'd make a piano trio," my brother says. "There's a great repertoire. I can already see it: the wilding, the Atsani orator, and the country radical."

"And Caleb?" I say. "In a piano trio?"

I'll be your impresario, he writes with a straight face. *I'll book your performances in the salons of all of Ashara's richest ladies.*

His mouth twitches, and we all burst out laughing. I never want this moment to end.

Too soon, it's time to go home. We get to our feet and brush crumbs from our clothes. We walk four abreast, Arik and I in the middle, Caleb on his left, and Hilah on my right. As we pass children playing in the street and factory workers returning home, it dawns on me that I'm doing what I could only dream of doing a few months ago: walking openly through Ashara next to my twin brother. And when we go our separate ways, the boys turning south toward Horiel, and Hilah and I continuing on to Firem, I watch my brother go knowing I can see him again tomorrow, and the day after, and the day after that.

Glossary

Aevlia: a temperate country southeast of the north lands

Aradi: the title for a teacher

Ashara: the city-state of the north lands where Rivka now lives

Assembly: the former governing body of Ashara, overthrown for trying to exterminate the halani with a plague

Atsan: the city-state of the north lands that Rivka is from

Banar: the title for an adult man

Erezai: a kingdom founded in the north lands by migrants from Xana five hundred years before Rivka's time; it split into the city-states

Fadra: a country south of Xana

Gadi: the title for an adult woman

Gadin: the title for a young woman

halan (plural: halani): in the north lands, a person without magical abilities

Ikhad: the largest market in Ashara, located in the city center

kasir (plural: kasiri): in the north lands, a person with magical abilities; a magician

Kiriz: a city-state of the north lands

Maitaf: the sacred text of the Maitafi faith, a monotheistic religion practiced in Ashara

medsha: an instrumental ensemble consisting of three violins, two violas, two cellos, two end-blown flutes, a lyre, a horn, and percussion

north lands: the part of the world where Rivka lives

Senate: the governing body of Atsan

sparker: in the north lands, an insulting slang term for a person without magical abilities

Tekova: a city-state of the north lands

United Parliament: the governing body of Ashara, made up of both halani and kasiri

wilding: in the north lands, a halan child born to kasir parents or a kasir child born to halan parents

Xana: a desert country across the sea from the north lands

Acknowledgments

I MUST FIRST thank Dan Lazar and Leila Sales for conspiring, however unwittingly, to convince me to make *Wildings* the book it is. I'm glad they did. Thanks to Leila for always supplying the crucial connection when I was stuck during revisions. Thanks to Dan and Torie Doherty-Munro for all their behind-the-scenes work. Many thanks to Janet Pascal, Jody Corbett, and everyone else at Penguin.

I am deeply grateful to Thandi Jobson and Juanita Poareo for their generosity in reading the manuscript and their insight in helping me portray Caleb's deafness. Thanks also to Christina Lisk for connecting me with them. I am responsible for all remaining inaccuracies.

Finally, thanks to my family, my friends, and my colleagues in the UCLA Linguistics Department for their enthusiasm and support.